Taken to Nobu
Xiveri Mates Book 2

D1714246

Elizabeth Stephens

Content

Pronunciation Guide & Glossary

Bo'Raku *(boh - rah - kooh)*
Ruler of the Drakesh planet, Cxrian; once an independent planet, but following a failed invasion of Nobu, the planet was absorbed into the Voraxian Federation

Cxrian *(ss - ree - ahn)*
The red planet, coined for its color as seen from outer space, as well as the red skin tone of its primary species, the Drakesh

Drakesh *(draah-kesh)*
Beings of Cxrian that were once autonomous before their failed invasion of Nobu; afterwards, their planet was absorbed into the Voraxian Federation

Hexa *(hex - ah)*
Yes

Kiki *(kee - kee)*
human name

Kinan *(keh - naan)*
Okkari's slave name

Kor *(kohr)*
Trading city located on in the grey zone between Quadrants 4 and 5; ruled by the Niahhorru species commonly referred to as space pirates; their leader is the feared pirate Rhorkanterannu

Nobu *(noh - boo)*
Voraxia's largest planet; ruled by Va'Raku; characterized by icy climates and long, brutal winters

Nox *(noh - cks)*
No

Okkari *(oh - car - ee)*
Principle warrior and traditional ruler of Nobu; see Va'Raku for alternate title in the Voraxian heirarchy

Qath *(kahth)*
An oasis city located within Voraxia; surrounded by harsh deserts, it is known for its extremely hostile plant and animal life as well as for being the training ground of Voraxia's elite warriors, trained and led by Krisxox

Va'Raku *(va - rah - kooh)*
Ruler of the Voraxian planet, Nobu, as decreed by Voraxian heirarchy; see *Okkari* for alternate definition

Va'Rakukanna *(va - rah - kooh - kah - nah)*
Mate of Va'Raku; see *Xhea* for alternate definition

Verax *(vair - axe)*
Explain

Voraxia *(voh - racks - ee - uh)*
Chief planet of the Voraxian Federation; base of the Raku; characterized by expansive werro woodlands and a sandy forest floor

Xhea *(shay - uh)*
Mate of the Okkari; see Va'Rakukanna for alternate title in the Voraxian heirarchy

Xhivey *('iv - ay) or (xhziv - ay)*
Good

Xok *('ok) or (tzok)*
Curse word used universally and liberally

Xora *('oh-ruh) or (tzoh - ruh)*
Cock, dick, penis, or your word of choice for it

To women.
Our untold power and unsung resilience.

elizabeth

1

Kiki

I'm swimming through syrup. Like the kind we harvest from the trees within the Droherion Dome. Jaxel and I used to go with our mothers to collect it during the cold season when we were little. Jaxel looked up to me back then, even though at just three rotations, he was already taller than I was. *He still does, I just don't give him that chance.*

I inhale deeply. Mmmmhmmmm. Everything is warm. The syrup is the same temperature as the rest of my body making it impossible to decide where my skin ends and the syrup begins. It's so comfortable. What did I ever do to deserve to be so comfortable? I've never been comfortable like this before, or if I was I can't remember it.

Plagued by twin suns and almost no atmosphere, if it wasn't too cold in our human colony, then it was too hot. The windows of my mom's tiny adobe and tin hut didn't close so there was never any insulation against whatever extreme temperature the outside opted for that day, and there was a draft that let in a ceaseless stream of sand. Mama always liked the gap in the windows. She said it let the stars keep an eye on us.

I'd believed her then. And then I grew up and I was hunted by aliens, viciously claimed by the worst of them, left for dead, and Mama tried to remind me that the stars were still there, still watching...but I know the truth. The stars don't care about us.

The Hunt. Running. My legs pumping. Jaxel hadn't started training me then so running was all I had. I thought I could outrun *him* — the red demon with the wicked face that they called Bo'Raku — but I could hear him behind me cackling with laughter.

He chased. I ran. I stood no chance and I refused to let what happened to me next happen to Miari, my best friend, a hybrid human-Drakesh, and the product of one of the past barbaric Hunts. This day every three Earth cycles red-faced aliens called Drakesh swoop down onto our human colony and demand their right to breed our women. And then they do it. Unforgivingly.

Last Hunt, Miari was targeted by a big brute — *he was blue though, wasn't he? I'd never seen a blue one before...* He wasn't a Drakesh but a Voraxian and apparently king of all the alien fuckers. He's coming back for her this Hunt, or wait...did he already come?

A sharp shard of a memory cuts through my passive bliss. *It's the day of the Hunt and Miari and I are crawling through the sewers, trekking outside of the Dome covered in shit. We find a cave to hide in while Svera, our best friend, takes Miari's place in the Hunt. She'll distract him long enough for us to find a hiding place and when she reveals herself to the king, he'll leave — or he'll search for us, but he won't find us. He'll leave either way because we've found the perfect cave. Sunken into jagged black cliffs, it's dank and wet and when we barricade ourselves inside, I know we're going to succeed. All that's left to do is wait...*

Tssaaaaak. My whole body jolts at the sound and the memory the sound brings to life in livid, gruesome color. *We didn't account for the monsters.*

The syrup thickens around me, becoming claustrophobic. *Kind of like the cave, filled with shadow monsters who have blades for fingers, seven arms and two mouths. Miari doesn't know the first thing about fighting, but I do. I take my sharpened spear and battle the thing. Pain lights up my abdomen as I'm stabbed by one of its claws. The serrated blade rips across my stomach, halving my belly button. I'm going to die. But I'm going to save Miari first. I stab it in the eyes and when I stab again, I kill it, or so I think. But when we flee the cave, I see that there are at least three more monsters closing in. I take the amp Miari built and I press the button, sending monsters scattering in a brutal explosion — one that takes me with it.*

I feel sharp rocks come up against my back and tension flee my muscles. I'm going to die here. Yes. Finally... *I sink into the smell of hot, metallic blood. And then nothing.*

And now warmth. Wet syrup sliding over my body. The smell of a deep, fragrant spice, like the blossoms of a cactus in a faraway desert. One I've never been to before. One without any rain. One without any storms. It's pure comfort where nothing can get to me. Not the monster in the cave, not the monster in The Hunt. There are no aliens here. Just a cactus and its bloom, and a pressure in my chest right below the beat of my heart that tells me one thing: Death will have to wait.

2
Kiki

I wake to the sound of my own teeth chattering. I'm cold. I remember the fuzzy goop clutching my bare body, my hair floating off of my neck, suspended by thick purple syrup, but when I open my eyes, the memory is gone like it never was. Like a bad dream. *No. Like a good dream.* I just haven't had one in so long it's hard to recognize.

Whispers. I hear them softly at first before they gain in volume.

"She's awake. The chosen…"

"The alien you mean. The weak one…"

"She would not have been chosen if she were so."

"She is to be our Xhea!"

"Shh! She can hear you."

"Who cares if she can hear me, she can't understand. She's useless. Speaking only her stupid, alien speak…"

"I…" I lick my lips, voice cracking from so many rotations of disuse. I haven't spoken in rotations. Is it worth it to speak now just to level insults? *Yes.* "I can hear you, you stupid bitch." I swallow hard, coughing into the floor, which is soft beneath my cheek. "I can understand you too." My throat hurts, like the chords have been cut. Like I've been choked by hands hotter than the sun.

One female voice titters nearby, but just the one. And then a voice says softly, "What did our Xhea say?"

There's a slight scuffling before a deeper voice projects, "It is not important. We only have a matter of moments before they raise the gate. Before we run the mountain. We must prepare. If we do not present well, we will not be chosen."

There's a pause, a few more whispered words. I use the lapse to find my fingers, to wiggle my toes, to shift my legs back and forth. They're stiff and trapped and for a second, I panic. *What did the goo do to me? Am I paralyzed?*

Then I blink. White light spears my eyes, but they water and clear and water again. Eventually I'm able to see past it. Black on white. Shuffling feet on stone, white walls beyond them…no, not walls…something white… something foreign…something cold.

What's clear is that I'm in a cave full of aliens and that it's light out and the light is natural even if it's made so harsh by so much white. It falls in light flurries, reminding me of springtime on the colony when the cotton fields bloom and little pieces of white are sprinkled through the world. It was always my favorite season. *Miari and I used to try to catch them.*

I shudder and block the memory out as I do memories of all things good. *There is no good anymore.* Just as there's no electricity in here, no wires, no heating. There's just a black stone ground and white surrounding it and aliens filling the space around me.

My hackles rise. I'm ready to fight. But none of the females are looking at me — well, they are looking, but only sparing quick, hesitant glances. Like they're more afraid of me than I am of them. *As they should be. I'll kill any of them who tries to touch me. Maybe I'll kill them just for fun.* I hesitate for a second as my head fully clears, wondering if I could really take on so many.

I quickly tally eleven females, most of whom squat in a circle near the gate that blocks us in and some, but not all, of the cold white stuff out. All but two in this cave are squatting, huddled together in what looks like concentration. Me and the one who paces.

She glances down at me and I meet her gaze squarely, knowing that this is the one who bad-mouthed me. I can tell by the look of her alone. Quickly raking my eyes over her frame, I see she's unarmed, wearing a strange combination of hide and fur-lined leather. The other women wear the same. I glance down at my own clothing, shocked to see I'm dressed identically to them. *Who the fuck dressed me?*

I exhale shakily, push that thought aside and shift to my knees. There's a furry white blanket under me and I catch myself on it, waiting for the cave around me to stop spinning. When it finally does, I shove my feet under my knees and rise even if it does take me a couple tries. I hate that. *Now they've seen that I'm weak and they'll use that weakness against me. They're aliens. They won't hesitate.*

I lift my arm, the ceiling so low I can touch it with my gloved fingertips. With all of the other females seated or kneeling at the mouth of the cave — except for the bitchy one — I feel seriously tall. And powerful. Ready to take them all on.

I take a step towards them at the same time that the bitchy one barks, "And what would the *human* know of the Mountain Run? She knows nothing. Look at her. How small she is. She's *puny*. She won't be any use to us at all. It's likely she won't even be chosen."

"Hush," one of the women says. *No, they're not women. They're females. Others. Them.* She looks over her shoulder at me and she's smiling. *Why in the stars is she smiling at me? Doesn't she know I'm going to slit her throat?* "We welcome the Xhea and any input she wishes to provide."

I glance at the two females who have spoken, and then all the rest, trying to decide what in the stars this particular selection has been gathered for. It's clear that these aren't warriors. From their waif-like limbs to the way a few cower, struggling desperately to meet my eyeline, the better part of them look like cowards.

And it's not like they're great beauties either. Some are tall, sure, but some are fleshy around the jowls, while others look so thin, they're barely more than color draped over bones. And they *are* brightly colored with skin tones ranging from the lightest lavender to the darkest cobalt.

While most have hair as black as tar, there's one who's bright green with hair whiter than the cold coming in through the gate. I meet her gaze for a moment and she tries a smile, but I bare my teeth and grunt low under my breath until she bows her head and looks away.

I refocus on the female who spoke with authority and brace myself, knowing that I'm going to have to speak with them if I'm going to get any answers. That means doing two things I vowed never to do again — speaking, and interacting with *them*.

"How…" I cough to clear my throat and when I edge forward tentatively, I can see a crude outline of sticks and rocks on the ground between the females. Instinct tells me it's a map, but I can't identify any of the markers they've placed.

"How long have I been asleep?" I bark, infusing my tone with authority that I only half feel.

The leader opens her mouth, but the bitch cuts in. "That isn't important. We need to prepare a good chase!" She shows me her back and flips her hair, trying to block me out.

Slowly, I step around the circle. I'm careful to keep the gate in my peripheries as I move around the group — who the fuck knows what else is out there — circling far enough that I can see the bitch's face again and no farther than that. She glares at me with all her severity, but I don't back down. Her face is cut like a diamond. Eyes high and wide, nose narrow and low. She has a petite chin and high cheek bones, ears sharpened to points. *Alien bitch.*

The alien on the ground who seems to be leading the congregation snaps, "She is the reason we are here. Do not dishonor yourself. If you do not wish to help, then step aside. Time is dwindling." She returns to the map.

Following her gaze, I work to make sense of what I'm seeing laid out so crudely, and as my pulse picks up its pace and my mind begins shifting blocks of understanding into place, I come to a single conclusion so startling and so horrifying it makes my bones hurt. I want to laugh — I *do* laugh, drawing even more attention to myself.

"We're preparing for a Hunt, aren't we?"

"A Hunt? Nox, my Xhea, not quite. We do share Drakesh ancestry, but Nobu's Run on the Mountain would test any Drakesh. It is far more severe. A test for true warriors." She pauses then and takes a moment to look up at me, her features masked, though her forehead *glows* as if lights have been switched on underneath her transparent bones. "We have heard that you too are a warrior."

Too many things jump out at me. I can't grab hold.

Even though whatever translation equipment I've been plugged into gives me insight into her words, I still don't know what they mean. What is drah-kesh? What is noh-boo? What the fuck is a zshay-uh? And how the fuck did I end up here? And where is here anyways? *Does it matter?* All I know is that here is nowhere I'm meant to be and I'm going to get out of here no matter how many I have to fight and hurt and kill.

"Where are we?" I bark, the sensation in my chest like thrown stones. I feel myself begin to sink as the idea of being tested in another Hunt, this one even more brutal, dawns on me. *Kill anyone who touches me. Kill everyone who tries.*

A slight, impatient sigh from the lead female before she turns her seemingly sightless eyes up to me. "We are on Nobu, my Xhea."

"She is not Xhea," the bitch snaps.

"Not yet."

"Perhaps not *ever*. Perhaps the Okkari will know through the Run on the Mountain that a *worthy* female awaits him."

The leader's face morphs into yellow this time. She seems to cede, but there is something in her words I can't interpret. "All shall be revealed." She nods slightly, then turns to me. "You are named Va'Rakukanna by Voraxian rights, but here on Nobu we observe tribal law. It is ancient law. The laws of first strength and first right.

"Eligible females participate in the Mountain Run to be awarded breeding partners. When the gates are lowered, we must run. We are given a quarter solar's head start before the warriors and the Okkari are loosed. Once they are, they will run the mountain in hunt for females. They will fight for coveted females. They will certainly fight for you."

"And if they catch us?"

The woman's forehead flashes an alarming white. I angle myself away from her, in a fighting stance, but the color fades just as quickly. "They will breed with us. It is said that when both parties are stimulated equally from the chase, that it is most like to be a successful coupling. More kits are produced from the Mountain Run than any other season."

Several other aliens murmur their assent, nodding vigorously *excitedly*. That's when it hits me: they *want* to be here. They *want* to be hunted. My blood heats but I clamp my mind vice over my mounting panic and focus. *I've trained for this. For three rotations, I've waited for the moment to exact my revenge against* him. *I won't go quietly into the night.*

"Why run? Why not just sit here and wait for them to come?" I ask.

Again, white flashes in the woman's face and I wonder if this isn't some sort of surprised expression. It would help if it were, because otherwise, there is no expression to their faces whatsoever. Just sculpted cheeks and sideways blinking eyes that freak the shit out of me.

"As a ruse?"

As a way to save our strength and plan a concerted offensive. "Sure."

Her head tilts in a way I find weird because it's so human and finally says, "It could be intriguing. To confuse them, perhaps? But certainly, all of us couldn't..." Her brow bone flashes grey then blue then the palest cream. Several of the other women begin to whisper. Some shake their heads.

I don't understand and unleash my frustration. "I'm just saying, what is the point of running? Why would we separate and run off like idiots when we could prepare now to fight?"

"I..." It's as if the thought has never occurred to her. Maybe it hasn't. She shakes her head. "We cannot fight the Okkari and his warriors. It is unheard of, besides. We must give good chase. If we are too easy to catch, then it will be assumed we are too weak to bear, raise and protect our kits. We will not be chosen, even if there are unmated males left."

"So if we do nothing, we won't be chosen? Is that a guarantee?"

The female's ridges blaze another color, this time bright fuchsia. "Nox. Nothing is guaranteed in the Mountain Run..."

"Then we can't risk it." My next words stick in my throat as I realize what I've said. *I said we.* "*I* can't risk it. So if you can't fight and staying put accomplishes nothing, then what happens when we do run and outlast the males?"

Her hands rest on her thighs as she kneels on the hard stone ground. No one else seems to have a blanket here but me. "It would be too dangerous not to be found *at all*. The Mountain Run can take to the end of the solar, and by the lunar, the temperatures are too stark. And even if somehow one managed to survive the lunar temperatures, it is likely that a night beast would find you quickly." She raises one hand. It has six long, hideous fingers. "They are not possible to kill bare-handed."

A fist tightens in my chest. I punch it down with aggression, plowing straight through it. "Where is the next village? How far?"

"Too great a distance to travel," she answers hesitantly. "Not without provisions."

I hardly wait for her answer before I fire off, "So there's no way to avoid this Hunt without being caught? Not if we want to live." *I said we again. Fuck me. Fuck them.*

"If a female were to evade capture altogether and return to the village after the final horn is blown, then...I suppose she could choose not to select a mate, as none were suitable for her. She may then be given the opportunity to participate in a Mountain Run in a different tribe so that she may find a stronger, more worthy male but...Va'Rakukanna, your concerns are unfounded. Never has this happened in the history of the Run on the Mountain."

I feel my insides pitch and my lips twist, as if biting down on sour fruit. "So I must either outlast the males or kill them."

"Kill them?" White ridges ripple around the cave. Six-fingered hands cup around hard, abrasive looking lips as low words are traded between the females. The white in the cave intensifies and it has nothing to do with the cold outside.

"I fear I do not understand. This Mountain Run has been called in your honor. We never thought we would be so lucky to have our own Okkari — the Va'Raku — discover his Xiveri mate on a Drakesh moon; however, he did and now that you are well, he wanted to organize the Mountain Run immediately.

"Even if you are not able to present an adequate chase, and even if another male vies for you — which is likely to happen given the interest of our males in the *human* females," she says, trying out the word in my own human brogue. Hearing our language on her tongue feels slimy and an unnatural chill shoots down my spine. "...the Okkari would not allow himself to be bested in this. It is a true test for him. And he will take you no matter how you present. It is known that you are overcoming your injury, my Xhea..."

"Don't call me that," I say, dropping to one knee beside her in the circle and slamming my fist onto the floor where it makes a muted thump. "Don't call me any of these stupid fucking alien names. Don't call me anything. Just tell me everything about the terrain."

She seems to search my face with her gaze, but I shut down, becoming as blank as she appears to me. All I hope to communicate is that I hate her. I don't want to be here. I want to see where my friends are and I want to know that they're alright. I want to go back to my mom and Jaxal and the shitty colony we live on — comets, I'd even take my dad and his new family at this point — but first I need to survive the night.

"Alright." She nods and proceeds to show me the crude outline of the mountain that they've sketched with twigs and rocks and snow. There are a few known hideouts, so naturally I'll be avoiding all of those. There's a copse of trees that looks promising. A mire that looks equally promising and what she describes as a stone labyrinth of *chenag* nests that also looks good.

When I ask her what's beyond the mire, she says, "Nothing. Just the endless ocean on top of the mountain. To the east. As far as the eye can see."

As if on cue, another wind gale whips in through the metal gate, bringing more of the white cold and with it, promises of a slow, torturous death. "And how do the males hunt?"

"By scent. They have been through our cave to track the scent markings of the females they desire most. Several stopped by to tag your scent while you slept, including the Okkari."

What. In. The. Actual. *Fuck.* I stop breathing until pain punctures my lungs and I feel sick with the taste of it. I glance around the barren cavern, imagining the huge, red giant who hunted me those three rotations ago leering over me while I slept, a big blue giant like the one who's probably torturing Miari now as I speak, right beside him. *Why didn't they just rape us again then? Why go through with this sick pageant?*

I shut down my thoughts, refusing to think of Miari because I can't help her now. Or Svera. Whatever gods Svera prays to will keep her safe. They have to. Because I can't get to them here on this planet full of white and cold and aliens. I *need* to get free so I can see them and make sure they're safe. Make sure they're not ruined like I was. *But first, I need to kill the red one.*

The thought of seeing him again makes my whole torso shake and goose pimples break out along the back of my neck. Sweat glosses my palms and I blink wildly, trying to shake the sudden hollowness in my stomach or the wobble to my knees. The women are busy trying to decide how best to traverse the labyrinthine cave system, but I've got half a plan and a lot more questions. *And a promise, one made to myself: I'm going to kill the red one.* That means that there's nothing to be afraid of. I won't let him hurt me.

"If they tag a female they want, but they don't find that female, what happens?"

Some of the women glance at me, colors visible in their faces but I don't know what they mean any more than I understand why we're being hunted like this in the first place.

Still, the leader patiently says, "They may choose to accept another female they have found, but more times than not, they will keep hunting. It is known that most — if not all — males will not participate in the Mountain Run in the hopes of finding their Xiveri mate, but their Xanaxana may still take a shine to one or more of the females. In this case, selecting one such female will be acceptable..."

"And you say that one of them in particular is going to come for me." *Just like last time. Just like every time.* The shakes threaten to overwhelm me. I feel bile shoot up from my stomach and into my mouth. My whole body heaves for a moment, but I swallow, throat burning with the taste of it.

"Hexa, you are his one true mate. His Xiveri mate."

I'd rather burn alive. I turn to the map, hating the female, and open my mouth to tell her every single thing

I think about her precious red alien and what he did to me in the last Hunt, but the bitch cuts in. "She is *nothing*. She is no Xiveri mate. She hasn't been claimed yet. She hasn't done the Mountain Run. She may *think* she's something special because she is this human aberration, but a human will never be our Xhea. Least of all this one," she spits, her last sentence coming out as a nasty, twisted whisper. It almost sounds like a challenge and I *almost* rise to it until I realize that she and I are in agreement about everything. In fact, she's the *only one* I've agreed with so far about *anything*.

I glance at the female whose forehead is as red and menacing as her words are and say, "You're right, but fuck you anyways."

"You disgraceful..."

"Shut up," I bark, loud enough to startle two of the other females, including the slight green one who sits off to the side, looking very small and very terrified. I hate her, yet my protective instincts flare anyways. *She's too young to be here. Just like I was, my first time.* "We don't have time and we need to work together if we're going to outrun — if we're going to present *adequate chase*," I say through gritted teeth.

"They tag us by scent so we need to disrupt it. Everyone, take off your clothes." No one moves. Everyone shines. Rising up to stand, I shout, "Take them off!" My voice is brittle and tortured.

My outer layers are bound around me in ties and knots I don't know how anyone is supposed to be able to get through. They make for slow progress, but I don't let any of the alien freaks help me. That would require them touching me and my stomach rebels at the thought.

Once the first two of the women are in the nude, shivering and turning blue — well, an even bluer blue — I bark, "Trade. Take each other's clothes. Tear bits of yours off and give it to someone else. The more people you can trade with and the more scents you can wear, the better."

I tear off strips of my own suit and hand them out to the females. As I reach the leader, I thrust a strip into her hand and ask, "You get what I'm doing here?"

She grins and nods, her ridges shining a weird funky orange, marred by silver streaks. If I had to guess, I'd say she was excited more than anything. "You are clever. I see now why the Okkari has organized the Mountain Run for you. He wishes to win you. He wishes for you to know that you will be well provided for by your Xiveri mate."

She drops her tone and leans forward, but I recoil, unwilling to get too close. Her breath forms clouds as she speaks, shocking and white and hovering between us but only for a blink before the wind steals them away.

She says, "He has told tales of you. Of how you are a warrior who battled a khrui. I see such tales are not so tall after all. You also honor us now. For with your scent marking us, it will make us desirable to more of the males. It is said you human females are very fertile. Perhaps the males will scent fertility between us, and perhaps, by Xana and Xaneru, it will be so."

I bite back the insults on my tongue and the urge to punch her right in the center of her stupid face. The one who pulled me up into a fucking tree like a scarecrow is telling stories about me now? Singing my praise? He has the audacity to run his mouth about me and call me *heroic* when all he did was destroy who I was? I *liked* her.

I liked her so much better than me, whatever this *thing* is that exists now.

"Just take it." I drop the scrap of fabric between us and thrust away from her, turning to the last woman left. The bitch. "Give me your suit."

Her ridges flare black, but I see the hesitation in her gaze.

"Give me your fucking suit. Your woman here says we don't have much time. You want the Okkari for yourself, don't you?"

"How do you know this?" She rasps.

I laugh and she winces, though I can't fault her for it. The sound of my own laughter disgusts even me. It didn't used to sound like that. It used to be high and light and draw stares from colony boys and smiles from the elders. It used to infect everybody. Now laughter comes out of me as infected as disease, snarling and hacking.

"I can read your fucking mind," I tell her, "now give me your suit."

She falters. "Humans have such an ability?"

I roar out my irritation and lunge for her, dragging her suit away by force. She issues a weak scream and lets me take it, putting up no resistance. I don her suit as quickly as I can and watch her try to fit her much longer limbs into mine. Hers bunches up around my elbows and ankles, which would slow me down if I planned to do much running, which I don't. *No running this time.* This time when I see him, he'll know that only one of us will leave this planet alive. Or neither of us. *Both options suit me just fine.*

"I'm heading for the swamps. I need to disguise my scent as much as possible. I need two women with me, four need to brave the caves, and four need to head to the trees. They'll provide the least cover, but are there climbers in this group?" Five of the women raise their hands tentatively.

"Good. You four will go there. You'll go to the caves," I say, pointing to the one I've singled out. "I need three more to go with her. Make sure you don't go in a group with someone whose scent you're wearing. We need to disperse them, muddle our scents as much as possible. Make it hard." A few more hands go up. "Fine. That leaves you with me." I point to the leader and to the one alien who hasn't spoken yet. The green one. *Is it a surprise I've chosen to bring her with me? To look out for?* I feel my insides crumble at the thought, the tower of swords I've built around my shriveled mass of a heart, tottering.

I look away from the girl, grateful for the leader and the distraction she presents. "Your plan is to hide in the mire?" She says.

"Just until nightfall. Then I make my way across the forest and to the village. You said there's a village at the base of the mountain, right?" She confirms and before she can interject whatever miserable tidbit of information she'd like to, I assert, "Then there must be a skyport. Some kind of transportation center to other planets and worlds. I need off this one."

"We among the Okkari do not believe in such things," the bitch snaps, stepping closer to me and my little group. As she does, her tone gentles, "But you were brought here on the Okkari's private transport. He keeps it here," she says, pointing to a spot on the map at the end of what looks to be a valley. "It is not far, but you couldn't seek it out now if you wanted to. This is the way the males will come from. You will need to get there under cover of darkness."

"Good," I tell her.

Meanwhile, the leader's face glows an unsettling color — something like pale pink and yellow and a much darker red. She opens her mouth and says something, but the sound is immediately swallowed by the gates creaking as they open. They slide to the side, stone on stone, sounding very much like thunder. A shockingly white world assaults my senses and I step through the crowded females, going to meet it head on. I bark out a few last orders before gathering the leader and the green one and taking off into the white.

We run and as we run, I understand a new pain. The wind whips my face, cutting into it in a way I've *never* felt wind cut before. It *hurts* whatever this cold white is, spearing me like the pointed blades of miniature warriors. My whole face feels like it's bleeding. My lips are swollen, my nose doesn't stop running. I can taste the disgusting flavor of my own snot whenever I lick my lips. My feet are weighted stones. My lungs burn. I can't get enough air. This atmosphere is too thin for human lungs and the gravity feels greater. I've never felt so heavy.

The leader looks at me worriedly several times, but I refuse to slow our pace. I thought I was a warrior, but I'm realizing that even if I could outfight either of the females with me, they were *born* in this place. Or at least they know it like a parent, and they treat it like kin. Even when the white powder falls in our path and we sink into it up to the knees, they just calmly wade through it, like the cold white is nothing more than dry leaves dancing in a summer breeze. It doesn't seem to matter to them that we're going uphill *and we're always going up a fucking hill.*

They call it a Run of the Mountain for a reason.

The mountain is a bold and treacherous thing, knobby and stark. Mostly cold layered atop stone. There are no trees to be seen in the haze of the thickening storm. It just gets thicker, until I can see less and less of the world around me. Until only the dim vision of a far horizon remains.

But I can feel the calm of the females beside me, marred only by their excitement when the sky starts to darken and they're sure the males are on their way. My heart is a spike in my sternum, punching and clawing and biting and shredding as I imagine being caught by *him*...I promise myself that I'll fight — that I'll die — before I let him laugh at me like that again. The memory only amps up my frustration and my determination. I set the pace. I lead them in the direction the leader dictated on the map and for all my human weakness, I am the first of us to reach the mire.

It looks like a living thing — the only thing we've come across that isn't white. Instead, it's *pink*, a color that on the human colony would be considered unnatural. Moving slightly, it bubbles in some places. I avoid those as I wade into it up to the waist and am pleasantly surprised that it's warm.

"What is this?" I say, scooping up a handful of the stuff and letting it plop from my gloves to rejoin the rest. Steam spits from the thick mud around me in some places, while around the entire mire, it rises to meet the cold white to create a white world with no end. There is no sky. Nothing beyond this mire, this moment.

I try to keep my arms out of the pink goo. The effort is useless and reminds me of something. *Helping my grandfather knead dough as he tells me a story. It's hot by the ovens, even under the shade, but I'm enrapt as he tells me his tale about a man who once tried to push a boulder up a mountain only to keep slipping back again. The boulder was too heavy for him.*

I was too young then to understand the point of the story, but I was horrified when my grandfather told me that eventually the man got his insides pecked out by crows, or maybe he was burned by the sun, or maybe that was somebody else. All I remember is that I never, ever wanted to be like him.

I release my arms and sink into the mud real slow and when I surface, it's to the sound of laughter — the leader and the green one both. Only the leader looks at me though, while the green one tries to cover her mouth with her hand. I squish pink gunk back from my face, feeling so much heavier for it as it sticks to my hair and coats my fur coverings without penetrating. The edge of my mouth tilts up threateningly, but I quickly remember where I am and squash the sensation.

I wrap my mud-wrecked hair up in my fist and knot it at the base of my neck and as I work, I feel myself starting to slow. My mind skips, like a rock over packed sand, and my ears cock back. *It sounds like thunder.* I turn, but everything is the same. Just white, even if a strange smell is calling me forward. That startling fauna is back again, bringing an oasis with it. Minerals and rich, fragrant earth. It smells like something ancient. *Like something known.*

"Xhea," I hear the leader call. *Known, but not by everyone. Known by me alone.* "I think we have gone far enough. Soon we will be out of the mire and on the tundra. We may be too far for even the most fearsome warriors to follow…"

"I thought you said we were supposed to be far."

She considers her answer. "There is *far* and then there is dangerous. It is expected that we want to live, and since we do, we should act accordingly. We shouldn't go onto the tundra. There are creatures there far more fearsome than a few males."

There is nothing more fearsome. I plunge ahead without answering.

She tries again. "There is a place we can rest…" Her voice cuts off. She hears it. I heard it a few seconds before. The sound of pounding. There's a scream — no, not a scream, a cry of rage. A deep, booming cry. A resounding decree that makes my toes curl and my tailbone tuck under. It's a roar that hearkens only death and demands. *He's here. He's coming for me. And I'm supremely fucked.*

I don't know who I am anymore, all I feel is my bones start to unravel. Jaxal wanted me to be strong but he didn't prepare me for this. For seeing him again and the horror that it would bring because right now it's washing over me like a frontal assault. I can't stand. I can't fall either. The mud holds me in place and I feel carved into it now and I don't dare move as the mist to my right shifts and parts.

I duck down lower, quickly trying to kick up into a horizontal position so that the top of my head doesn't stick out of the mud. I kick and stroke the mud, but I must make too much noise because I can hear the male roar, his cry different and more imminent than the last had been because he's right here, right on us.

The green female squeals, giving away our position entirely and I hear thrashing in earnest now. It feels like eternities pass in less than a heartbeat. I lie there, still, hoping not to be found. Hoping he doesn't find any of the others either. *Where did that thought come from? Just leave them. They're* aliens. *They'll probably enjoy it anyways.* But when the leader lets out a shout and I hear the sounds of struggle return in earnest, my whole body is propelled into motion.

I come upright to see the leader just a few paces from me, though the mud made it feel like she was so much farther. There's an alien — a male one — curled over her. He has a strip of my fabric in one hand and seems to be staring between her and it in confusion. I feel lightning rip up my spine at the understanding that *I'm* what he was looking for, but I also feel an equal lightness. His skin is blue. Not red. A little balloon bursts just below my lungs and suddenly I can breathe again. *And if I can breathe I can fight.*

The male isn't armed, which sucks because I'd been counting on being able to take his weapons away from him. Doesn't matter. I wade closer towards him and see that he's got the same idea, only he hasn't let go of the female even though he's looking at me. Like he thinks he'll be able to take the both of us. *Fat chance.*

He stretches his other hand towards me, intending to grab me by the neck. I block with my left forearm and upper cut with my right. He's tall so it takes some effort, but I reach his chin with my fist.

When his head whips back, I feel like I'm alive. I also feel grateful for my fur lined gloves because otherwise I might have broken a fist. Jaxal luckily had me practice on wooden boards until my hands bled. He said their skin would be stronger, tougher. That they'd be hard to kill. And I'm ready.

I grab the leader's arm and wrench her out of his grip. "We have to fight him together!" I shout to her without waiting for her answer.

I turn back to the male and watch pink mud spray across his stupid lit up face when I hit him again and then a third time, and then another. Frustrated, he swipes both claws for me, catching my forearms and tearing through the leather covering them.

Nicking me, he doesn't wound me or slow me down. There's too much mud between us, and I'm wearing too many clothes and him, almost nearly as many. His hides look thinner, more agile, but are no less tough when I try to gouge them with my nails. Fleetingly, I long for claws. The fact that they have them puts me at a severe disadvantage.

The fight lasts ages. I'm alone. The other females don't help. I hope that they're running away but somewhere in the fray, I catch a glimpse of them. They're just standing like twin pillars in the mud wearing mud on their cheeks and white on their foreheads.

"For fuck's sake!" I shout, "Do something! Anything! Move!"

I don't have time to watch and see if they scattered, but turn and punch the male again. This time when his head flings back and he manages to right himself, he's got copper blood smeared across his mouth and nose and a forehead that's red and angry. He cocks a hand, I block, but then his other makes contact.

I knew it would hurt. Jaxal hit me a thousand times in preparation for this moment. It wasn't preparation enough. It *hurts*. His fists are made of marble and I feel my whole body take the hit all at once.

Suddenly the females are shrieking. I can feel someone's hands on the front of my suit, pulling me out of the mud, but I lift my feet to my chest and kick with my whole being. An *uff* puffs out of the male and I start to backstroke as fast as I can across the mud. He grabs my ankle. I kick with my foot, feeling as my heel makes a lucky connection with his throat. He curses. I curse louder. He curses again. I'm still cursing.

Then both our cursing and our fighting is punctuated by a roar that stalls us too. The sound lights up the white sky, effulgent and deafening. It's louder this time, closer. I glance up towards the perimeter of the mire and as soon as my vision settles, I see something that numbs my withered core.

Like a treeline sprouted in the beat of a breath, there are at least eight males standing there, shrouded in shadow. The one I'd been fighting moves swiftly ahead of me, wielding a swatch of fabric from my hood like a sword. He stands in front of me, blocking my body with his own, and shouts something to the rest that my translator doesn't catch.

"Oki phondaeron!"

Hisses sputter through the males, and even the females behind me gasp and whisper. But then there's a silence. The fog stirs. The men glance around between one another and I can see foreheads flashing in nature-defying colors, and I can hear meaty fists pounding against plated chests, and I can feel masculine energy whipping through the air like a tornado, that riotous undercurrent.

But then my heart catches and the fog clears just enough for me to be able to see a male even larger than the rest, more terrifying, more imposing, more *severe*. He steps forward, slashing a line through the amassed crowd that does nothing but part to make way for him. A few of the males actually scatter until only three remain.

"Taka'ana," comes the booming, terrible bass, the one that seems to let loose something inside of me as I drink in all of his form. Alien and huge and imposing and decidedly male, I know that my first thoughts of him should be of hate, and yet, only one thought comes to me.

He's purple.

He's not red, which means I was wrong about something — many things — that the females said. The male they spoke of before — the one who says I'm his mate, the one who told them stories about me — isn't the one who broke my soul.

Instead the male they spoke of has arrived before me now in all of his glory and as he looks at me with matte black eyes that angle towards his hairline, the world goes quiet. *He's not the red one. He's not red.* He has black hair instead of white. A single white streak runs through it right at the front in the middle. It makes him look like a blade, a knife that will cut me through to the bone, if only he could reach me. But he won't. I won't let him.

I break his gaze and turn back to the mud, ferociously charging through it now. I can see the other side. From there, I'll make it to the tundra. From there, I'll be able to make a stand. My final stand. He may not be red but he's still an alien and what I said was true. *No alien will take me alive, no matter if they're pink or green or red or blue.* Or purple.

"Oki phondaeron Xiveri. Taka'ana!" His roar chases me and makes the ground shake. Or maybe it's just me. A strange vibration sizzles through the air, electrifying it, and a pulse beats in my chest that I swear hadn't been there before.

I reach the other side of the mire and as I pull myself free of the pink, I think about the words he said and what they could possibly mean as the translation turns over in my mind. "With this challenge, I claim my Xiveri."

Fuck it. Now it's time to run. I take off into the tundra, into the cold white.

3

Okkari

Where is she? I am savage in my need now that the battle is ended. The males who vied for my human lost. I took the plates of the one who refused to yield. He crumbled before me. By my bloodright. By the right of Xana.

The rest competed over the remaining females and at my last count *nine* pairs were made. It has never happened before in a Mountain Run. There are always many females too feeble to fight or run or too afraid, or males that are bested by other warriors and left too injured to proceed. Too often, the Xaneru within awakens for no one.

I wonder if it was not because of the decoys that my human gave to the others on this solar so many pairings were created — that even one Xiveri mating revealed itself between Tre'Okkari and Vren'Hurr. I came upon them in the act of their first coupling, distracted by the scent of my own female's clothing in Vren'Hurr's possession. I know it was *she* who gave them. The only she in existence. Who else would have had such cunning but the same carnivorous human who defied our Raku and helped to withhold the Rakukanna from her mate?

Pride surges in my breast, only heightening the desperation of my Xanaxana, which could not be less at rest. I am a calm, calculating male. I am a male who abides by order and tradition. I am a male who needs not seek understanding for in my thirteen rotations, I have seen and experienced more than the elders. I have fought battles. I have shed blood. I have commanded a nation. I have guided our current Raku and his Raku before him.

But now as the fiery winds become threatening, battering me as I charge across the snow, I understand something new. Something *more*. Everything that scripts have ever told me of the Xanaxana and its power were weak analogies for what I feel burning in my chest. It has demands. *They will be sated.* I do not care if I have to tear the mountain down stone by stone.

I pass by males in rut and feel my own xora's steel shaft brush against the barrier concealing it. Given the severe temperatures, my fur coverings are constructed to allow only my xora release for this first rutting. It is late in the season for a Mountain Run. Too late. But it could not be avoided. The moment she woke from the merillian tank, I knew I needed to organize such a run, no matter the conditions or how extraordinary they are. Because nothing about finding my Xiveri mate on that meager, nondescript moon was ordinary. Nothing about *her* is ordinary.

When I returned for her on that moon, it was to find that she had battled khrui, vicious creatures that my own warriors avoid for they demand respect. And even here on this Mountain Run she battled the warrior who came upon her before me. Of the fight I saw, I was impressed.

Humbled, even. When I take her to our den, I will need to tend to her wounds, for she fought like something from the depths of the sea. A she-beast, a gift for our nation. *A gift for me.*

I have been favored by Xana and Xaneru and by the Okkari ancestors to have been given the fiercest of all females — a warrior — for my Xiveri mate. Among all females in the universe, I know that I could have no better. Because there is none.

Every male on the mountain vied for her.

Every male. And I defeated every single one.

My injuries are not enough to stop me from hunting her scent, marred by the mire, towards the tundra. I wonder if she seeks to lose me in the mist. If so, fortune does not favor her, because it's thinning, the storm settling as it prepares for the icefall that will come upon us quickly and with reckoning.

As soon as I am free of the mud, I arrive at the tundra's closest edge. I peer into the dark, watching as white ice and falling snow swirl to meet the darkening sky. A deep maroon, it can scant get any deeper. This is the night here. Almost, but not quite deafening. But not quite.

A scrap of movement floats between ice and sky, as if carried by the mist herself. I charge for it, using my skills on the ice developed and honed since I was a kit when I learned to glide atop water and swim beneath it at the same time that I learned to walk. My chest is burning with the Xanaxana I have so cautiously repressed this past rotation without my Xiveri mate. Now it is fully unleashed and unrepentant.

A snarl disintegrates the composed male I once was. I feel light burst from the ridges above my eyes in an unbecoming display of emotion, but I do not attempt to tamp it. I will let her see just what it is that she does to me.

She cloaked her scent from me, and I am still savaged by the fact that I was not the first male to root her out. I sate myself with the knowledge that though I may not have been the first male to have found her, I will be the last.

Thoran'El discovered her first in the mire and was the male that delivered the bite in my side, but I do not know what he was thinking, attempting to challenge me for her. Did he not know that it would take much more than claws ripping through flesh to slow me in my pursuit? Did he not know that I would take his plates just for his attempt? I will not be shamed by him or any male. Not before her.

Nox, my Xiveri mate, my Xhea, my Va'Rakukanna, my warrior queen, does not demand weakness. I must be worthy of her and this I must do in the *human* custom. I must not only defeat males of my own tribe, but I must best her in battle as well. The thought makes my chest swell. The custom is not mine, but I feel honored to be able to meet her on the battle plain and prove to her in her own traditions that I am the male that she seeks.

Wind whips my hair into a rage around my face as I close the distance to her by half, and then by half again. She must sense my approach for she glances over her shoulder and begins to slow. I slow in response, proceeding with greater caution as I watch in wait for her body to face me. When it does, I am not prepared for it. Neither for the heat of her fire nor the depth of her beauty.

Even caked in pink mire and the copper blood of my kind, the sight of her catches me. I stumble. I am my nation's Okkari and yet, I stumble before my queen like an infant.

I could say it is her eyes, as dark as screa and just as cutting. Hard. Scalding. And somehow that makes the beauty of them all the more potent. The sharpness of that heat-filled gaze against the delicate curve of her cheek. They sit slightly rounded and high before tapering to a smooth chin.

Her mouth is large. Obscenely so. I have never seen a female with pillows on her mouth like these. And stranger still, they contrast the darkness of her skin with a lightness not found in Voraxian biology. Much lighter than the mire, they are the palest pink — a color that could be interpreted as either mild anger or fear, even embarrassment. It makes *me* embarrassed to see it, as if I am seeing something sacred, a permission not yet given. But I do not look away.

Even in her swollen garments, I have seen no greater beauty. The cloud of her hair is tucked away inside the hood of her coat, but I remember what it had been like to see it, and the rest of her, fully bare on the hot, gritty sands of that human moon. Full breasts, a taut abdomen, delicate collar bones...

My Xaneru had wept for her and the Xana had pulled at me, daring the Xanaxana to come forth. I had locked it down and battered it back, knowing that my Raku would never have allowed me to take home my Xiveri bride when he was denied his own. I am a strong warrior, a disciplined Va'Raku and a fair Okkari and it had taken every ounce of power I had to not challenge the younger Raku there. But I had resisted. And I have already used up the reserves of that resistance. What is left behind is but a tendril, a thread, diminishing smoke.

My xora is in a state and all three of my stones pulsate beneath it. Clenched hard against my body, they do not care that the winter winds of the tundra are enough to douse even the brightest flame and take life from the strongest warrior. I had never been foolish enough to consider braving it, but for her, I'd have continued on until the last breath left my lungs. Not even for her, but for the promise of her. For her in the flesh, watching me with the hatred in her eyes that she carries, I'd do much more. I feel as if I am Okkari no longer. *Nox, I am Kinan. The male I was before I took my title. The boy.*

"What are you waiting for?" Her voice rips from her lungs and even though I can sense she is shouting, the words arrive to me bitter and torn. They are a battle cry, I sense, a challenge. My Xiveri mate is not to be disappointed.

I charge.

She jerks, as if surprised by my speed, but she does not run. Warriors far larger and more fearsome than she have withered beneath the coming of the Okkari. I am known. But she does not know me. So she fights me without context, without history. A fight I have not fought since I was a kit. *Since I was Kinan.* I am impressed, proud and above all else, grateful.

My human lunges out of my path. As she dives, I snag a swatch of her muddy sleeve. She brings her right arm across my wrist hard enough to break my hold. I feel white flash along my ridges, followed by a splash of black and on its heels, a wave of green — surprise, bloodlust, amusement — before finally my ridges settle on a fierce orange pride.

The wind picks up speed and when I grab for her, she ducks and I catch only fluttering ice crystals. She holds both fists at her chin, just below her eyeline and though I understand the posture, I have never before seen a female assume it. This is why, when she strikes, my hands are lowered and my torso is left exposed. She strikes me. *My warrior queen is savage.*

The pressure is enough to slow my advance when she strikes me again with her other hand, I realize she is a *dual handed* warrior. I am impressed. Not all of my most seasoned warriors are and yet she attacks me with both hands and with confidence.

I block the second attack with my forearm, but she uses her legs. She kicks up — or tries to, but she is limited in her mobility by the thick padding that covers her, weighted by water and filth. I had feared it was not enough when I allowed the elder females to clothe her for the Mountain Run and I worry still.

She comes from a planet equally harsh but entirely opposite, plagued by suns that whither their fauna to sand and dust, whereas we on Nobu almost never see Voraxia's suns for our world has been claimed by ice that covers everything. Even the sky. My warrior queen is likely cold down to her bones.

Her eyes are slits and I see the way her lower jaw trembles, teeth chattering against the upper in a way that resembles the younglings in their first encounters with weather like this.

She grunts when she kicks and I can tell it is work for her. She is too slow to make contact with my groin and as her left leg lifts, I sweep her standing leg and lurch forward, catching the back of her head and her waist before she hits the ground.

She does not attempt to dislodge my hold on her body — my Xhea is too smart for that. Rather, she punches up, striking me squarely in the face. Immediately after her first strike, she repeats her attack until I feel the skin around my mouth break open on her fist and I taste my own viscous blood. White and then black, green and then yellow are the colors of my ridges once more. *This combination of my emotions will know her well. She pleases me to no end. Even as she strikes.*

I do not dare drop her, but let her punch me twice more — once against my right eye and I feel the skin above my ridges tingle at her punch, but when she hits my left cheek, I hear a slight crack and watch her expression twist into one of pain. Furious that she would bring injury to herself, I growl out my displeasure and the delicate hairs on her eyelids flutter in a way that sends pulses fluttering through me.

I hiss so loudly she flinches, and in her hesitation, I lower her all the way to the icy ground below and plant my palms on either side of her head. Her momentary calm lasts only until I position my lower body on top of hers and she registers my weight.

She resumes her fight in earnest now, body ripping from side-to-side, fingers forming claws even though I know they are not tipped by them. Her hands attempt to score my skin, but she is injured. I snarl. Her bottom mouth pillow shakes.

A momentary grapple ensues, in which time she is able to lift up one knee and spear it into my thigh. She makes contact with sensitive flesh and the pain is palpable, but fleeting. I feel green again, and then orange. And on my tongue, I do not taste the blood of the other males on my skin or the mud from the mire on hers, I taste zxhoa, that delicate, flowering herb. A desert canyon bathed in sunshine. The dizzying dazzle of a faraway star. I hallucinate the Great Ocean of the After and for a moment, bask on the tide. *What is she doing to me? What has already been done?*

Her grunt of frustration drags me into the present as I settle my weight onto her once more. My xora presses against her stomach and I feel my eyes roll back into my skull. The pressure is not something I instinctively know how to fight through. Rather, every instinct in my body is screaming its demands. Demands for release. The Xanaxana in my chest is pitching. It wants to find unity with its pair. And I am the male. The one responsible for guiding the mating. I need to move quickly or rutting fever may grip me and I need to remain in control if I am to satisfy us both for our first time together. I want to satisfy her. I want nothing more.

I reach down the length of her body, finding a small panel taught to us males that will allow my xora entry, but before I can unlace the binds, she slips her hand from beneath mine and swipes for me. I release her covering to snatch her wrist mid-air. Taking precious seconds, I fasten both of her arms over her head and hold them down at the wrist with one of my hands, careful with her injured fingers.

She continues to struggle, to seethe between her teeth. She bites at me and I have to lurch back out of the path of the strike. When I do, she wriggles more fiercely and that's when I see and feel what she's done.

She slips her arms free of the sleeves and jolts forward *out of her coverings. Is she mad? Is her fight truly so desperate she would endanger herself?* Rage swims through me as I take in the sight of her beautiful ioni body surrounded by so much white. The wind is strong, the ice, unforgiving. In trying to stop me, she will kill herself.

Cold fury rips the plates clean off of me. I level my forearm across her chest and press her back. I grab the arms of her suit and force her into it, one wrist at a time, and when I have the front of her suit secured, I yank up on her hood, and use it to cover her thick, mud-sodden hair. The need to claim her quickly dawns on me. I *must* remove her from the cold and take her back to my nest where I will warm her, clean her of the filth caking her skin and tend her wounds. *And then mount her again and again, into the next solar.*

I take her wrists and hold them to the center of her chest with one hand. I find the flap covering her core and untie the strings. My fingertips press forward to find damp fur and beyond that, a searing heat.

Shock.

I did not know what to expect but it was not this. Too curious not to continue my exploration, I delve one finger forward, careful not to cut her with my claws as I explore this mystical fur and this tantalizing heat. My spine stiffens as I finger something wet and so soft catacat silk traders would be jealous.

This cannot be the place where my xora will enter. It cannot be… Withdrawing my fingers, I bring them to my nose and breathe deeply.

Miaba is a winter flower with large, blood red petals and even more violent red thorns protruding from tough, black stems. Rare and highly valued, the flowers carry the most intoxicating scent. But they are deadly. The poison takes effect over days, slowly making it impossible for its victims to take in sustenance until eventually, they starve. A violent death, I never understood why anyone would risk so much for a scent.

But I understand now. My entire body shakes as the Xanaxana rages through me unchecked and unbridled. A scent is worth the risk. Worth coming too close to the thorns. Worth raking them over my flesh.

I inhale again, press the tips of my fingers to my tongue and shudder. *This is what the universe smells like.*

My Xiveri mate has been watching my vulnerable display, but there is little else I can do except hope that she understands the Xanaxana and that she feels it too. She continues to fight until the moment I bring my fingers to my lips, needing to taste that miaba nectar. Then she stills, watching me with enormous, rounded eyes. My fingers slide against my tongue and I suck *hard*, unwilling to let so much as a droplet of her miaba go to waste, for it is just as sweet and bitter as its scent promised. And even more deadly.

I moan. She whimpers.

"Shh," I tell her, stroking her mud-soaked hair back from her face. "I will not leave you to this pain."

She blinks rapidly and begins to fight again as I pull the strings to my own covering and release my xora. I guide my xora forward, finding first her fur before gliding lower to reach the exquisite softness I felt on my first exploration.

I glide the bloated head of my xora over the plump, fat mound of her sex and then delve inwards, through the first of her folds. They part exquisitely around my xora as I stroke up and down and up and in becoming softer and softer the closer to her core I come. *Am I truly supposed to slide my xora into this softness?* Even my xora, softer than the plates on my body, is no match for this. I will surely tear her. The thought makes me cold. One hand in her hair, the other on her hip, my body stills.

Her eyes blink and they are full of gloss. Like the surface of still water, subtly rippling. Seeing me, or sensing my hesitation, she surges up again as if to strike. But this time she speaks — snarls — and I am surprised by her.

"Just do it already! Don't you dare stop! Don't you dare *let* me win!"

There is some hidden weight in her words I fail to understand, though their meaning is clear. I am failing her as a warrior male, for I have not yet fulfilled my right of conquest. And yet...she is so soft...

I position myself fully over her and snarl brutally as my xora presses forward, diving past the first of her folds and reaching a fountain of fire and silk. The pleasure is inundating. She must feel it too because she turns her face to the side, ripping back and forth. Her breath forms in clouds. Her eyes, she shuts.

"Xiveri," I whisper, hating the tint of a question coloring my tone. Okkari does not question. He commands. Yet, I have never been less sure.

The pounding in my chest is riotous but the honeyed thread of the Xanaxana beneath my breast sours and stills. *Something is not right.*

"Xiveri, I wish to look upon you for the ritual mating."

She shakes her head and her bottom jaw sets fiercely. "No. Never."

I frown. This is not the way. I have never completed the Mountain Run before this, but I have heard the tales. I have seen Xiveri mates in each other's presences. The connection between them is visible to anyone within sight. Yet she turns from me as if she attempts to shut such a connection out. *She is human. Perhaps she does not feel Xanaxana in the same way we do. If this is the case, then what I attempt to do to her here will not be a union. It will be a rape.*

A hiss barrels out from between my teeth and my xora shrinks at the thought. Rape. A scandalous, treasonous thing only for those with no honor. I am Okkari. I am its very definition.

I lift my hips and quickly cover my xora, still straining for her. When I settle against her again, I move one hand to the side of her face, the other to her neck. We lay still for some moments while the wind gains in intensity and the cold of the night rises around us. But no matter how gently I stroke her clear, unblemished skin, or how calmly I inhale and exhale — showing her that I am a male in control of his inner beast — she does not release the tension that warps and rattles her frame. She does not stop shaking.

Something is very wrong.

I reach down for the panel still open at the front of her coverings and very carefully tie them back into place. As I work, the backs of my fingers brush against the outside of her mound, finding soft fur there, slick with wetness. I try to swallow my desire, but a haggard groan escapes me, one full of male desperation.

My xora bucks against her thigh and I can feel cream bead along its tip. I am tortured by it, yet it is she who releases a tortured sort of sound. She must sense her defeat is near. She does not know that I will not claim her. Not like this. Not *ever* like this. I have waited all my rotations to claim the female the universe created for me, not even knowing if I would find her. I will not spoil this moment. Claiming her when this sensation of *wrongness* hangs so heavy between us I can scarcely breathe its cloying air, would ruin everything.

Pressing my weight down onto her, she tenses even more, but this cannot be helped. Ice crystals form on her skin. I need to warm her. I need to remove her from this. *But the Run has not been completed. My Xiveri mate remains unclaimed. This is not the way things are done on Nobu. This is not tradition.* A flash of irritation. A thimble of shame. *Tradition is not worth keeping if it causes pain.*

"My Xhea," I say and she winces at the sound of my voice. *Wrong.* This is wrong. Against tradition. Against Voraxia. *But she is not Voraxian.* Perhaps this is not her culture.

Perhaps she has never heard of a Mountain Run or a Hunt as is practiced by the ancient Drakesh, once rooted here on Nobu before migrating to Cxrian. The Drakesh left behind many of their genetic traits to mix with those of the Voraxian populations that remained, resulting in the varied skin tones of my people. And then they left this. But if she is not Drakesh and is not Voraxian, perhaps she does not know of this. Perhaps, to consummate our Xiveri union, she needs something else. Wants something else.

"Xivoora Xiveri." I sound pained as I speak. Realizations have not in any way dimmed the desire coursing through me, threatening to unbecome the male that I am. It is painful, but for her I would suffer through the vilest of tortures, drown in the deepest of seas.

I push her matted, freezing hair from her face and arch my body over hers to try to bring up her declining body temperature. Our foreheads touch and in the quiet space between our mouths where not even the savage wind can reach, I whisper, "Warrior, what do you need?"

4
Kiki

"Warrior what do you need?"

My thoughts are fucking haywire. Every emotion and nerve ending and sensation and thought and breath in my body is wired to stay alive. To block this out. To fight. *Fight! Don't stop fighting!* But I do stop fighting because I've lost. Now all that's left is to wait for him to do to me what the other one did. What he brought me here for.

Then why did he stop?

His huge fingers invaded me against my will and then he tasted my insides. He'd looked wrecked by the taste, like it was some exquisite meal, and me, the full fucking feast. I tried to ignore the heat of his passion. I tried to ignore everything about him, but his scent. I just couldn't block that out. In a way that can only be described as ancient and primal, it called to me.

The oasis. A lush green plant, that rich fauna, a gentle heat. *No. Don't get sucked in. Fight! Kill!* But how do you kill an oasis? Not even the desert can do that.

I moan — sob. *Pathetic. Weak.* To silence the sounds slipping out of me, I bite the inside of my cheek until I taste blood. Pain is better than fear. Pain is better than capitulation. Anything is better than capitulation. I'm supposed to be fighting. *But I'm so exhausted.* And the scent. I just want to give up and dive in.

"Xiveri, what do you need? Speak to me."

"No." He's the enemy. He positioned himself between my legs without my permission. He was going to rape me. He's *still* going to rape me. Why hasn't he? I'm so confused. The smell is cloying. I can't breathe through it. I blink in the sight of his face. He's staring down at me and his strange purple face is illuminated by fuchsia and pink lights beaming from his forehead — a lamp to the counter of the dark red sky behind him and the white swirling through it. The cold white. *But it's so warm in the cage of his arms.*

He frowns and starts to pull back. Hope flares for a second that he'll leave me be — *that he'll leave me to die* — but when he sits back on his heels, he grabs the front of my suit and drags me up.

I try to push him back, but my hand stings from hitting him earlier and I'm slowing down. *No. I trained. Endurance. I can do this.* But I've been in that syrup for who knows how long and I haven't eaten or drunk any water in a day at least and I've fought warriors and battled this beast of a male and somehow none of this matters as much as the scent of his purple, alien skin and the havoc it's wreaking on my mind and will and body.

"Are you injured?" He says and there is a strain in his tone I *hate.*

I try to push him away. "Get away from me."

"Kiki, desist immediately. Stop fighting. You cannot seriously have expected to come out victorious on this day. It is not the Xanaxana's way." *Kiki. He called me Kiki. He knows my name.*

Tears come to my eyes but I refuse to let them fall. *Pathetic. Weak. Small.* Oasis. I grab onto his suit, which matches mine except that it's a hundred times larger. He's huge. What good is fighting? He's right. I was always going to lose. *No!*

His black hair whips in the wind, spraying across my arm as the next gust of cold charges against my skin. It burns. It burns so badly, but it's nothing compared to the strange pain bubbling up inside of me. It's the smell. *Get away from it!*

I try to stand, but my body buckles and I fall into his outstretched arms. "Are you injured?" He says. "Tell me this at least."

I shake my head, willing him to stop talking because the more he says the more potent the smell gets and the more the pain flowers and blooms, but I don't speak. I can't speak. And he doesn't stop speaking. "I will take you down the mountain to the healer. Do not attempt to fight me on this. Your life is too precious to me. I will not risk it."

He starts to stand with me cradled in his arms, but the moment he moves, it hits me. A pain so surreal it's unlike anything I've ever felt before. And I have felt the purest torture. No, this is like that, but a thousand times more painful. *I'd rather be tortured again by Bo'Raku than feel this sort of pain.*

No, I wouldn't. No, I don't.

Because it isn't *pain* that rips through me like a hundred knives through cloth. It's a pain that isn't painful. It's a pain that's demanding something of me and I know exactly what it is but I'd never in a million years do what it wants. It's a pain that says, this monster is mine, bound to me across every lifeline, across every lifetime and there's nothing I can do to prevent it. Nothing I can do to stop the pain. No thing, but the one thing.

"No..." I moan, grabbing hold of his collar to stop him from standing. I look into his pure black eyes and take in his purple face and I commit it to memory. Here is the male that I will hate most for the rest of eternity, and it is because of what I will say next. The words that barrel out of my throat like a bruise as the barbed wire in my abdomen tightens and a surge of liquid and heat spills from my core and wets my suit, all the way down to the thighs.

"Fuck me," I say, and I mean it with every fiber of my being.

5

Kinan

"No," she says, pulling me down to the snow and ice when I attempt to lift her. "Fuck me."

My xora steels, my thoughts blur into nothing, my stomach lurches into my chest. Pain tears its way through me and it is only painful because it is so desperate. Finding myself buried beneath layers of reckless inhibition, I wrench back. "My Xhea, you do not mean these words. I felt your tremors. Tasted your terror…"

"You tasted nothing," she rasps, her voice full of a hate whose provenance I cannot fathom. *I am her Xiveri mate.* And like a Xiveri mate, she clings to me even when her words say something else.

I shake my head. Another burst of wind brings with it threats of the impending storm. The first frost of the season will be sharp and cutting. I cannot have her sensitive human flesh exposed to it. "You are wrong. I tasted *you*."

Her eyes, squinting against the frost, widen slightly. She lifts a hand to shield against the wind, but I switch my body around hers, blocking her from the worst of it.

"And I will tell you what you taste like."

Her lower mouth pillow trembles. She shakes her head, but I can *feel* her arousal floating through the air, the scent of it impossibly potent and impossible to ignore. It burns down my throat as I swallow. "You tasted like sweet water...and I am thirsty."

With no warning issued, I grab her legs below the knees and wrench her body back so that she falls prone beneath me, her knees spread wide. So inviting. I ache to tear through her coverings and take her in fully, just as fully as I ache for her to take me. But she is still frightened. And I do not know why. But I know that I can still help her.

"I can help calm the pain of the mating call, if you give me this permission."

"Yes! Fuck. Please. Fuck me..." Her vulgar words displease me, but I must assume this is the fault of the Xanaxana. It can make even the most stoic of beings desperate, and I am sure that my Xiveri mate would be a stoic creature.

I make the pleasure expression as I cup her mound through her clothing and watch her head fall back on a moan. "Oh stars, please help me..."

I feel the need calling to me and I imagine that for her slight figure, it must be even more torturous. "I will help you. But only on one condition..."

"Fuck...oh fuck, what?" Her head tosses back, her eyes still squeeze.

Gently, I whisper, "You will need to look at me."

She doesn't speak for a long, shaky moment, but when she finally releases the tension of her mouth, opens her lips and her eyes in the same beat and looks down the length of her body at me, she catches her breath. It is as if she sees me for the first time and I cannot help but inhale, hoping to appear naught but strength before her. I roll my shoulders back and massage her core with the heel of my palm.

"Do not look away."

Water comes to her eyes then and I am made curious by it, but not curious enough to stop and root out its meaning. It is enough for now that she looks at me, even if I can still feel the tremors running along the insides of her thighs and the tension radiating throughout the rest of her body. Even if she still carries this strange fear with her that is just as alien to me as she is, she faces it for the sake of the Xanaxana.

My hands reach for her covering and I do not have patience for the ties fastened on either end. I tear straight through them and her whole body jerks, but she still does not break my gaze. I offer her my pleasure expression, an expression I have not made in some time.

"You are brave, my warrior." I wrench her hips up to meet my mouth, inhaling the scent I find there. So strong, my eyes nearly roll back into my skull — would have, had I not vowed to her not to break the connection. "My Xhea."

She opens her mouth, but when no words come, I plunge forward, mouth catching her core and devouring it. She moans so loudly it shakes her whole body. She also closes her eyes. I wrench back, immediately severing the connection between us even though it pains me. Her eyes flutter open and she squeezes her fists, reaching for me.

"Why…please…why did you stop?"

"You looked away."

She clenches her teeth, but nods and I feel the pleasure expression on my mouth again at the unreasonable nature of this pact we have bartered. But I don't care or question it. I lean in once more, this time licking a line from her rear sex up through her folds to a mysterious nub that sits at their crest.

Her hips buck hard enough for my hold to slip. Voraxian females are not so responsive as this and I am surprised by her, as I seem to be perpetually. I concentrate on this nub and her groans grow louder, deeper, and more desperate. Feeling powerful to reduce my warrior queen to this, I lathe her full sex with the ridges lining my tongue, tasting her insides. In a fit of urgency, I blunt one of my claws between my teeth and mercilessly plunge the length of my finger inside of her core. She is *tight*. A feeling of uncertainty sweeps over me, even as I drink from her miaba ocean. *Will I harm her when I seek to enter her?*

"Oh stars...oh stars..." She is writhing madly now and my pumping becomes more frantic. The ridges of my tongue flick at her nub, my finger slides deeper into her, reaching a desperately tight wall, and I feel her suddenly, all at once, clench. *Her core can tighten even more?* I cannot believe it. She is the tightest thing I could have ever imagined and yet, here she is shuddering and moaning and gripping and pushing and kicking as spasms warp and twist her slight form.

Covered in mud, screaming into the frost, she is pure fire. Heat. Warmth. *Mine*. An honor to worship.

A gush of liquid floods her sex. It crashes around my finger and coats my mouth and chin. It *drips* onto my hides, onto my neck. I pull back and stare at the dark brown of her beautiful body and with my blunted fingers, I open her lower lips. Just as shocking, she is pink here too, an even brighter color than that which lines the insides of her mouth. Her core pulses with its own heart, and the sight has my own heart stuttering a beat.

Her hips spasm and she jerks back when I lathe her nub once more. "Oh no, please. It's so sensitive." Her eyelids flutter and she meets my gaze and I cannot help the pleasure expression from taking over me. My Xanaxana is more at peace than it once was, even though it was she and not I who found some small measure of release.

I reach forward and she is slow to react, as if she is swimming through the mire once more. She does not move away from me in time and I touch her face. "You are cold," I say, concerned.

She shakes her head and bats my arm away. "I don't care." Her breathing is heavy. Off. "I just want more." She licks her lips and spreads her thighs wider. "I need you to fuck me. It hurts. Everything still hurts."

I nod at her. "Hexa, the Xanaxana is strong."

"Then please, just do it. I know that's what you brought me here for. It *hurts*." I understand her meaning, even if I do not understand her words.

I swallow, for the thought of what she has asked of me leaves me dangerously close to trembling. "Lie back."

She does, body flopping down as if it has no elasticity. She tries to turn her face from me again, but with my finger — blunted and still covered in her juices — I tilt her face up. I lower her hips to the ice and cover her body with mine. Releasing my xora, I position it at her entrance, her wet heat scoring me like a candle pressed directly against flesh.

I cradle her face in one of my hands and hold her hand in my other. I twine our fingers. I stare deeply into her glossy, haunting eyes. And yet…I find myself unable to proceed. I do not know enough about her anatomy and I *need to know…*

"Will I tear you?"

She whimpers but does not answer me. I know she knows what I mean.

"You will answer my question."

"Why do you care?"

Shock. *What could she mean by this?* I do not know. And so I harden my grip around her. "Answer me."

She blinks quickly, breath puffing in white clouds between us. I fight the urge to taste it, to taste her mouth. The pillows she has there call to me on a primitive level, the sensation akin to the urge to rut. I do not understand it.

"No. You won't tear me." Her voice croaks quietly, lodged as if from disuse or extreme emotion. That is when I notice that she is not fighting. Quite the opposite. Her small, five-fingered hands are holding me back.

"Are you certain? I have read that untried females often feel pain."

She shakes her head, and a single droplet of water escapes her gaze and winds its way over the curve of her cheek. "I am not untried."

I do not feel disappointment, but rather, a seed of doubt. She is so strong. Worthy of an Okkari. *But am I worthy of her?* I have not mated before this, but I hope to honor her. I nod once, firmly and assuredly on the outside, while inside I can hope only that she is right and that she will feel pleasure from this and no pain and if there must be pain, then only for an instant.

Just before I press forward, I hold for one final moment so that I may hold it in my memories for all of time, crystalized. I wish to forget nothing. From the smell of the mud freezing in her hair to the snow crystals balancing on the tips of her curling eyelashes.

I then speak the ancient words and I do so slowly, knowing that she can understand them but that she will not understand their significance. She cannot. Not yet. "I cover your flesh with my flesh. I cover your heart with my hearts. With this union, you are claimed. To serve as Voraxia's Va'Rakukanna. To serve as Nobu's Xhea. To be my Xiveri mate. With this union, I am yours. To be your Okkari, to be your sword, to be the sire to our unborn kits, but to be your servant above all else."

"Are you ready, my Xhea?"

She nods jerkily. "Yes."

"Do not break my gaze."

So softly I almost cannot hear her, she replies, "I won't."

With nothing else between us, I press my hips forward to meet hers. My xora shifts past the first of her folds, driving deeper…and deeper until I can proceed no further. Something is *blocking* my forward progress and as soon as I reach it and test its elasticity, my Xhea gasps, surges back over the ice and grabs my shoulder with her free hand. Fear passes across her face and it is so violent, I feel my hackles rising, as if there is an opponent before me I could slay.

Steeling myself, I take a deep breath and press one hand to her forehead to calm her while the other continues to grip her trembling fingers. *She said she was not untried. Why would she lie about this?* And then I remember… "It must be the merillian. It healed you inside and out. Your barrier will have grown back, so I must break it if we are to continue. You will tell me if you wish for me to continue or stop."

She doesn't say anything, just watches me with an expression I cannot put name to. I feel frustrated in these humans' lack of ridges, but there will be time for questions and understanding later. For now, I struggle to hold true to my words. I struggle not to slam into her and break her apart.

"I'm a...virgin again?" She stutters.

"Hexa, you are untried. As am I," I tell her, though I do not know why. "This will be a first for both of us."

Her eyes close for longer than a standard blink, and I feel something small burst in my chest at the realization that her eyelids do not close left to right, as mine do. *So alien. How could I have ever wanted anything other than her?* "I want you to continue," she says in a small, pinched voice.

I exhale, relieved. *Exhilarated. Frightened in my own right.* "Xhivey, my Xhea. I will break it now."

I push forward as gently as I can, but realize quickly this causes her more pain. Her eyes close but I command her to open them, and as she does, I thrust forward, impaling her cleanly. I feel the barrier break as my xora slides home and bellow out a moan. Gasping and whimpering, she grips my upper arms in her hands and I hate that I cannot feel her hands on my bare flesh.

I hold her steady as she squirms, trying to get comfortable. I press my forehead to hers and exhale heavily. "You are safe. It is over. From now, there is only pleasure."

Her voice catches. More gloss builds in her eyes as she watches me. And as she watches me, her hands come down onto my shoulders. Her touch turns tender and with that encouragement, I feel a multitude of colors blast over my ridges. I thrust again, moving as gently as I can, even if this defies all of my instincts to mount and rut and breed so savagely.

Moving gently in and out of her gripping, desperate heat, I feel supernovas explode behind my eyelids on each thrust. Yet our gazes never break, even as I see starlight. Even as she gasps and her back arches.

I feel as if we have only just begun and yet her mouth opens on an inhale, distending, her hips jerk up, she fists the hides covering me and bites her bottom mouth pillow so hard I fear she will break skin, even with her blunted teeth. And then I feel the pressure. Her core *squeezing* my xora to the point of pain, making me realize with elation and with horror that the battle is not yet complete. It is a full-out war not to find my release right after hers — one that I lose.

I cover her body with mine, circling her shoulders with one of my arms so we cannot get closer. I stare into her eyes and feel her thighs tighten around my hips. My xora is bathed in the rush of her wetness and my Xanaxana explodes through me in relief just as my seed explodes into her, pumping into her core, filling her. I black out as I transcend this plane and enter another and when I come down I feel my weight settle onto my Xiveri mate below the waist, while my arms continue to support my torso.

I glance down at her face and see that she wears a shocked expression, yet one corner of her mouth is tilted up for a moment before the moment fades. I touch her cheek, watch her shiver, remember where we are and feel the chill of the outside air. Without waiting for her to react, I pull my stiff xora from her wetness and rip the coverings away from her body so I can tuck her cleanly into my suit. She is cold, and I am warm. *It has nothing to do with my needing to feel her close against me. Nothing at all.*

When she does not fight me and she does not protest, the Xanaxana rumbles in my chest, satisfied that this human mating tradition is clearly now complete. I cannot help but be pleased to have honored her as I gather her muddied hides and drape them over my front to provide her with extra covering, and take my human prize down the mountain to the village where my people — where *our* people — wait, eager to meet their Xhea.

6
Kiki

Shock. It must be shock. That's the only explanation I have as to why I'm no longer fighting. Why I'm not even running. Why I'm just...waiting.

I feel less like a human and more like a puddle, sunken into the white floor. Everything here is white. Why is it so damn white? As blank as the thoughts firing inside of me. I've got nothing. Nothing but a desperation not to feel like this. I'm so hot I *hurt.* I hurt *bad,* and it has nothing to do with the cuts on my arms or the swelling bruise on my face that makes it hard to see out of my right eye and it has everything to do with the unsteady lurch of my stomach when I hear the door whoosh open behind me.

There he is. The male who carried me down the mountain. The one who tucked me into his clothes, his enormous dick *dripping with my orgasm and his own* pressed against my stomach. The one who took me down into a valley of white so that we stood amidst so many glass homes that looked as if they were cut into the surrounding mountainside, and meticulously arranged.

There, we were swarmed by more of *them.* Aliens. My enemy — each and every one. So many jewel-toned faces staring in at me, and I hated the slash of fear that cut across my chest like a blade and the way I'd clung to the one the others called Okkari. I hated clinging to him the most. Because it felt way too much like need. *Like safety.*

Trying to fight my panic, I'd bared my teeth and met each of their gazes wild-eyed to let them know I'm not afraid *even if I am petrified* and that I don't think anything about them but the hatred I feel coursing through my blood like a sickness. I wanted them to know I hated them and so that's how I hoped I looked, but...they didn't seem to care. For all my attempts at savagery, they just stared at me in awe.

Because the big purple male had unwrapped some of the bindings holding me to him, exposing my chapped and battered skin to the elements down to the neck. He'd pulled my hair, thick with mud and frost, away from my face and though he hadn't spoken to me, he spoke *of* me, regaling those gathered with the tale of his Run on the Mountain as if it were ancient lore, instead of just ended.

His voice had been deep when he spoke of my cleverness, telling them how I'd marked the other women, cloaking my scent. He told them how I'd bested him.

How I'd. Bested. Him.

He told them that he hadn't been the first warrior to find me, but when he did, I'd stopped and turned to face him and I'd challenged him with my words, daring his approach. The congregation that pressed in on us from all sides gasped at that.

He even told them...he even told them of...when my...when my insides... He even told them about my pussy clenching around his dick — *the treacherous, evil bitch* — robbing him of what he called his *zah-nah-zah-nah* first mating. There had been murmured whispers, sounds of adulation, of admiration. Murmured words that, despite how hard I try to deny it, had been wreathed in respect.

My chest clenches. I haven't ever been talked about...not like that. Because when he spoke to the people around him, he didn't tell them about my beauty. He told them about my might. *Warrior, what do you need...*

And then the purple brute carried me off to his house where I sit now, fully naked except for the ruined white fur I've got clutched around me, covered in filth that's mostly pink. My muscles are soup, but they're also clenching in little spasms, lightning pulses that are telling me something that can't possibly be true. *Need. I need him again.* But I'd rather cut myself down first.

Meanwhile, he just stares in at me, limitless gaze filled with a lust that I know well. It intensifies the longer he watches me and I know I need to fight it. Forcing myself to break his gaze, I quickly scan my surroundings. Like many that ringed the white valley, the front half of the alien's home is glass while the back half is buried in a mountain made of hard black rock. Through the clear panes, I have a view of the entire village below, which is now just scattered orange lights glowing against a backdrop of shadows — and white.

The cold white falls from the sky slowly, in huge star-shaped lumps each as big as my palm. *They're stunning. What would Svera think? What would anybody on the colony think? None of us have ever seen anything like this before.*

I shake my head and focus on the steps I need to take. One after the other, just like I'd place my feet *if I could feel anything besides pulsing need below the waist.* One. Get away from him. Two. Get away from this house. Three. Get away from this planet. I should probably find some clothes somewhere in there, but fuck it. I'll hazard the snow if the docks are close. *But where are the docks? Where are the transporters? How did we get here?*

For a moment, my thoughts flash to my mother. *Sitting between her legs. Her fingers yanking tangles out of my hair unforgivingly.* I wince from the memory, and from the realization that I don't have a way back to her. *Does it even matter? You've been dead to her for rotations.*

I clutch at my chest as my gaze finally lands on a small table against the far wall. A few objects lie scattered across it and though none of them look sharp enough to stab, they could be heavy...if only I could reach them. If only I *would* reach for them.

But I don't. I just...sit there.

It must be shock. That's the only way to explain it. *Shock doesn't account for lust.* My gaze flicks back to him.

He holds onto the frame of the door as if it's the only thing keeping him anchored, from tearing his way forward. The muscles in his corded arms ripple and muscles I'm sure human males don't have slither and pulse down his neck, across the plates slathered across his chest where pectorals should be. The top half of his suit is bunched around his hips and his black hair hangs in thick, mud-locked chunks all the way down his back to tickle the sharp V-indentation that starts at his abdomen and disappears below the edge of the suit where I can no longer see it.

He's covered in strips of brown mud and darker smears of grey that I *think* is the blood of his own kind. It covers his breadth — and he is broad. I knew they were broad. I've always known. But he seems bigger. More powerful. Maybe it's because that's how he is. Or maybe it's because that's how I see him after what he did...or maybe, after what he didn't do. He's huge. And powerful. I can't believe I fought him. I can't believe he felt, at any point, defeated. And I can't believe that at no point, I did.

He took me. He took me in the way I feared the most. In the rough way I'd once been taken. In the way the red alien ruined me.

But he ruined me more. This purple alien with a single blazing streak at the front of his hairline just as white as the outside's cold must have broken something in me when he looked me in the eyes and whispered his words, that unholy incantation, that blasphemous rite. *Warrior,* he called me, *Kiki.* He asked me if I was untried, but I...I felt it break. I felt it go. *I got to try again. I got to start over.* And when he took my *virginity*, I hated how much I loved it. Because I loved it so much it hurt to breathe. It still hurts. *And I regret nothing.*

Never, I promised myself, *never again with any male. Kill,* I promised myself, *kill any alien that I come across.* But I helped alien females and I even defended one and I helped males find alien females — even if that was unknowingly — and when I was down in the village, I saw the leader wrapped in the arms of a male, covered in pink mud and smeared in a brutal happiness that brought tears to my eyes and heat to my cheeks. *Never again*...but I started over again and I started over again with him and he's as alien as they come.

"My Xhea," he says, voice low and deep. It pulls at my insides. "I will...take care of you." His words are full of implication that draws an unfettered moan from my throat.

He closes his eyes — eyelids blinking from the side — and seems to struggle to open them, despite the commands he's given me. "I will first tend to your wounds. These are your new hasheba. They are honored to tend to you. Kuana and Kuaku, take your Xhea to the baths."

The soft patter of footsteps against the soft white floor pulls my attention away from the male. There, two female aliens stand in the doorway and I'm shocked to recognize both of them. They were both with me in the cave and I think again of Svera and her Tri-God for a moment. Of *course* these two females would be here. The bitch and the green one.

"The hasheba are here to assist you. Do not be wary of them."

As he speaks, I lock eyes with the bitch. Somewhere along the way she's been cleaned up and freed from her hides. Now she just wears a leather, fur-lined skirt and nothing else. Her chest is flat, just plates studded by little nipples slightly darker than the rest of her, and even though I can't search her expression for tells, I can feel the bite of her claws in my flesh when she reaches forward to grab my arm. I break the hold with one upward cut of my wrist and she stumbles back, ridges flashing white and then pink.

"I don't want them to touch me," I say, but my throat is gravel and sore and I don't recognize the sound of my voice. *It's been too long.* Since the last Hunt when I was hurt, I hadn't spoken a word until the Mountain

Run. *So much hard hating work, undone.* "I don't need any help."

There's a lag, in which time the male just stares at me passively. How can he be stone when I'm melted wax? I feel *ashamed. Get ahold of yourself! I'll fight.* I'll lose. *I'll fight anyways. Until the end. That's what I've been searching for all along, isn't it?* I wince because a seed of doubt has now been planted. I still want the end — whatever end — but in the meantime…I'd like some more of what I felt on top of the mountain too.

Deep rumbling that you can scarcely call words reverberates behind me when I turn away. "Whatever your Xhea wants. And when she is prepared, bring her to our nest with the medical kit."

"You do not wish for us to fetch the healer?" The bitchy one asks.

"*Nox.*" The pressure of his voice fills the entire room and I close my eyes. It's too much. All I see in the darkness of my eyelids are black stars hanging against the backdrop of a blue moon. *Paradise must not be far…*

"I will not have another male in our Xhea's presence until the Xanaxana is settled, not unless absolutely necessary. Now go. Move dutifully, and quickly. I can smell her blood. I need her wounds clean and free of infection before I will suture them. She may be a warrior, but she is still human and human skin is more delicate than I believed possible, so please exercise extreme caution with her."

"Come with us, my Xhea," comes a small voice in front of me. The little green alien is standing halfway across the room, gesturing at another doorway with her six-fingered hands. "We will show you the way."

"I don't need help," I blurt out reflexively. Her forehead blares yellow like a beacon and she quickly looks down at her feet and I feel something horrible rise up within me — a desire to treat her some other kind of way, any other kind of way. A desire to be different. *That would mean getting rid of hate, but without hate, what is there? What's left of Kiki?*

Nothing.

"Do not be long, my Xhea," says the voice behind me. The one who is my enemy. The one who calls me queen.

I grit my teeth as a nail bomb erupts inside of me, devastation increasing in impact with each step away from him I take. *Does he feel it?*

He releases a growl and I hear the whoosh of a door, and then a second from the one we pass through. The green alien shoots me tentative glances over her shoulder as we walk down a wide, white corridor, lined on either side with doors like the one we came through. *No, not tentative. Frightened. She's frightened of me.* It occurs to me then that to them, there's only one alien in the room.

"Move." The word is accentuated by a sharp elbow to my spine. I stumble, this time, catching myself on the green alien. She winces when I touch her and I open my mouth to apologize on instinct before thinking better of it.

I jerk away from her and snarl over my shoulder, but the bitch is unmoved. Continuing, the white walls give way to black stone and I start to wonder if the little bit of mind I'd saved hasn't also gone, because I *swear* that the walls have started to heat. I nearly jump out of my skin when I step down on a spot that's hot to the touch.

"Have no fear, Xhea. The dagger mountain has many underwater pools. They are heated and as such, warm the Okkari's house by way of the stone. Screa. It's a conduit for heat." She speaks so softly I can barely hear her and my hatred only grows. *Hate her. It's easier than admitting the truth...*

I say nothing and when I feel another light shove against my spine, I am filled with renewed purpose. Thank the stars for the bitch behind me, because without her, it would be even easier to forget. Too easy. *Maybe that's because I want to...*

Eventually, the black walls have swallowed us up and strange coiled lamps fluttering with light are all that we have to illuminate our path. Cut into the stone walls in intricate shapes, I can't even fathom what could make light like that and for a second, I think of Miari. An inventor as much as she is an explorer, she was always distracted by the way things were put together.

Coming home from training with Jaxal, I find Miari sitting on the stoop of our shack. She has a package in her lap and I appreciate that she doesn't try to smile at me like Svera's always trying. Like the world is good. When Miari opens the long, wrapped gift, I see what she's done. She's attached some kind of electrified blade point to a long staff — one made out of steel, *though comets if I know where she got the metal for that. It's a beautiful gift. The first time I really felt like a warrior.*

My thoughts jump back to the present. *Where is she now? How quickly I've forgotten her...* I'm ashamed yet once again, and at the same time, reminded of where I am and what I am. *I'm human. Not one of them. Never one of them.*

The small green one turns left, stepping through a large archway cut into the stone. I turn towards the misty darkness beyond it, peering into the chamber hesitantly, but when I don't move forward I'm rewarded with another light punch to the spine.

I jerk forward and the green one releases a little chirp. "Kuaku!"

"Don't. call. me. that," comes the acerbic response.

The green one flutters around me, but doesn't try to touch me again. Instead, she steps between me and the bitch and the horrible sensation I felt before returns in force. *She's protecting me...*

"It is what you are," says the green one in high sing song, "A hasheba. And it is a very respected position."

Red surfaces in Kuaku's face and looks wretched against her dark grey skin and the even darker walls behind her. It makes her whole forehead look like it's bleeding. "I am no one's hasheba, *Kuana*," she sneers.

"You are," Kuana says, a little less confidently this time. "And I am proud of my title."

"You are weak. You *should* be proud of your title because it's all you'll ever amount to..."

"Hey!" They both turn to me, white on their faces, and it takes me to that second to realize the word was my own. *And now I'm protecting* her. "For comet's sake, shut up. I just want to get this mud off me."

"Of course, Xhea, apologies." Kuana rushes ahead and pulls aside a heavy black curtain that I'd mistaken for a wall. Beyond it, the white in the air is thick — too thick to see the far wall through. It looks...well it looks like steam. But how can it be? I've seen steam before on very hot days and over boiling pots of water — there were pockets of steam floating above the mire — but I've never seen so much of it at once.

"Is that a *bath*?" My mind blanks as I approach Kuana. She holds the curtain aside and a very small smile quirks on her face.

"Hexa, my Xhea. It is."

I inhale deeply, moving towards the black basin nestled halfway into the room's rocky floor — the steam's provenance. "What's that smell?" I hear myself say, speaking as if the voice is not my own.

"It contains healing and cleansing minerals, to help you ward away infection."

"I can smell them."

"I hope they are to your pleasure, my Xhea."

"Yes," I whisper, lost. And then because I forget to hate her for one singular moment, I whisper a vulnerable truth, "I've never had a bath before."

Realizing what I've said, I glance up, embarrassed. White flashes again, only this time is followed by something darker, the color of cinnamon. She bows to me slightly, breaking my gaze. "Baths are an everyday occurrence here, my Xhea, you will have many. As many as you like and as often. We have no shortage of hot water…"

Her voice is killed by the bitchy one's laughter. "That doesn't surprise me. You're a filthy species, covered in all that disgusting hair and sweat. I can still smell you through the mud. Unfortunately, I don't think a bath will ever help you be rid of it…"

"Kuaku," Kuana says again in a surprised tone. As if she can't imagine anybody ever doing anything evil to anyone. As if the universe is truly a good place in her eyes. "You shouldn't speak to the Xhea this way. Okkari would have you banished for it."

"And who will tell him? You? You are a coward and this flimsy little wretch here is little more than an animal. Would he even believe her?"

I round on her and try to force some elasticity into my limbs, which are hot soup at this stage and little else. Her bug eyes widen as I advance and I can see my reflection in them. *I look like a monster, like the animal she says I am.* I falter, but only for the second it takes me to remember that she's the enemy and I'm meant to fight her. Lifting my arms, they're too weak to level a proper punch so I throw my whole torso forward instead. I smash my forehead into her mouth, butting her like a beast. She shrieks and stumbles back into the hall and I grin when the automatic door glides shut between us.

I turn to where Kuana cowers by the entrance, clutching the heavy hide curtain to her chest. After a few seconds, she says, "Are you alright, Xhea?"

"Don't call me that," I mutter.

I approach the massive black basin sitting in the center of the room, water rendered black inside of it. I twirl my fingers over the steam that coats it and my heart pounds harder when I lift one leg over the edge, and then the other. I sink in. *Paradise...* I close my eyes and give up for just a little while.

Time passes. I don't know how much of it before a small voice finally disrupts the quiet. "Sorry, but what should I call you then? Va'Rakukanna?"

Heat that has nothing to do with the hot water enveloping me licks up my spine. "No. Call me human or nothing at all."

"Human. You wish that I call you *human*?"

"Yes." It's a good reminder. Them. Us. We are not the same *even if she does smile so tenderly it reminds me of Svera.*

"I...alright." She inhales, then exhales shakily. "Human, may I help you remove the mire from your hair?"

I think of my mother and what she would say to me now and wince. I almost say no. Almost. Instead I choke out, "Do what you have to."

Alien fingers in my hair. Running diligently through my locks and over my scalp. Running water — hot water — through my muddied locks... And I don't stop her.

It must be shock. It must be what keeps me from rebelling and killing her and finding my escape. It must be shock...

"I will need a stiffer comb to get through your hair, my Xh...I mean, human. Let me fetch one. I will be right back."

I don't say anything. I don't even open my eyes. She doesn't deserve it. *No. She doesn't deserve this, the way I'm treating her now.* I flinch again and only when I hear the curtain rustle do I dare look up. The room bowls around me, all dark rock with those strange lights switching across its craggy surface. They pulse, making me wonder if they aren't *alive*. It's frightening. *It's incredible*.

I follow the traces of lights until one meets another, then I follow that. I follow the patterns they make until I can't follow them anymore, even tilting my head all the way back.

Wondering how in the comets the water stays hot even though I feel myself shriveling up inside of it, I paw at its surface, watching air bubbles bloop and blip as they rise. I can feel dirt lining the bottom of the once clean basin now and am shocked when I reach back to touch my hair to feel how soft it is.

"I should just drown you now."

I start at the sound of the bitch's voice but refuse to let it show. Instead, I glance dismissively over my shoulder at the female standing against the wall, a white rag to her mouth to staunch the flow of copper, nearly orange, blood. I smile a little at the sight of it.

"What happened on the mountain?" I ask, not because I care but because I want to know why she's here.

Her ridges burn an even brighter red even though her expression doesn't change in the slightest. "What do you mean, what happened? I wasn't selected. The hunters who found me smelled my clothes and ran off again. *You* gave me your filthy human clothes and like the pathetic savage you are, you ruined my chances!"

"You weren't the only one carrying my scent. So why were you the only one who wasn't chosen?"

"I..." She falters.

I grin. "So now what? You're his slave? Or what? A whore?"

"*What*? The Okkari's...if you weren't...I would... you dare insult me!"

I try to revel in her pain but something painful breaks across my sternum. *Shame again. A new friend.* And something else I refuse to name. Because the thought of the Okkari's other women makes me restless. I don't like it.

I shake my head, ready with another insult, but say instead, "Whatever. You're not even worth it."

Her jaw works. It takes her a moment to speak and when she does, her voice is shrill. "You're evil. You are the most dishonorable being I've ever met. I wish that the Great Ocean of the After drowns you and your whole filthy human colony!"

Yes. Good. Hate is good. I inhale, letting it fill me up like a cistern in the rain. Hate I understand. Hate is easier. *Hate is all I have to my name.* "You can go fuck yourself. Why are you even here anyways?"

She scoffs in disgust. "You heard what Hurr said. The Okkari organized the Mountain Run *for you.* Tales of the great warrior Xhea have been spreading for solars. The one who fought khrui. Who helped the Rakukanna escape her Raku in this strange human ritual where you ugly females fight the males instead of accepting the Xiveri bonds the goddess Xana has so generously gifted you. He claimed *you.* He thinks you're his Xiveri mate and he has named *me* hasheba. A disgrace."

Her voice rises. "I have known the Okkari since we were kits. I watched him swing his first sword. I was there when the Drakesh invaded, seeking to claim Nobu females. I was there when the Okkari before him fell and he rose up to take command of our warriors to fight the brutes off even though he was hardly grown. I stood beside him at that chamar and laid down the second to the last stone," she says, colors flaring in her brow — some grey, some blue — before her gaze flicks again to me and the colors dim, becoming less vibrant.

"I even know his slave name, the name given to him as a kit." There is implication in her tone and I hate that I feel myself rise to it. I grip the edges of the tub to remain where I am and my toes all curl. *What is a slave name? What is a chamar? A Drakesh invasion? These beings suffered at the hands of the Drakesh too?*

I bite my lips together and hate the way her expression twists. She can see me and knows that she's gotten under my skin. "You don't even know it, do you? You're his *Xiveri mate* and you don't even know his true name. Does he know yours?"

Yes, because he called me Kiki on the mountain and I loved hearing my name in his voice. "No. And he doesn't need to. I don't need to know his either. You can have him." *Over my dead fucking body.* I jerk, startled at the onslaught of that particular emotion. *I can't be jealous. I don't even know his name, the one given to him as a boy.*

"I'm not his anything. Not his ziv-air-ee or whatever you want to call it. I'm not the szhay-uh of anything." Watching her face, I grip the edges of the tub so hard my knuckles lighten.

Something in my tone — more so than my bad pronunciation — must give her pause, because she uncrosses her arms and stares at me now with unblinking eyes, slack-jawed and in a way that's totally and utterly human. "You...you do not feel..."

"*No. I don't feel anything.*" *Does she hear that my voice is higher pitched than it had been?* "I just want to know where my friends are and how I can get to them. But I need to escape first."

"You would escape the Okkari?"

"Yes." I lick my lips, the rich taste of the water reminding me of something I cannot place. "And if you help me, I'll be gone from here forever."

When she hesitates, I bark out a laugh and the sound is a horrible, tortured thing. I never used to laugh like this. "Whatever you're talking about with humans fighting in a ritual — it's a lie. We fight because we don't want to mate with you stupid, alien fucks. We just want to be left alone in peace on our colony.

"Instead, I was transported without my consent off-colony and dragged up onto the top of a freezing cold mountain where I had to fight for my life in order to escape a male who I'd never met before wanting to hunt me down and fuck me. And that's exactly what happened. He hunted. I fought. I lost. We fucked. And now I want to go home."

The bitch fires back, "The Xanaxana reveals itself in pairs, demanding that they breed. It is nature's way of helping us ensure the continuity of our species, since kits these days are so rare. Even our stoic Okkari speaks of it at length — he says that he knew you were his from the moment he saw you on the filthy little moon you humans occupy."

That makes me start. *He was there?* I'd been so focused on the evil red one that I don't remember seeing him. Knowing he'd seen me and that he'd recognized me and felt something for me then makes my stomach flutter. *If the Hunt had happened, he would have come for me.*

"In the tales he tells, he had every intention of participating in the Drakesh version of your Hunt to claim you — to fight Bo'Raku even, for he knew that Bo'Raku wanted you too. However, he left with the Raku when Raku was unable to claim his own Xiveri mate.

"One rotation later, he brought you back to Nobu to participate in the Run on the Mountain to *honor* you. He paid more credits than the entire wealth of Voraxia's smaller planets for the merillian you so casually bathed in after you fought khrui monsters on your human colony and yet you show him scorn. Do you have a surplus of merillian on your human colony? Do you have healers who could have done a better job?"

She's red again and advancing on me now and I'm ready to fight. Trying to be ready. Trying not to be made to feel so small. She says words I don't understand and others that I do. *Bo'Raku. Does she know him?* Bo'Raku. Okkari wanted to fight him? I shudder, wishing something strange. Wishing something terrible — that the Hunt had happened one rotation ago, just so I could have seen that battle. So I could have seen the Okkari shred my tormentor to pieces. Purple beats red. Maybe I could have gotten away in the aftermath. *But would I have wanted to?* He called me warrior. He called me Kiki. And even back then when I didn't notice him, he *knew*.

She balks, "I do not pretend to understand you, but for the Okkari's sake I will help you escape from here. He deserves better."

The words sting like a slap in the face and I hate that I break her gaze first. Breathing in and out heavily, I say, "I never asked for him."

"The Xanaxana does not ask for permission. But if you choose to turn your back on it, perhaps it can be undone. Perhaps Xana will choose another for his Xaneru, for his spirit. Someone more worthy of a male of his caliber."

To this, I scoff. "Let me guess. Someone like you?"

"Of course. I have tried many times to win the Okkari's affections." Her lips pucker at that. "He has resisted, and though I would have liked to have been his first and only female, I will content myself knowing that I am his last."

A balloon expands in my stomach, coming to fill my chest. I freeze for an instant and don't breathe, but words I do not dare speak, squeeze out of me, "What do you mean his first female? Surely he's had many if he's the leader of this place." *And since he knew exactly what to do to please* me.

She makes a clicking sound in the back of her throat and comes to the edge of the tub where she settles onto her knees. "He is an honorable male and would take no females unless they revealed themselves to be his Xiveri mate. And yet, all of that waiting was wasted on you. Now hold still."

She picks up some sort of comb, one that looks like it's made out of bone, and lifts a clump of my hair. She teases the bone through it slowly and as she works, she drops her pitch and says, "You cannot escape now. The Xanaxana mating has not yet been completed and the Okkari will hunt for you until it is. You will need to mate with him and complete the Xanaxana union. Then, when he is at peace, you will leave his nest and take the hall to the left. Where you reach its end, I will be waiting. I will show you the way to the transport pods and then you will be gone from here..."

I nod, mute, hardly hearing what she's said. Because all I can think about is the fact that I took his virginity. He said something about *firsts* on the mountain top, but I didn't understand. Or maybe I just didn't want to. Because knowing that he waited his whole life to give his virginity to the one he thinks is his true mate — and then gave it to *me* — burns.

I took his virginity with hate in my heart and have every intention of betraying him. *Then maybe I will have something in common with him after all.* His first time will be also be ruined by an alien. And unlike in my case, it's a moment he won't get back.

7

Kinan

I approach the door to my nest — *our* nest — clean, wounds tended, the Xanaxana firing through me in intervals as rapid as the infant water skubbs enjoying their first thaw. The hasheba wait, as commanded, in the corridor, their faces illuminated by the ioni in the walls. Kuana's head is bowed, nobly, while Kuaku meets my gaze, boldly.

Inviting these two to be hasheba was a move atypical of an Okkari — normally, the Xhea would select her own — but as she does not know our customs or the members of this tribe, I made this selection for her. Kuana appears to have been a good choice, while Kuaku has behaved in a manner that has been somewhat difficult to interpret thus far. If she does not improve, I will need to remove her.

"Your report on the wellbeing of my Xiveri mate, hasheba," I say in a low tone, not wishing for my Xhea in the next room to hear us.

Kuana bows more deeply then, honoring herself, before rising to stand. "She is well, Okkari. The healing salts have already done wonders for the wounds on her forearms, the few that she had. I have placed bandages on your table. She waits for you there." Kuana makes a pleased expression, a display of emotion I would not tolerate from one of my warriors, but here and now from a hasheba, I feel my own expression threatening to mirror hers.

"You have done well."

Her ridges bathe in an orange glow, her pride well deserved. I fix my attentions on Kuaku then, who quickly averts her gaze. *Petulant as a child, as she always has been.* "You will tell me if you have anything to add, Kuaku."

Her ridges betray no color, but there is a tightening in her jaw that I will need to address. Not now. Certainly not now with the Xanaxana hanging over me like a threat. All I desire is to forget formalities and forsake restraint and go to her. My title be damned. I am Kinan for her anyways. Always.

"I have nothing I wish to add."

"Xhivey."

I start past her, but she jerks and says, "She did express some degree of emotion when I told her that you had not been with a female before. I believe the emotion may have been one of dismay. She spoke highly of human males who had been with many females prior to finding their Xiveri mates."

I stiffen. My gut sinks and my spine arches back. My fingers form fists but I flex them and attempt to ease control back into my muscles. "You will tell me why you spoke of this with her," I say in a growl, tone dark and intentionally obliterating.

"The human asked me questions about Voraxian couplings and male anatomy. I believe she found ours strange."

Rage. Doubt. I feel my ridges threaten emotion but reign it in. "You dare address her as such. You are hasheba..."

"Apologies, Okkari, but she asked us not to address her as Xhea or Va'Rakukanna. She wished to be addressed as human. I believe she views herself above us."

Doubt swells even greater. I switch my gaze to Kuana. "You will confirm whether or not this is true."

Kuana's mouth opens. She meets my gaze with difficulty. "I was absent for a time, fetching the combs you provided, so I did not hear this conversation." *Xhivey.* I exhale, allowing myself to believe that Kuaku manufactured or exaggerated this.

Then little Kuana severs such a hope cleanly. "However, she *did* ask me not to refer to her as Xhea or Va'Rakukanna. She wished to be addressed as human. I do not know why."

Sorrow. I feel shame but I do not show it. *Have I failed her in some way?* The sibilant hiss of a serpent could not sway me more into disbelieving in myself. I am Kinan. I am a weak boy who watched the Okkari before me slain.

"You are dismissed."

They bow and I watch them until they disappear down the hall, taking calming breaths. They have little impact. When I turn towards the door, I am a cacophony of emotion unbecoming for a warrior and even less honorable for a leader of this federation. I feel helpless and weak in the face of a threat to my union that I do not know how to fix. I will need to be straightforward and confront her.

Clenching my jaw, I start forward, the sensors opening the door before me. The room is not large, but intimate. A cave with ioni slithering across the walls. As such, my eyes are drawn to her instantly and the threats of inadequacy I felt before are reinforced.

I have never seen anything more lovely and I feel but a humble worshipper at the altar of his ethereal queen. Drawn forward by her to her, I wade into the space, sucked into the cavern of her gaze, which is harsh and unyielding. A warrior yes, but there is also something vulnerable in her human expression as she sees me. I wish I knew more about these humans and how to interpret their facial cues and ticks.

Her full mouth pillows fall open and she releases a small exhale that sounds like pleasure. *But perhaps I am wrong. Perhaps this is the dismay Kuaku spoke of.* Meanwhile, the sight of her is enough to make me shake. Entirely bare now and free of the mire she fought through, her skin shimmers. She is ioni, brought to life.

A dark jewel harvested from the depths of Nobu's deepest oceans, calling it brown would not be doing it justice, for the outer shell may be made of eons'-compressed earth, but the inner contains small mites that burrow down beneath the layers of compressed screa sediment.

Inside, they glow, becoming brighter and brighter in color until the dark brown becomes amber and then gold before they burst. The mites, fat from the minerals contained in the stone, move on to the next until they too dissolve to dust, made brilliant by their own gluttony, but also ruined by it.

My Xhea's gaze rakes over my own body, traveling from face across my chest and abdomen to the covering I wear over my xora. I remove it and she gasps again. In pleasure? Or in dismay. I do not know and not knowing wrecks me, but as honor dictates, I allow her to look upon her Xiveri mate unencumbered by clothing, just as I look upon her.

My xora is stiff and unyielding, small tendrils of color illuminating it that I can no longer control. I am a calculating male, yet I am nothing but raw emotion before her. Deep indigo desire, blue pleasure, canary uncertainty, a darker shame. Her eyes are round again and she stares at my member unflinchingly. She seems uncertain. *Perhaps dismay then.*

I move forward and take the seat placed before hers at the small wooden table, medical equipment dutifully laid across it by the hasheba. They were correct in their assessment. As I take her right forearm and begin applying salve, I can already see that her cuts have begun to heal.

As I work, I feel her fidget. Her thighs clench together, knees hugging one another so tightly I cannot help but wonder if she does this to assuage the need coursing through her, or if she attempts to conceal herself from my gaze. I glance again to the thatch of hair between her thighs and inhale the faint scent of her arousal before looking to her face.

She starts and looks away quickly and I feel myself heat. *Dismayed. Dismayed with her Xiveri mate.* "We will not breed on this solar," I say before I can sensor myself.

She jerks at the sound of my voice, flinching back. I wonder if she does not attempt to retract her arm from my grasp or if it is merely an involuntary response. I cannot be certain. *I am certain of nothing.*

"What? Why not?"

I am startled by the sound of her voice. It is so pleasing. Deep for a female, and throaty. I glance at her mouth and a scandalous vision assaults me. *Her mouth on my xora, sucking it into her as she stares up at me, wet gaze full of wanting. Full with a desire to please me.*

"I have been informed that my performance in the Run on the Mountain was not to your satisfaction. I will need to first inform myself of how to please a human female before I again attempt to breed you. If I feel pleasure, then so too should you. And I *did* feel pleasure." I meet her gaze and press my meaning onto her, willing her to see this truth. "My first rutting with you was paradise."

As I wrap another layer of gauze around her right forearm, she stares at me unseeingly, as if caught in a dream. Her lips mouth a single word, too quiet even to be considered a whisper. "Paradise."

Clearing my throat, I speak when she does not. "I will leave you then, unless you would debase yourself by informing me how you would like to receive pleasure in the human way, and describing to me how human males are able to deliver it to their females." The request is both selfish and humiliating, but it is what will allow me to expedite this process and remain close to her.

She blinks quickly and glances down at her bandaged forearms, then shakes her head. "Yes. I...I mean no." *Dismayed again.* "No, I liked the mountain. I mean, being with you up there. And we need to do this now. I mean, don't we? For the zah-nah-zah-nah?"

I cannot help but be pleased by the human lilt she gives our language, unable to make the clicking sounds herself. *She will need to learn.* But there is time for that. For now, I would like to take my time with her.

"I do not wish to displease you and I am aware that my anatomy differs greatly to that of a human male's."

"No, we need to do this now," she says with some force. Her gaze is shifty. She shakes her head again. I wonder if it is the Xanaxana again confusing her. If so, I need to know the truth. I will not allow her to be blinded by it.

Leaning forward on my stool, I cup her chin with one of my hands. I see her chest inflate as she breathes a little harder, a little faster. I can smell the scent of her miaba arousal, thickening in the air. "You will tell me why you told Kuaku that you did not enjoy our first mating. You will tell me why you asked the hasheba to call you human, Kiki."

She starts at the sound of her own name, the small black dot in the center of her eyes widening until it consumes almost all of the color. "I didn't. I mean, I didn't tell her that I didn't enjoy the mating." She licks her lips. "And I don't understand the titles. We don't use them back home."

I am interested in what she says. Far too interested. And yet, something tugs at me. *Something is wrong again.* It is the last thing she said. *Home.* I am her home now just as she is mine, yet she still speaks of another place. Of her human colony.

"You will tell me why Kuaku led me to believe you were dissatisfied."

"Probably because she's in love with you," she says and I realize there is so much I do not understand about humans because immediately afterwards, she looks frustrated that she has said this. I will need to speak with the human-Voraxian advisor, Svera, and learn more. Quickly.

"What is love?" I ask a question, something an Okkari does not do.

"What do you mean?"

"It does not translate for me."

She sucks in a breath. Small bumps form on the outsides of her arms. Curious, I brush them with my fingertips, only to be startled when she shivers all over. Despite the screa surrounding us, she must still be cold. Quickly, I pull a zyth fur from our nest and drape it over her shoulders.

"Thank…" she starts, then falters, hair where her ridges should be scrunching together over her nose.

"What is mine, is yours."

She looks down at her lap and inhales. I do too. The potency of her arousal is cloying and I hiss. She glances at my xora and I feel my own seed bead at its tip. It takes all of my control not to fist it and demand my right to rut her then.

Instead, I say, "This beast is called zyth. You find it further west, in Nobu's forests. I hunted this creature in my sixth rotation in honor of my future Xiveri mate." She blinks at me widely and I cannot help my pleasure expression, it cracks across my face and for just a heartbeat, I see a corner of her mouth quirk up too.

"I have enough to cover our nest and those of our future kits. It was the largest kill any have seen since." *What am I saying?* I have never uttered words in such shameless self-aggrandizement before, but it is because I suddenly, very desperately want to impress her, that I say them at all.

I clear my throat. "Now tell me of this love."

She sucks in a breath, holds it, and speaks on a rapid exhale. "When two people love each other it's like the whole rest of the world isn't there. They'd do anything for each other. They want everything from each other."

I make the pleasure expression again and gently, boldly, place my hand high on her thigh. I do not miss the way she spreads her legs slightly, or whimpers almost inaudibly at my touch. *Kuaku, the treasonous hasheba. She does not deserve the title. And yet, what could she hope to gain by attempting to deceive me in such a way? Is my Xiveri mate correct in her assessment of the hasheba's feelings towards me?* I feel pride and relief. Nox, my Xiveri mate *does* want me. She is pleased by me. And she is clever to have seen in Kuaku what I could not.

"I was not so naive to think that Kuaku did not want to be made Xhea. Many females vied for such a position. But my sires were fortunate enough to be Xiveri mates and I desired to replicate the depth of their union with a Xiveri mate of my own. So I selected no mate, choosing instead to wait for her. To wait for you. I thought that, upon finding you, the interest Kuaku has shown in me over the rotations would resolve itself and that she would understand that her place was not in my nest. That is only for you."

I slide my hand up towards the juncture of her thighs. She spreads them for me and her eyes flutter. She grips the edges of the zyth fur draped around her and bites her lower mouth pillow.

"I have this love emotion for you, Kiki."

"How? We don't even know each other." She says, voice breaking as I reach forward to touch her heat with my hands. I have blunted the claws of two fingers carefully, so as to better explore her folds without hurting her. And I do so now.

"Oh stars," she whimpers.

Purple pleasure beams down my arms, radiating through my chest and up the length of my stiff xora. "We will. With time. For now we can only listen to the Xanaxana. It has guided me to you and I know with absolute certainty that I would do anything for you."

"But I'm a human. And you're an alien," she says with eyes closed. Her legs are wide now and she is pumping her hips in a way that appears subconscious.

My control slips and I growl out a question. "Why does that matter?"

"I...I..." My fingers slip through the wetness that coats the furs below, balance on the tip of the little nub I have come to know so well, and finally push past the barrier of her outer lips into her hot, wet core. She rattles off a curse and shakes her head feverishly, clutching my forearm with both hands.

"I don't know," she gasps. "Fuck, I don't know..."

I cannot take it anymore and lurch up onto my feet. My xora is at her eye level and I love the expression that cloaks her when she blinks her eyes open and sees it. *Need.* I tilt her face up and meet her gaze with mine. Let her see what she has done to me.

"I will tell you the answer. It does not. You are my Xiveri mate and I treasure you more than I treasure my own life. Now you will tell me that you understand my words and believe them."

She licks her mouth pillows and I nearly ejaculate then. A vision of her large, dark breasts coated in my blue seed sends a spasm down my left leg. Seeing it, her eyes widen. She nods.

"Xhivey. Now you will tell me how you would like to be pleasured and I will take you to our nest and spend the coming lunar bringing this pleasure to you."

Her breathing comes in short, shallow bursts and she surprises me to my core when she reaches forward and takes my xora in her trembling fist. "Everything you do...did...up on the mountain pleased me."

She swallows audibly, as if admitting something wretched instead of the most beautiful truth. I have never heard words more lovely. And then I have never seen anything more lovely when she leans forward and licks her pink, ridgeless tongue up the length of my shaft, swallowing the seed that now coats the head. Urgent need slams into me. I cannot allow her to continue without emptying across her chest. I rise and sweep her with me.

She grabs onto my shoulders, looping one arm around my neck. I set her down on the edge of our nest roughly, drop to my knees on the stone floor and press my face to the seam of her thighs. Her fingers slide into my hair and I growl out my approval. Quickly, she pulls them back and I snarl. Looking up at her, I grab her retreating hand in one of mine and return it to where it was.

She does not need white ridges to express her shock, but I don't care. I am slowly sinking into the scent of her, which grows stronger at the juncture of her legs. I nose my way forward until I reach her mound glistening with moisture that smells of miaba and salt and spice and makes saliva pool beneath my tongue. My xora bucks, releasing more seed that should be spilled inside of her. *It will be. Deep inside of her.*

I glance up the length of her body to see her chest rising and falling in waves. "Your mound is already wet," I inform her. "Does this mean your body is ready to receive mine?"

She hesitates. Propped up on her elbows, she stares at me down the length of her body, then nods before she looks away.

"Kiki," I hiss, refusing to call her human or by any other name if she does not find pleasure in it. "You will look at me when I mount you."

She flicks her gaze to mine, breathing hard. I make the pleasure expression and bite down on the inside of her thigh. She chokes out a mewling whimper and I cannot help the Xanaxana from rattling through my entire chest, threatening to tear me apart from the inside.

In a tone so gruff it is nearly indiscernible, I ask her, "I am eager to taste you. Do I have your permission?"

She nods and breath jerks into her lungs, making the dark-tipped mounds on her chest bounce and jiggle. These mounds are so very soft, and with no plates covering them, seem so precious. I feel at a loss, wanting and wishing to explore them with tongue and hands... *perhaps even placing my xora between their fullness and using them to pump seed all over her ioni skin...* The thought is a pleasure as much as a torture to me. I need to feast.

I lick her slightly and her eyes roll back. She wavers, falling onto the furs but I nip at the skin above her hip, making her jerk. "Kiki, what did I say? You will watch me as I bring you pleasure." I place my hand on top of her lower stomach, just above the thatch of her glistening curls. Then I push up, pulling the skin away from her mound and further exposing that small little nub she found so much delight in earlier.

She moans so loudly I am startled. Startled and pleased. I splay her thighs apart with my hands until the point I feel them resisting. She moans louder and whispers, "Harder."

"Repeat yourself."

"Harder" she says, clearing her throat.

I spread her legs until I am sure I cause her pain and then pull back, but she says, "Don't. It feels...it feels..."

"I will not bring you pain."

"You won't."

I make the pleasure expression. *My Xiveri mate knows me.* And I cannot help myself. "You will give me your answer."

"What...what answer?"

"You will tell me that you want me to taste you."

As I wait, I feather light licks across her folds, delving between them to taste more of her essence. "I can't admit that...I can't."

"Then I will stop my wetting of your mound," I say, and I do.

"Oh stars...fuck," she curses, hands fisting the zyth fur below.

"That is not an answer," I say, pleased.

She groans and kicks her feet, "Yes, I want you to kiss it. Please."

"You need your Xiveri mate."

She hesitates, and then releases a tiny, strangled, "Yes."

"You need me."

When she does not answer, I pull back even more. I glance up at her and she has her eyes shut. "Kiki, do not make me repeat myself again."

Her eyes open slowly and she meets my gaze. She looks fevered and wild and in pain. My xora feels so sensitive the slightest stroke of the zyth fur against it sends electricity firing through me. I understand her pain, but before I can save either of us, I need her to tell me.

"Tell me you need me."

Water fills her gaze again. She reaches one hand for her chest mound and kneads it in a way I find mesmerizing. I blow very lightly onto her dripping core and her head kicks back on a gasp and when she returns her gaze to mine, I see the resolved set of her jaw.

"I need you," she says and I dive forward, mouth latching onto her mound.

I lathe her little nub with my tongue and I realize that with my tempo and touch and speed I can *control* the writhing of this little warrior's body. I know then that Kuaku was violently wrong. Because my Xiveri mate receives pleasure from me and it makes me feel powerful. More powerful than all my titles, all my lands, all my rights.

When I slow, she moans deeply, when I quicken, her fingers clench and her back arches. When I nibble the folds of her lips, she cries out to the stars. And then when I worship her little nub, she shatters. Her whole body shivers and shakes and I see liquid prick the corners of her eyes and drip down her smooth, curved cheeks.

Curious to see if this liquid tastes as good as the rush of salty, sticky cream that has spilled from between her lower folds, I finish lapping up the moisture at her thighs, careful to devour all of it hungrily, before prowling up the length of her. She is so beautiful. Lying there, arms splayed to either side, utterly defenseless and so vulnerable, ready and ripe for the taking. I reach a hand forward and sink it into the depth of her thick, rich curls. Her eyes are open, blinking slowly up at me.

I cradle the back of her head and tilt her face to mine. Gently, I press my mouth to the water on her face and take it away. She makes a troubling sound, but before I know what has happened she is pushing on my shoulders, urging me onto my back. Her hand reaches between us and I am stunned when she pushes my palm aside and again takes my xora for her own. Her skin is so soft around my shaft that my whole body lurches. Before her, I have never felt another's hand on my xora before. Not nearly so pleasurable as the raw, wet heat of her core, but pleasurable all the same.

"Kiki," I growl as she swings one leg over my hips. *What is this?* I do not know. I do not know but I stop her as I sense she will lower down onto my xora all on her own. I have to ask, though it humiliates me to do so, "Do I fail you in our rutting?"

She freezes, as if stunned. "No."

"Yet, you wish to lead…"

She nods.

"You wish to lead even though it is the male's responsibility to guide the breeding."

Her eyes crinkle. She makes the pleasure expression and I am so stunned by the beauty of it I don't hear what she says next and have to debase myself yet again by asking her to repeat herself.

"Human females are known to lead the rutting too, sometimes. I never have… But I just… I thought. I mean, I wanted to try." She poses her voice as a question and the request makes something tighten in my chest. I reach up and stroke the tip of her chest mound, her stomach, the edge of her jaw.

"Hexa. My body is yours." She blinks, but the water that fills her gaze does not spill down her cheeks. Instead, she makes the smallest pleasure expression as she rises up onto my xora and slides down onto it smoothly. She moans and this time it is I who grips the zyth fur below me, as if fearing that it will fly away or I will. Because as I fill her tight, wet heat, and issue a bellowed roar into our cavern, I am lost to her. Completely. Nothing more than driftwood, washed up onto paradise's shore.

8
Kiki

My dreams are wonderful. Paradise. Hallucinations of an oasis. *It's been too long stuck in the sand, thirsty and starved.* This dream feels like fullness. The essence of satisfaction. A wonderful aroma of salt, semen and sweat. He smells like the brown root spice we use most back home.

I'm two rotations old. My grandfather sits outside on the stoop we called a porch, kneading dough on a flat board. Instead of forming a ball, he flattens the bread, coats one side of the dough in root spice, the other in sweet water, rolls it up and bakes it. It's the first time I ever had root spice and cane bread, the first time I ever had anything sweet. I believed in magic then. That life was a perfect, treasured thing.

I lurch up, my hands reaching out and finding warmth. Cocooned in it, the scratch of inhuman plates against my back let's me know that I'm against his chest. That his thighs are cupping mine. He has a leg draped over my whole body protectively and an arm clenched around my torso like a vice. *Why did I wake up? Why should I ever have to wake up from this?*

My chest tightens. I can hardly breathe. A foreign energy flushes through me and I feel alive with it, even if

I am being dragged back into lethargy by the hands of sleep itself. Everything is just as it was. Nothing has changed. But everything.

I was on top. He let me take the lead. *I* rutted *him.* And he was so nervous about it... The thought crunches as I try to expel it, undigestible and hard to take. I have a decision to make then and it's too easy to make it. Get up and flee, or just...sink back down into the cocoon of the oasis. Wait for the solar. Instead of fighting, try to reason with him. *What am I saying? He's an* alien, *he can't be reasoned with! What is happening to me? Get away! Fight this...fight...*

A vision of my mom. A flash of a memory. *Some months after the Hunt, I'm still thinking about the red alien, fantasizing about slitting his throat. My mom sets a mug down on the table beside me. I smell the mint and bark spice wafting from the steam on top of it, masking the smell of the earth-rich water but I don't look at it, or her. Even as she says, "You can't release your demons if you keep them prisoner."*

I exhale, mind made up, and lower back into the furs *the ones he hunted for me.* His arms tighten around me but no sooner do I close my eyes and surrender to the dream, than a sharp sensation pulls me back into the present.

A flick against my forehead jerks me awake. I blink and it's hard to see anything in the low lights swirling throughout the room. They seem to have dimmed. But how? Miari would know. *Maybe if I asked him, he would find her and I could show her the lights and the cold white. I could even introduce them.*

The flick strikes again and the vision before me focuses. *Kuaku. What's she doing here?* I open my mouth to ask but she claps a hand over it. Her forehead is swirling red mixed with murky blobs of copper as she glances at mine and the Okkari's bodies, intertwined.

She gestures for me to follow her and silently makes her way to the door. Confused, I'm wobbly as I sit up and start to make my way after her. The moment my foot hits the warm rock floor and my last limb extricates itself from the web our bodies have created, Okkari jerks awake.

His forehead becomes white then pink then he looks up and sees me with a gaze that's sharp and not at all sleepy — one ready for battle. His chest rumbles and he starts to sit up. His ridges are a mutiny of colors now and my stomach lurches, an irreverent desire filling me up.

"Why do you leave our nest?" He says and his voice is low and sensuous.

I have a hard time standing up against the sound of it and hate that, when I speak, I don't sound half as sure and authoritative as he does. "Bathroom," I lie. And I hate that I'm lying.

And I hate that I hate it.

And I hate that, looking up at his purple alien face, hate is so hard to find.

He nods, the smooth ridges above his eyes burning blue and a little purple. "Xhivey. I will escort you."

"No," I blurt, scrambling as I remember Kuaku standing just out in the hall and the reason she's here. What I told her I wanted. What she agreed to help me do. "I'll ask one of the hasheba to help me if I need it."

He grins with one corner of his mouth and his white teeth flash in the low light. Bubbles fill my stomach and pop in small explosions, each one a symphony of sound. *Just lie down. Sleep. Forget about the bitch. She's after my man. Fuck her.*

"Xhivey. They are here to help you. I will eagerly await your return, Kiki."

I drop my gaze. He sits up until he can reach me, then slides one finger under my chin, forcing me to meet his strange, alien look with one of my own, even if I try to shutter it. I'm sure he can see through me though. I feel utterly transparent. I want to kiss him and lick my lips, hating my reaction, but wanting to kiss him all the same.

"Just sleep," I tell him.

He strokes the side of my face lovingly, and looks at me like I'm the sun to his universe. Heat begins to build between my legs and his rumbling gets louder. "Hurry back, or I will have to come and hunt for you."

I wince at the word, a memory of an alien — this one red and savage — loping after me across hard, packed sands, a look of gleeful determination in his eyes, making me cringe. I pull away quickly and go to the door, refusing to look back as I step through it into the hall. It's empty, but flashes of a half-heard conversation steer me to the left.

Careful not to touch the weird lamps that flicker with movement like glow-in-the-dark snakes, I run my hand along the wall's bumpy surface to keep myself steady and eventually, I hear rustling up ahead and come upon an open door.

Kuaku — *the bitch* — is standing just beyond the threshold and I can't imagine what she sees because her ridges are a mutiny of colors — everything from copper and red to grey and black. Colors I can't name seem to strip her bare. Even her shoulders are tense by her strange pointy ears.

I understand her shock. I would be shocked too. I'm *still* shocked even though I'm not the one in love with him. *Even though when he says he loves me, I believe he's telling the truth.* Standing before her covered in thick swabs of blue cum drying haphazardly across my skin, I swallow hard, open my mouth, but I can't speak. I have nothing to say in my own defense.

Her eyes slit and she hisses, "Don't tell me you're having second thoughts."

Is it that obvious? I shake my head. *Wait — what am I even here for?* "I'm not. I just...I told him I'd be right back."

"Don't worry. I plan on keeping him plenty distracted."

Jealousy warps my pitch. It comes out higher, more sure. "What are you going to do?"

"Why do you care? You don't even want him, remember? He's an alien. Beneath you."

I've heard as much from Jaxel and my own internal monologue for the past two rotations. They're all I've focused on. What I've built my new self and my new self's entire world around. But hearing the words from her now make them feel so trite. So worthless.

"Maybe this is too risky. And he seems..." *Don't say it.* "He seems reasonable. Maybe I can speak with him and we can figure out a solution." I look away, ashamed at my own uncertainty. What happened to me? A good fuck isn't worth abandoning Svera and Miari.

She balks scathingly, in a way that makes me feel worse than I already do. "A solution to what?" In the dim light, her pure, black eyes flash with murder. "You think he would *ever* let you return to your home planet? Or somehow try to interfere with the Rakukanna and the Raku's relationship? He would never let you near her — either of them. You are on trial because of what you did."

My heart feels like it's being dragged through coals. So much for hope. *Hope is a useless fucking emotion.* Everyone is just as bad as I think they are... "What trial?"

The colors in her face dim and she uncrosses her arms from over her flat, plated chest. "As soon as the first icefall is over, you and the other traitor who tried to stop the Raku from finding his Xiveri mate will face a trial by combat. You'll have to fight Voraxia's most vicious warriors and if you lose, you'll likely be banished beyond the tundra to Nobu's endless ice ocean where you can try to survive. Most don't and you're not equipped for it.

"And even if you somehow *do* manage to defeat your opponent which, let me repeat, will be impossible — then you *might* be allowed to settle here and keep your position as Xhea. Might. Perhaps the Raku will want to do something else with you for the trouble you caused him."

"But would the Okkari really let the Raku banish me?"

"Who do you think the Okkari reports to? Raku outranks him. He is leader of our entire federation. Not that the Okkari *would* try to defy him. Why do you think he left you on that human moon even when he *knew* you were his Xiveri mate? He is a soldier first and deeply loyal to Voraxia. Why would he choose *you* over an entire galaxy?"

My heart is pounding. My fists are clenched. "But the Okkari hasn't mentioned any of this. And he's made it seem…" *Oh stars, no. Don't even think it. Don't breathe it life. Don't be so fucking naive.*

"How can you believe that he thinks anything of you beyond your capacity to breed kits for him?" Soft, cruel laughter floats between us. "You need to escape now if it is truly your desire to see your people again. If you even value your own life."

Her tail flicks back and forth behind her and reminds me of the sand cats that used to roam the human moon. The last of them died out a few generations back but I still saw carvings of them. My dad used to make them out of petrified nightshade and sell them at the market. *Dry sand swirling through the air. Every other market conversation punctuated by my dad's rolling laughter.* But he left us when I was young. After my mom went through the Hunt. My parents started fighting then. Everything changed. Because all the Hunt does is ruin.

Energy drains out of my shoulders and fleetingly forgotten hate froths in my mouth. "You're right," I tell her. "What now?"

"Come." She leads me into the room behind her and then through a labyrinthine maze. She knows her way well, like she's been here before. A pang of treacherous irritation flares again, and makes me remember yet again why I need to be free of this place. *I can't believe for a second that I forgot. I can't believe for a second that I wanted to believe in him.*

My left knee threatens capitulation and my stomach lurches and sinks. The strange thread tearing through my abdomen has begun to unravel — not itself, but the rest of me. I force myself to plunge on, even though every step feels like wading through the mire. The temperature gets cooler the farther we go until finally, the walls turn white.

We enter a small room, the cold so desperately cold I can't imagine what in the comets this will mean for the outside. Thankfully, the bitch thought ahead and turns to me with a fur-lined outfit similar to the one I wore before. Shoving aside one last hesitation, I shove my feet into the in-built shoe holds, surprised that the legs don't bunch up around the ankles and hips like the last one did. I lace up the chest piece and throw the hood over the bushel of my tangled hair and as I hold up my now-gloved hands I see that there are five fingers on these gloves instead of six. *The suit was made for me.*

Emotion taunts me and for just a fraction of a second I wonder if this is the right decision, if I just shouldn't go back. *Why would I go back when he didn't even tell me about my trial? Unless...*

"How do *you* know about my trial?" I say, voice leveled heavy with accusation.

But the bitch just laughs. "Everyone in Voraxia knows about your treason. All anyone talks about are the tortures the Raku will devise for you for attempting to keep him from his Xiveri mate."

Xiveri mate. There's that term again. "If the Raku thinks Miari is his Xiveri mate, then that means that he got her, doesn't it?"

"Of course. Did you really think *you* could stop him? He is leader of the Voraxian Federation and a fearsome warrior. He cannot be stopped by the likes of *you*."

I hate the way she speaks to me. Like I'm *nothing*. It reminds me too much of the way the red alien looked at me, spoke to me, hurt me — and I could do nothing to stop him.

I bite down hard with my back teeth and try to keep myself from hitting her as I say, "And now? Where is Miari?"

She flashes yellow then and quickly looks away. "They are in Illyria, Voraxia's capital."

"And?"

"And what?"

"How...how is she?"

"How should I know?"

"If my trial is talk of the town, then she would also be. What do people say about her?"

The bitch waits for a moment, as if considering what or whether to tell me. Finally, she says four little words that change my life. "She is with kit."

Stunned, I let the revelation sink in, but only for seconds that take eons. *She's pregnant. Possibly forced to mate. Abducted by strangers — aliens — I've never even heard of.* I failed her. I failed her in every possible way. *Not again.* Hate flowers again in my chest, finding purchase in my doubt and hanging on. Turning away from the bitch, I swallow hard and look at the only other door in the room, the one that emanates such oppressive cold.

"Tell me where to find a transporter. I'm ready to go home." The bitch hesitates one last time, ridges flashing an unsettling peach. She seems uncertain herself, and I don't like it. Barking sternly now, I say, "Do you know the way or don't you? I did my part. If you want me to leave, then tell me the way."

Her features harden. Her colors die. She cocks her head to the door and says, "Follow the eastern sun until you reach the black screa cliff face. The door to the Okkari's private transporters will open for you as you are Xhea. It won't for me, so you have to do this on your own. Inside, you'll find the transport pod. You'll be able to take it where you need to. You'll have plenty of time. I'll keep the Okkari distracted. By the time you reach your pathetic human planet, you'll be a distant memory for him."

The thread in my chest opens up, forming a hollow gong which rings. I take another painful step until I can feel the cold breach the barrier of the door and my gloves and wonder if the temperature outside hasn't dropped even more significantly.

"How far?"

"It is a quarter span walk, not far. Though with your short, stumpy legs it will probably take you a half span at least."

"I don't know that measurement," I snap, ignoring the insult. "How many paces?"

She shrugs, her ridges swirling with a tendril of black. "Three hundred. Then you'll be free."

I turn to the door again and this time she presses her palm to a panel beside the door before it releases and slides open, letting in a burst of bright white light and a blitzkrieg of frigid, biting air. I take the first step outside of his home quickly, before it's too late. *Before I succumb to the oasis and let it drown me.*

"Human." I turn. Her ridges are calm once again, and I can sense a satisfaction simmering beneath her words. "Don't come back." The door shuts between us silently, with no great ceremony.

Putting the house to my back, I turn to face a shocking sky. Red strips shine through a limitless white, which screams down at me. Cold falls from it like needles and melts where it touches my skin. Squinting, I see the murky outline of cliffs in the distance, just as the bitch promised, even if they do look farther than three hundred paces. *Three hundred of their paces is probably five hundred of mine.* The world is flat everywhere else and there are no houses here. *We must have come out on the other side of the hill.*

I measure out forty paces and when I look back, the purple alien's house is barely visible. Ahead of me the horizon is still just a seamless white, only the vaguest outline of *something* up ahead to give me direction.

I take another twenty steps, then another ten, then another five. The wind feels like fire. I don't understand how something so cold could feel like this. It's even worse than it was on top of the mountain, and I hadn't thought that possible then. *Does that mean it can get even worse than this?* Meanwhile, the ground beneath my feet has shifted from plush, springy white to a hard, unyielding cold, like the tundra I ran onto, even though the female leader told me not to. *If she said not to run onto the tundra, why would they keep transporters here?* Maybe she lied. *Maybe Kuaku did.* After all, she wanted me gone. Why did I think she'd care if I lived?

A blast of cold cuts across my cheek and I can't push forward against it. I turn my back on it and even then, the needles seem to flutter around and even *through* my suit. It hurts and I feel the fluttering in my chest devolve to the first whispers of a very real panic.

I turn around, but I'm not so sure I'm facing in the exact same direction. Trying to orient myself, I look back for the house — gone — and then for my footsteps — but they're gone too, erased as soon as they're created. The wind is too hard. The white is too white. The cold is too brutal. *I need to go back to where it's safe.* I can fight him there about the trial. I can fight him there about Miari. I can fight anything in the warm, but in this cold white it's getting harder and harder to move and to breathe — both things I desperately need to do.

Picking a direction, I take a step, only to feel the hard cold beneath me rumble, the sensation almost *exactly* like when the red aliens touched down onto our moon colony in their large sky ships. Is there a port around here? I haven't gone three hundred steps yet, but maybe she just miscounted. I must be close. No other sound could sound so *large* or so exactly like an off-world transporter.

Hope lifts my chest and urges me forward, but where I walk, the ground beneath me darkens. There are no shadows overhead and it's too white and all encompassing for me to have created a shadow myself.

Confused as much as I am curious, I bend down and swipe away the top misty layer clouding the packed cold and jump — damn near out of my own suit and skin — when the shadow passes by below my feet. *Something is* moving *down there.* And then I feel it. A muted thump and a distant, terrible wail coming from *below.* From underneath.

The thump comes again and when I look up, it's without caring that I have no points of reference to guide me. None of that matters. I don't know if whatever is below the hard cold can get through it, but the thumping is enough to shake my whole body, to lift my feet off the ground, to make me stumble. It's *big.* And I don't want to be here to find out just how thick that hard cold is. I thought fighting khrui was difficult, but I'm in the alien world now where I know nothing of monsters. Because everyone is.

I take off running as hard as my suit will allow, stumbling every third step on the tremors the thumping creates. Exhaustion is forgotten. So is Miari, Svera, the colony, the differences between human and alien. All I feel is a fire across my chest and a desperation to live claw at me…and then the splintering crack of the hard cold beneath my feet.

A deafening shriek scrambles my brain waves. I slip and slide to my knees, but I only stay grounded for the length of a blink. Everything lurches. The cold hard gives way and I go flying as something huge — huger than aliens, huger than khrui, huger than homes on our colony, huger than ships to take me away — breaks free of the cold prison that had kept it at bay.

A singeing sort of heat sears my entire right leg as soon as I stand and I come down hard on my knees. I glance at my suit to see it shredded by some strange colorless goop. Steam rises from it and judging by the sudden inflexibility and immobility in my entire right side, I know it can mean nothing good.

Another screech blasts through the white and sends me flying over the hard cold, propelled by nothing but the wind it creates. I land on my stomach and when I look up, I see it, and seeing it, I pray to the universe for a quick death.

The mammoth of the *Hard Cold Below* has three limbs and is clawing it's way out of the water with strange smooth tentacles, bringing forth one giant body that's completely eyeless. All that sits in its round gelatinous center is one enormous maw.

The size I can fathom, but that maw is what makes me shudder. Round and wet, it has no teeth. It's only a gaping white and pink, inside of which I can see organs and flesh and the stuff of nightmares. *And I'm going to be inside of that.* The only question is how long it will take to kill me and how. *Will I suffocate? Or will whatever stomach acid this creature contains eat me alive?*

I stagger up to standing as the tentacles jolt forward, latching onto the hard cold and, with impossible strength, pulling the creature towards me. It moves slowly, which is the only advantage I've got at the moment.

Lurching in ungainly steps, I run for my life and as I run I scream, "Okkari!"

The word shocks me because it sounds so right that the thread in my chest settles, calm. As if in acceptance of something greater. And as I run for my life, this strange calm settling in my chest in spite of my terrifying and impending death, it's with the thought that funny enough, Svera may have been right all along.

I'm starting to think that there is a Tri-God, a divine force who rules the cosmos, and that the Tri-God has a bitter sense of irony and a funny sense of humor. Because right now, as I imagine being chewed alive by a beast with no teeth, devoured for eternities, I prefer the Hunt. And all I wish is that I'd stayed in the oasis.

9

Okkari

This is not my Xiveri mate.

The knowledge blankets me even before I wake. The body attempting to slide into my nest is not my Xiveri mate, she is not Kiki, she does not smell of miaba or zxhoa or crova. She smells of something foul. Worse than overripe fruit or rank meat, she smells like corpses rotting on a battlefield. My Xanaxana reels and my body begins revolving against the zyth fur, coming to life. The warrior in me flares.

"What have you done with my Xiveri mate? Where is your Xhea?" The female is one I recognize in the glow of the ioni. *Kuaku*. And she is as naked as her name-day.

"Okkari..." she says and there is a seductive lilt to the female's tone.

With neither mercy nor warning, I snatch her up by the throat. "Kuaku, you have lost your senses!"

She claws at my hand and I release her with a shove, sending her stumbling backwards until she hits the wall. Fear eliminates the pleasure expression that she had worn on her face. "Okkari, I did not mean to..."

"You did not mean to defile these furs, disrespect my Xiveri union, and dishonor me, my Xhea and yourself," I seethe, "Nox, you could not possibly have meant to do these things. But you will tell me now what you *did* mean to do, and you will tell me where my Xiveri mate has gone and why you appear to me now in her place."

She falls to her knees and places her ridges to the floor — an ultimate sign of humiliation. "Heffa, Okarri, heffa…"

"You must know that begging will not save you now. Tell me what you have done here. Tell me what has become of the Xhea." *Kiki, where are you?*

"I did nothing, Okkari! The Xhea…it was her. She asked me to help her escape. She asked me to take her place in the furs. She had no desire to be bred by you and wished to return to her people. I did not want to, but she is my Xhea. What other choice did I have, Okkari?"

My whole body turns to stone. Weakness assaults me and it is a crippling, alien sensation. I cannot believe it. I cannot dare to believe it. Not after what we shared. The previous lunar tore me apart. I am not the male I was when we began and and after our last breeding, I have never felt closer to another living soul. Her Xaneru speaks to mine as if they were, at some single, infinitesimal point in the creation of the universe, one whole. Is it possible that what Kuaku says is true? Did she truly mean to leave me? Or is Kuaku up to something much more sinister, just as she was before?

"This is not the first time you have lied to your Okkari on this solar. You will tell me where my Xiveri mate is now and you will speak the truth or I will not hesitate to banish you to the endless ice ocean where you may live out your few remaining days alone with the frost," I tell her in an even tone, colder than the first icefall.

"She just wanted out, my Okkari. I advised her that east was too dangerous, so I believe she may have gone west."

I hiss, "You are lying. Had she gone west, she would have stumbled into the village. The icefall has already begun. You know as well as anyone that the village is busy preparing and battening down. She would have been seen and I would have been alerted immediately."

Pink fear colors her face then before the emotion is extinguished. By her own ridges, she is betrayed. I lift Kuaku from the ground by her shoulders and shake her flaccid form. *Tell me where she is!"*

Pink flares again, the brightest I've ever seen, followed by a sickly shade. *Regret.* It will not save her. "East," she says, "she went east."

I drop her and she hits the stones below with a squeal. "And what of Kuana? Where was she in this?" I ask, already activating my life drive and sending a message to four of my nearest warriors and three of my best trackers to prepare my dreya and meet me at my home's east entrance. If she has gone out onto the eastern tundra, then we have few moments to waste.

Kuaku rocks back and forth and shakes her head, genuflecting before me like the coward that she is. "I..." She shakes her head. "She's in her quarters. I locked her in."

I roar out my frustration, unwilling to waste anymore words on this female now. Not when I have allowed this creature into my home, to care for my Xiveri mate and such an act has put her in direct danger.

I prepare myself at speed before racing through my home, down black and then white corridors until I reach the east entrance. The doors glide open as they sense my approach and I am assaulted by the first icefall's earliest breaths.

While we on Nobu are suited to this weather, she is not, and it will soon come down much more severely. At its deepest point, winter drives even the most bold of our villagers back into their home. For Kiki, mere instances could mean the difference between life and death.

I leap the steep steps of my home and sink into plush snow up to the shins. I charge through the white to where my dreya await, fastened to their ice glider, the first of my trackers already arrived and awaiting me in the transparent hull of his own glider.

Fierce beasts, my dreya stand on six legs and measure the height of a Voraxian male. Covered in shaggy fur and with short necks, but square blocks for teeth, they make for fierce battle companions and swift carriers in times of peace. Travel by transporter is forbidden in these temperatures, which often cause even our most advanced technologies to freeze.

By the time I am ready and strapped into the ice glider's hull, my remaining warriors and trackers have gathered. I give only one swift signal before beginning to carve a path east. She has had little time and in these conditions would not have been able to move at speed. She would not have been able to reach the next village of Tannen. *Unfortunately. There, she would have been found and I would have been alerted. She would have been given quarter, shown hospitality, and been kept warm in the time it took for me to come for her. Now she is exposed.*

"Okkari, don!" Comes Cal'El's hail from behind me. I rear up on the holo reins I carry and come to a sharp stop. Through the clear fiber shell of the hull that carries me, I see the dreya in front of me impatiently stamp their feet. They are loyal, hardened creatures. The storm would not usually put them on edge like this...

And then I hear it. An ancient beast's wail followed by a female's scream — *my female* — and she screams for me. *"Okkari!"* Chills rocket up my spine and an explosion goes off in my chest.

"It's a hevarr!" My tracker, Cal'El roars over the sound of the storm.

I do not answer him, but snap my reins, taking off further east than the course we had set. Kuaku, the sniveling welp, the treacherous hasheba. If what she has said is true at all and my Xiveri mate was looking to escape, she would have needed help. Someone to guide her. Someone to tell her where to find the transporters. Kuaku knows where they are, just north of my home, cut into the mountain. She would have had to give direction to my Kiki to come here with the express intent to kill her. *She lied to her*, just as she attempted to lie to me. And a sick, distant part of me feels relief that just perhaps my Xhea does not revile me so much that she wanted to run, but that she too was deceived.

Another scream lights the bright sky and the ghost of a pain ripples up my right leg as we ride. I ready the ice spear I carry as well as the ion blaster I keep strapped across my back. It has been many rotations since our hunters have faced off against a hevarr and it is likely not all in my war party will survive.

When we arrive at the source of the screech, I am sure of it.

The hevarr here is fully matured, easily visible even against the wind and mist engulfing it. My Xhea, on the other hand, is not. I bellow a battle cry as grief shatters through me and my warriors roar out their response. The collective noise, undampened by the snow, startles the hevarr, which hunt blind and rely solely on sound and vibrations to source their prey.

It turns towards us and as it shifts, my gaze flits rapidly over the white tundra, swept with ice and gales of wind carrying thickening snow. And against so much white, a small dark smear. She lies on her back, staring up at the creature with an expression of horror — one that recognizes that even if she were armed, which she isn't, she alone would stand no chance against such a creature.

But all that matters to me, is that she lives.

"Kiki," I roar, and I would never have used her slave name and disgraced her in such a way were it not so urgent. But it is effective. Across the gulley that separates us, she looks at me, and I can see her human gaze struggling to hone in on my features where my vision remains unaffected by the distance and can see her perfectly. I can see how her chest quakes. How she mutters her funny, human curse that she sometimes says in the heat of our rutting. *Oh comets.* And then, *Thank the stars. Thank the stars. Okkari…*

The Xanaxana in my chest beats harder for her as rage and fear and honor and duty and something greater than all of these disparate parts overcomes me. I roar out another battle anthem and charge the feral creature. It releases a screech of its own and then the white world around us shatters as the Okkari within me rises to defend his own.

10
Okkari

The sweeping tentacles came in violent blows, like the crushing arms of Xana herself, while the acid ink spewed like the deadliest sleet. Three of ours fell before I was able to kill the creature — a kill that would not have been possible without Re'Okkari's sacrifice.

In the end, he engaged two of the creature's limbs at once while the remaining warriors severed its third. His attack put him close to the creature's mouth in a position where he was unable to avoid the hevarr's acidic saliva. Still, he remained planted where he was, even as the saliva chewed him apart.

Using the distraction of all the creature's limbs at once, I was able to come in at Re'Okkari's side and stab the creature through with my black glass and Droherion spear — a new design by the Rakukanna. The end of the blade seared as it cut, cleaving a hole through to the hevarr's small brain.

It fought, even as it died, splintering my spear and releasing one last gale of spray that I caught with my left forearm, flaying the skin from my flesh where it landed. Flopping desperately against the hole in the ice it created, it dislodged several shelves. Va'El's body went down, but another of my warrior's dove after it. I swept Re'Okkari aside and helped Cra'El and Ren'El secure the hevarr and afterwards, I issued terse orders to the rest to secure the fallen soldiers and dreya while I tend my Xiveri mate.

I remove my left sleeve and pack the raw skin with ice before jumping from floating ice-shelf to floating ice-shelf until I reach the other edge of the hole the hevarr created. There, I find my Xhea standing in wait — I might have said proudly, if not for the tremble in her chin.

"Are you hurt?" Bitter anger and deep grief make it difficult to speak.

She shakes her head and flinches when I reach for her. Snarling, I grab her nonetheless and run with her back to the other side of the broken ice, where my warriors and dreya prepare our return. I set her down in the hull of my glider where she is shielded by the wind.

As I climb in after her, I cannot control my wild and untamed pitch. *"What were you thinking!"*

She starts to shake — quite badly now — but she does not look at me. Nox, her gaze remains fixed to Re'Okkari's body. It lies prone but a pace to her right, already prepared for transport. I curse this day, for it has claimed the life of one of my warriors and two dreya at least — I still do not know the status of Va'El or the injuries of my other warriors. And right now, I just need to know *what for*. Even if I must debase myself and ask her question after question, I will have answers from her.

I slam my fist onto the slick floor, my hair shaking loose around my face in wet locks. "Answer me! Why did you run? Were you deceived? How did you end up here?"

"He's dead?"

The grief that shines in her too wet eyes overwhelms my Xanaxana. I falter before her now, even though in front of a fully matured hevarr, I did not.

"Hexa," I answer her through gritted teeth. If she ran, she needs to be punished, but I find that I cannot do that either.

She is tight and huddled and reaches out to touch a shredded strip of the covering that binds him. The flesh that contained his Xaneru but a quarter solar before is now still. Hands cross over his chest, his body is wrapped securely in the vestiges of his hide coverings. Having been lashed by the hevarr spray, it disintegrated the outside of his suit before tunneling inwards.

"It is thanks to him that the creature was slain. Knowing he was going to die, he advanced on the creature, delivering the blow that distracted it and allowed me to get close enough to the creature to kill it. Without his sacrifice, it is likely more would have died, or been gravely injured. And it is because of you. Because you *lied to me* and then you ran," I say, lashing out — not because these are truths but because I aim to hurt her. I am to hurt my Xiveri mate. I am a proud male, yet in this moment, I do not feel it.

Shocking me suddenly, she smashes the heel of her left hand into her forehead while the other wraps around her middle. I reach for her wrists to stop her but she blocks my hands in a well-practiced motion. Furious that she would try to fight me here, I bare all of my teeth and lunge for her.

She gasps, and then she does something very small. Something damning. She lifts her right arm, splays her fingers, and uses that elbow to shield her face and head.

She prepares to be struck like someone who has been struck before, many times, and could not fight back.

Time stands still. Outside of the clear shell of the hull, the white world rages. In here, in the warmth we share and create together, I take her suspended arm in one hand and I pull it against me. I pull her against me and onto my lap and I clutch her to my chest so tight so that she might know that she is a part of it and I would no sooner strike her than I would my own flesh.

I allow my Xanaxana to purr its relief, filling the entire hull with its vibrations. Her muscles begin to ease and she hiccups, then covers her mouth with her hand. Her eyes are shut tight and she is clutching at her chest.

"This wasn't supposed to happen," she finally says, words bursting out of her in a tempest, "An alien wasn't supposed to die trying to save my life."

My anger flares as she makes such an inane delineation between us, and I snarl into her hair, "Alien or human. Voraxian or alien. We are all the same. You dishonor his sacrifice by reducing him in this way."

She clenches harder and trembles now with vigor. Turning into my suit, her fingers clutch at the fabric, pulling desperately. I maneuver around her, caught off guard at the sight of warm water coating her face.

"You make this water again with your eyes..."

A sob wrenches out of her before I can say more. "Just leave me here. Please..."

What does she mean? What can she mean? "Do you suggest that after I risk the lives of four warriors, three trackers, three dozen dreya and myself, I should throw you back out in the snow? *What do you think?*" I seethe, my voice threatening to shatter the fibers of the hull around us. "You are my Xiveri mate! You are our Xhea."

"Don't call me that," she says and I start.

Of all the things to say to me. Of all the things to say. I release her and rise to my feet and as I look at her kneeling there on the plastic floor of the hull, a surge of emotion comes on so strong, there is no hope for control. *I am a controlled male. I was. But not anymore.*

"You dare!" The words rip out of my throat like a strip of bark torn from a tree. Scarringly.

She jumps, her bottom jaw trembling. She looks up at me glassy-eyed, but only for an instance. In the next, she rights herself and fumbles for the broken shard of staff I used to kill the creature. Lying there beside Re'Okkari's body, she snatches it up and lifts it as she rises. In the impossibly small space, she squares off against me like I'm nothing but another hevarr. As if we had not traveled the galaxy's most distant pleasures just the lunar before. As if we are not all exhausted and wounded and in pain.

"Lower your weapon immediately."

"No." She lunges at me, but I bat away her first strike with the plates lining my forearm, and then her second. I back away from her as she advances and when the hull doors open, step out into the snow. She chases me into the falling ice, but does not make it far when her right leg gives out. Plunging staff-first into the snow, she nearly skewers herself when her lower half spasms and she cries out. She grabs for her thigh, squeezing it in her gloved fingers. *There are five, yet she calls us alien…as if somehow five and not six makes any difference at all.*

I dive down to meet her and wrench her small body across my knees. I reach where her hands are reaching, noticing now tears in her coverings that I hadn't before. She tries to stop me but I push her hands aside.

"Get away," she says. *She begs.*

"Xhea, what has gotten into you?"

"Don't call me Xhea. I don't...I don't deserve... Xhea. I don't deserve it..." Her head falls back on her neck. Her muscles become slack. There is water on her face carving paths through the ice that has formed. Her lips are blue and her skin is ashen. My Xanaxana writhes wildly in my body and I suddenly cannot breathe. *She is dying.*

Fear and panic become me, but I do not have the capacity to staunch the rush of color to my ridges as everything she does denudes and flays me to my bones. "Cra'El! Ka'Okkari!"

My tracker and warrior come to flank me just as I again lower Kiki's body into the ice glider, my remaining dreya stamping their feet before it. They lost a brother and a sister today, two who had grown up with the litter since birth. They too will feel their own form of sorrow.

"What is it? What is killing her?" I say. My fingers fly over her body, unwilling to remove her coverings but unsure how to proceed without. Ka'Okkari answers my question as he finishes fastening her legs to the stabilizers.

"Okkari, here. The hevarr's spray has maimed her. It has chewed through the top layer of skin." As he speaks, he takes snow from outside of the glider and packs it against her wound — an effective counter to the effects of the spray.

Though it may slow the effects, it will not bring back the skin that was already stolen. *Not like merillian will.* I am overcome by shame. Twice that I will have to place my own Xiveri mate in a merillian tank to save her, because it is twice since the Xanaxana named her as mine that I have nearly allowed Voraxia's creatures to take her life.

I draw my holoscreen and issue quick commands to the healers. At the same time, I command my trackers and hunters to disperse and take the remains of the hevarr to Hurr where she and the xub'Hurr will prepare it and treat it for use during the coming icefall. Such a bounty will go a long way. The hides can be tanned and used for a number of purposes. The acid can be reduced for medical supplies and weaponry. The blubber used for soaps and oils. I should have said this and more to my Xhea. To my strange, wounded Kiki who mourns for those she calls alien. *It is as if she hates us, yet still grieves for us.* I do not understand…

"Okkari," she says suddenly and I drop to my knees, allowing autopilot to control our direction for the moment as we fly over the ice, racing towards our home.

"Hexa, Xiveri. I am here."

Her eyes are closed and she is thrashing. The temperature of her skin is raised already from the effects of the poison, which are much farther along and seemingly more destructive to her than they are to me. Delirious, she says a name, and then repeats it. "Mom… mom…"

"Kiki?" Beads of sweat are already formed on her smooth, rounded cheeks. The color has darkened around her eyes, yet the rest of her is so pale it is as if the Mudan who guides the way to the Ocean After has come to collect her himself.

Emotion chokes me. I am Okkari yet I could not stop this. *Just as I could not stop the Drakesh invasion then either. Weak. I am weak.* I bellow a roar to no one but the dead warrior in my ice glider and the dying Xhea beneath me.

She blinks and her eyes are bloodshot, half-moons lowering. "Okkari?"

"Hexa, Kiki. You are alright. You will survive the effects of the acid. I will restore you in merillian..."

"I don't hate you." Startled, I have no answer for her. She blinks up at me. "I hate me."

I plunge my fingers into her hair and shake her, furious *but only because I fear so deeply*. Low, I growl, "Kiki...you are feverish. Calm yourself. Save your breaths..."

"And him."

Stalled, I freeze again. "Who?"

She licks her lips and nods. "Mhm. Bo'Raku. I hate him too. I hate him the most."

She quiets, leaving me alone to stew and to fear and to seethe. *Bo'Raku. What could she have with that putrid conspiring welp? The one who tries to sell human females to the vicious warlord of Kor and his pirate Niahhorru.* I don't understand and I try to coax more intelligible words from her — to keep her lucid, hexa, but also because I. need. answers. — but she is unresponsive after more than a few mumbled words that speak of the living and the dead.

My home comes into sight and as I gather the Xhea to my chest, I call up my life drive. Orders are issued to my tribe with how to treat the injured, the fallen and the hevarr. And another two requests are sent. These go to Rakukanna and to Svera, the human advisor and female who conspired with the Rakukanna and Kiki. They will meet with me on this solar because I have never needed answers so desperately. I need to know everything about my Xhea. Why would she run? For whom does she grieve? Why does she speak Bo'Raku's name? Why does she fear me? Why is she sick with a hate that poisons her?

I shake my head. My hair hangs forward as I stare down at my Xhea's face, so tortured even in sleep. My soul shivers and shakes. *Answers.* I will have them despite my exhaustion. If it takes me through the lunar. If it takes me the rest of my life.

11
Kiki

Warm. I'm swimming again. I'm swimming so slowly. *Don't they know I don't know how?* I smile to myself and my cheeks pinch. I haven't smiled in a while.

My toes zing. Pins and needles. *Pins and needles. Svera sewing a dress — one for me this time. That year, me and Miari got matching ones for Christmas from Svera and her family. Miari made hers into some gadget but I wore mine and everyone told me I looked beautiful in it. It felt good to feel beautiful.*

It feels good. Syrup coating my limbs. Slow wakefulness. I'm comfortable. So comfortable. *Wrapped in the arms of a male. His skin shimmers in the low light from the strange decorations zigzagging across black walls. Coccooned in a nest made from the skin of an animal he hunted, his breath warms my neck as he breathes, Xivoora Xiveri. It doesn't matter what the words are. I know them already. From another time, from another galaxy, one much gentler than this...*

I take a breath and air punches into my lungs like I've been beat. I gasp and try to find my arms, but they're lost. I'm touching...ah stars, it's more of the goop. *The goop is real?* It clings to my body like stains do, like scars. Goo. Purple weird goo that tingles every place it touches, and it touches me everywhere. My skin, my eyes, thickening my hair, making my head feel even more weighted. I can feel it even on the *inside of my body*, making my privates feel like they've just been rubbed in peppermint.

Get the fuck away from me, I think, but I open my mouth and I choke. *Fight fight fight*. I cough and focus on getting my feet beneath me. From there, I can find a weapon. With a weapon, I can kill just about anything. Maybe not the goo, but anything else.

But I just fall back into more goo. My head goes under, and when my face breaks the surface of the liquid, I gasp in air that tastes like sour licorice. Can I breathe? Am I breathing? *Fight fight!* Just calm down...I need to calm down...*Fight! Now stand. Stand! Open your eyes.* No. I'm scared. *I'm not scared of anything.* I'm scared of everything.

"Shh. You're safe. You're safe..." Soft fingers touch my hairline and my eyelids flutter.

"Svera?"

But my fuzzy vision reveals a face that isn't light brown like Svera's is, but green. As green as the sacred trees that grew outside of the human colony in the uninhabited place. That grow there still. *How would I know? I'm not there anymore.* And then it comes back to me. The Mountain Run. Defeating him. Being defeated. The need. The pain. The monster on the ice. Aliens dying in my name...

"Fuck. What is this? Where am I?" It's so dark in this room. There's a few of those weird lights swirling across the ceiling and the smell of minerals. *I've been here before.*

"You are in the bathing chamber, in a merillian bath where you have slept the past several solars. Your wounds were not extensive, so you healed quickly. Apologies, but it is deep in the lunar now and the ioni are at their darkest. I have been informed that it is difficult for humans to see in dim lighting." A bright lamp is illuminated against the far wall, this one looking very much like an oil lamp we used once on the colony before the oil ran out and Merdock started charging too many rations for more. "Here, is this better?"

Kuana's face comes to life before me. Wide, black eyes, bright white hair, soft lips, so unsure as she watches me, fearing me.

The purple that coats my arms looks like jello. Big, fat globs of it. Only it feels the teeniest bit like...it's *moving*. "Merillian?" *I remember this word. He said it before, up on the ice, when he was delivering me the most intense pleasure I'd ever felt...*

"Hexa. The microbes contain healing properties. They are responsible for saving your life when you were brought from your human moon to Voraxia. The healer has informed me that you were then in the merillian for thirty four solars. Your wounds were extensive. The Okkari says it is because you fought khrui in order to save the Rakukanna's life — and that you succeeded in killing two. Please excuse my impertinence but I would like the honor of asking if this is correct."

"I..." I'm still dizzy, but sitting up, I manage to recline against the edge of something hard. As my head spins momentarily, I blink and focus only on small green face. Kuana... I lick my lips, feeling...comfortable... whole. Fixed. "I did."

Tsssak. Tsak. Tsak… Enormous grey beasts advance on Miari and me. They're all claws and all I've got is my grabar, an amp that Miari made with only one pulse, and a willingness to die.

"Wow," she breathes, lips curling up but it looks like she's trying to fight it. "That is so impressive."

"The Rakukanna," I exhale.

Her ridges flash grey. Her mouth turns down. "Why do you seem so sad? The Rakukanna is well. She is in Illyria where she rules Voraxia alongside Raku and nurtures their growing kit. It will be the first Voraxian-human offspring born since your earliest Hunt with the Drakesh. Our entire federation is extremely excited to hear more news of the kit."

A deep grief fills me. "I failed her."

Kuana, as irritatingly upbeat as Svera always was, shakes her head. "Nox. You have not. But I have been informed by the Rakukanna's closest advisor, Svera, that you are unaware of such developments and am honored to open communication to her for you. Would you like to speak to her now?"

Shock. It must be shock. Because I have nothing to say but, "Now?"

"Hexa. Now. You may also wait for a moment of your choosing."

"No…no. Now is good."

Kuana grins and passes one hand over her left forearm and a whole host of holographic numbers and symbols appear, seeming to hover in front of her face. "Communication line E6FV8." A pause. Silence. Then the holographic numbers disappear and in their wake Svera's two dimensional form appears in stark clarity, as if she's here, watching me through a clear window pane.

"Kiki! Oh my stars, oy Gewalt, Alhamdullah you're okay. Are you okay? I've been speaking to the Okkari for the past two solars and he told me everything. You were brought to Illyria after you were injured. He wasn't supposed to take you out of Illyria until you woke up and had a chance to speak to Miari and me but he did and now we're stuck and we can't get to you — apparently the first frost of Nobu is too harsh even for our transporters. We'll have to wait for it to pass before we can come and see you or before you can leave and come see us, or go back to the colony if that's what you really want.

"I'm so sorry, Kiki. This is all messed up. He told us that he forced you to do another Mountain Run and that he...that you two..." She huffs and looks torn, tortured on my behalf. "He thinks you're his forever mate — that you have something called Xanaxana and that it would cause you to respond to him...physically." She struggles with the term — Svera, who worships the Tri-God and knows nothing about desire or sex or a man's body — and her voice breaks. "He doesn't know that humans don't feel the Xanaxana like they do. He thought you would."

I do.

"And I'm sorry Kiki, but I had to make him understand. I told him what happened to you before. What Bo'Raku did to you during your first Hunt. Va'Raku — the Okkari — he feels deep remorse. He did not know, and the cultural differences...I'm saying a lot but I know it's no real consolation."

A soft clearing of a throat. Kuana stands and with a few flicks of her fingers she moves away from the edge of the basin, but the image of Svera remains. "I will leave you now. Please do call me when you have finished. I will help you prepare a bath."

I nod at her, struggling with words, with what I'd even say. *Thank you?* She's an alien. *Fuck you?* She's as kind as Svera is. *And she's an alien.*

I sit up little by little and grip the edges of the tub. "Oh Kiki, please say something. I know you probably hate me right now, but write something if you don't want to talk to me. Gesture. Just, please tell me." She clasps a hand over her mouth and I see tears fill her eyes. They fill mine too.

I open my mouth. Eternities pass. Lifetimes unravel. *Lie. Tell her that I hate her. Tell her I hate him. Tell her that they've all abandoned and betrayed me. Tell them that I want to kill still. That I'm glad the alien who sacrificed himself for me died. Tell her that I feel nothing. That I feel nothing!*

"I feel..." *Nothing. Nothing is what I feel.* "I do feel it."

My voice breaks. The hateful demon writhing within me dies. The river in my body dries. I desiccate, squeezed dry. I'm shaking all over. I open my mouth and a horrible mewl comes out. And then a half sob.

I close my eyes and I tell her the horrible, terrible truth. "I felt it from the first moment I fought him. I feel *everything*. I feel everything but hate. I don't hate you. I don't hate Miari." I don't even hate him, the one who calls himself *mine* even though I know nothing about him. Nothing but the oasis he takes me to, that impossible cane-and-root breeze.

12
Kiki

I'm out of the purple goop. I'm out of the bath. I'm in a small dark room where a pallet lies. I'm shaky. It might just be the product of a good meal and a good night's sleep. Or it might be the memories of the conversations I had with Svera and Miari. Knowing that they're both somehow happy here off-colony with the males that they've been assigned to. That Miari is even in a union with one of them. That she's a queen. That she's pregnant. I shudder. *What if that happens to me?*

With a firm set of my jaw, I get up from the small table where Kuana brings me things to eat. She's been waiting on me in a way I find uncomfortable. We're both uncomfortable. Me, because I don't know what to do with her — I've never had much and what I have had, I've had to fight for. I'm not used to someone helping me do things...not for free...

Her, because she doesn't know what to do with *me*. I've behaved erratically since arriving here — at best. And when I tried to run, she apparently got locked up by Kuaku. *And I didn't even ask what happened to her. So focused on me, at the expense of everyone else around me. I* wince.

I have a headache I can't seem to get rid of. A fear that pulses through my body, sending pins and needles up my legs through my toenails. An itch to fight something to slake my aggression. *An urge to say sorry to every being I come across, even if they are alien. Maybe then especially.*

I sigh, exhausted by my own thoughts. Gathering up my stone dishes, I take a steadying breath and approach the door. It opens on a sensor of some kind and as quietly as I can, I wade out into the hall. As soon as I reach the white part of the hall, the temperature drops and I regret not having worn the slippers Kuana laid out for me. My dad always called me petulant. So did my mom. By the end of their being together, it was the only thing they ever agreed on.

I enter the big white-and-glass room that overlooks the village and am so distracted by the sight of the storm raging on its other side, rendering the whole world white and lifeless, that I don't immediately notice Kuana. I start when she rises from a pile of white pillows near the black basin set into the floor and bows slightly.

Grunting, I turn from her and cross the room, heading for the door. I'm not surprised when Kuana intercepts me. Instead of letting me pass, she tries to wrangle the empty plates from my hands, but after an awkward dance that I gather is frustrating *for both of us,* she lets me pass.

"Just show me how to do it," I snap at her, wishing I knew how to gentle my tone. It's not her fault. I know that, and yet it changes nothing. *Even without the hate, I'm still this horrible beast.*

Her ridges trickle with color that I can only assume means she's terrified or she thinks I'm crazy. We've done this dance before, and just like those other times, she finally nods and leads me through the doorway to the next white room which has a sunken pit in one part of the floor and inside of that, a raised dais.

She takes me down into the pit, then past the dais to a patch of black against the all white wall. It juts out at about hip level and there's a trough to one side of it. Kuana removes the stopper at the base of the trough and surprisingly warm water gushes out.

"You can use these crystals for washing," Kuana says softly, taking some round colorful balls from the ledge that juts out at eye level and rolling them in her hands until they form a rich lather. My eyes are wide — I can feel them on my face. I can also feel when my lips quirk at the sight of her taking a black scrubber and holding it out between us. Looks just like the wool ones we use back home.

I reach for it, but she hesitates. "It is an honor to serve you," she says and it's about the fifth time she's said it the past two solars.

"Yes," I say stiffly, "I know that." I can feel my cheeks warm. I don't know what else to say. "I just...I'm more comfortable doing things for myself."

Her face turns down. "I understand, my Xhea."

"And tomorrow I want you to teach me how to use these other things." I point to the dais with its strange marbly surface and then the whole host of white paneling that stretches across the wall at my back. There are silver boxes interspersed inbetween that I've already fumbled my way across several times — I'm still unable to figure out how to open anything.

Her face falls even further, grey and cerulean trailing across her brow bone. "Of course."

I feel guilt and self-hate renew and the worst part about it is that I know exactly what I'd do and say to stop it, but at every turn, I choose not to.

I wind my way back through the house feeling like a shell of a person. At least, until I reach *the* door. My palms start to sweat and a drum beats in my lower half. I don't give into the temptation to seek him out though. *How can I, after what I've done? What does he even think? What could I even say? I'm sorry I ran and they all died?* Fuck me. *I wish he would just fuck me.* And fight. I just want to fuck and fight until I'm numb.

I speed up as I pass it only to be shocked and horrified when I hear the door glide open at my back. *Faster. Move. Get away.* My feet slow. Cold causes the hairs on the back of my neck to stand on end. I turn and my stomach flies up into my throat. This male isn't one I know. He's blue — not red — but he still isn't the Okkari. I canter back, hitting the white wall behind me and wishing that I had a weapon.

"My Xhea, it is good to see you well."

I freeze and my head whips around as I look up at him, inspecting his face for the first time. An ounce of steel eases from my bones. "You...you were there. Out on the cold white."

His mouth quirks making me wonder what I've done wrong this time. "Hexa. I am Ka'Okkari, warrior and hunter of the Okkari and this tribe."

I feel nervous. Nervous and terrified. He saved my life *but he's an alien.* I can't attack him, as is my first instinct, and since he's one of the aliens who saved my life, I can assume he won't take it. Not after all that was lost trying to keep me alive.

Grief surges inside of me, mingling with the regret and fear and shame to create a potent combination. "I... dont..." He blinks at me and I know I've slighted him even though his reaction betrays nothing at all. He just smiles and the expression makes tears of frustration sting the backs of my eyes. "I'm just going back to my room."

"I know, Xhea," he says and his smile stretches even fuller. "And I was hoping to catch you. The Okkari has informed me that you desire to visit the homes of Va'El and Re'Okkari. He told me you wish to honor their sacrifices. Once you are properly outfitted, I am able to be your guide."

I am completely stalled by his offer. Nervous-bordering-on-mortified. I do want to do those things. I do want to apologize to the families of the aliens who gave their lives to me, that's what I told Svera. She must have told him. *They've been speaking?* I hate that. And not for the right reasons. It's not because he's an alien and she's talking to him behind my back. It's because he's *my* alien.

He's mine. He once called me his. But that was before I ruined everything and got his people killed. Why would he still think that?

I glance past the broad beast of a male, but am unable to see anything of the Okkari's office. "Is the Okkari there?"

"He is, but he has duties to attend to. There is much to be done before the first icefall sees its end. Organizing the preparation of the hevarr that was slain, repairing the grain stores damaged in the storm, continuing warrior training. He also has the chamar to organize on behalf of Re'Okkari."

"Chamar?"

"In honor of his death, we will celebrate his life. On your human moon, do you also carry such a tradition?"

I jerk back as if struck, then nod slightly.

Ka'Okkari gives me a small bow and I feel rattled at the sympathy he emanates. "Fear not, Xhea. It is understood that you were without induction into our culture and that you suffered in the past." *What does he know of my past?* Panic grips me.

"I am not here to torment you, and I assure you that the Okkari is not either. We are here to protect you. And it is only on Re'Okkari's honor that he should meet Xana knowing he has done all he can to protect you, and to protect the tribe. The hevarr will make it possible for us to survive the impending icefalls well. It is a rare day that hunters are afforded the opportunity to take on such a worthy opponent and live to tell the tales. I am sure songs are being written of Re'Okkari as we speak. He will receive a warrior's rest in the Great Ocean."

His words make my insides cramp and I have to hold onto the wall behind me *hard* otherwise I feel like I might die. I blink rapidly and say in strangled notes, "Alright, I'll go...I mean, I'd like to go...honor them. Let me just get dressed." I turn and find Kuana standing in front of my door, already holding a heavy fur-lined jumpsuit out for me.

"I thought you might need it," she offers in this timid, heartbreaking way that only heightens my agony. These beings aren't like the Drakesh. They aren't even like the humans. Humans are mean, nasty little things. *And since I've been made by humans, and reshaped by the Drakesh, what does that make me?*

I hastily pull on the jump suit and the additional fur pelt that Kuana gives me and follow her to the front door where Ka'Okkari waits wearing a small smile. I notice that his skin is bluer and darker than the Okkari's, his face not quite so angular, giving it a softer slant. I don't know why, but I'm not *afraid* of him like I thought I'd be. I feel no urge to fight.

"The temperatures have risen just enough this solar for this weather to be safe. Still, coming from your desertous moon colony, I imagine the icefall will still be bracing. Are you ready, Xhea?"

I nod, surprised again that he could know so much about my colony and say, "Yes."

"Xhivey," he replies before opening the front door to a world of white. "Brace yourself."

I follow him down the black stone steps, surprised to note that they're the only things out here that aren't white and cold. The cold white is coming down heavier now, flakes bigger than my face, even if they are flat like bark. Their size and ceaselessness makes it hard to see more than one house away. Luckily, we don't travel far before we arrive at a dwelling carved into the same stone mountain as the Okkari's.

It has a glass-plated front, but being further down the mountain, it lacks the same impressive view of the village that the Okkari's house has. Stuck deeper into the mountain, I'm not surprised to find that most of the house is black stone, rather than white when I step inside into the warmth. And it is warm. Warm and welcoming with a distinctly feminine touch.

Where the Okkari's home is all white and black everything, this house has rich red tapestries woven through with gold scattered across the dark rock floor. Lush green plants that seem as if they'd grow only in much warmer climates sit on stone daises, hang from the ceiling in large black rock basins or seem content to merely lick their way directly up the walls.

As I take a step further into the room and the doors shut behind me, I can't help but be drawn to a whole shelf that's just full of holo images trapped in pink and green and beige frames. In every one is smiling face. A smiling *alien* face.

Sometimes in snowy environments, some in ones more lush and green, some inside buildings, some with other aliens, but in all of them are the same two aliens — Va'El and a female — and in all of the images they look incandescently happy.

"We are honored to receive you, Xhea," a female voice says and I tear my gaze away from the holographs and refocus on the female alien by the fire pit who's holding Va'El's hand. The female from the pictures. The sight of them sitting there so obviously in love with one another makes my chest sting. I rub the space above my heart with the heel of my hand even though it does nothing to dispel the sensation.

Va'El is sprawled out on a divan, his leg propped up on a stack of plush furry pillows. Even though his leg was broken in three places and acid from the hevarr venom chewed through a lot of the muscle in his calf, he's still smiling. His guiless contentment makes me wonder how it can be that in a house full of aliens, the person I hate the most in that moment is me.

"I just..." *Stop sounding like outer dome trash and speak.* I try to hone my inner Svera and inhale deeply. I exhale just as deep. "It is I who is honored," I say finally, though it takes some will. Some force. It's the first kind thing I've said to any of them and it hurts, but only because it feels so good.

Va'El and his female exchange a look. She seems slightly amused, but inclines her head nonetheless. "It is gracious of you, Xhea."

"Most gracious," Va'El echoes.

When I don't continue, and they don't either, I feel heat rise in my cheeks. I don't know what to do. I don't know what to say to these people. To these aliens, I mean...No, to these *honorable* beings. "I um..." *Stuttering fool.* "What you did, Va'El, it was really brave." *Idiot.*

"It was my duty, Xhea. An honor. And if my own Xiveri mate had been in the same position, I'd have counted on the Okkari to do the same."

That surprises me, and I feel the heat in my cheeks hold. "You two are Xiveri mates?"

"Hexa," Va'El says and his ridges suddenly pop with radiant colors. They remind me of the Okkari's ridges and the way he looks at his woman reminds me of the way the Okkari looks at me sometimes. *Used to look. Now he doesn't want to see me.* "Tre'Hurr and I discovered our bond during a Run on the Mountain between our tribe and a neighboring one. Two rotations ago, it was one of the largest runs we've seen yet."

The alien — *Tre'Hurr* — beams. "Hexa, we are most blessed by Xana and Xaneru to have found one another. We hear that you and the Okkari are also blessed. I must say that I find it even more remarkable that Xana and Xaneru would have placed you in each other's paths from so far away. Even if the circumstances that brought you two together were most unfortunate. I grieve for your human females."

"Drakesh muxung," Va'El spits, before his ridges radiate a soft yellow, scattered amidst a much deeper red. "Apologies, Xhea. It is simply too unforgivable not to want to speak on the subject."

"You...you know about our Hunt?"

"We know that the matings were forced, hexa," Va'El says.

"And how the human females' lives were forfeit unless unborn hybrid kits were discarded." Tre'Hurr makes a trilling sound in the back of her throat while her ridges beam grey. I wonder if grey then doesn't mean grief, for I see it echoed in the ridges of many of the aliens in the room. *All* of the aliens.

A stone lodges in my throat then, making it hard to speak. I blink many times, hoping to keep the emotion from my tone. *They grieve for us.* "How do you know all this?"

"We have received the first broadcasts from the human advisor to the Rakukanna — *Shuh-vair-ax*," she says, mispronouncing the name so badly I can't help the twitch to my lips. "They are very detailed reports on human culture and recent history. The Okkari requested the information be disseminated across all of Nobu so that we may better understand our Xhea. He has also informed us that you were not immune to the unfair pact created between your human council and the Drakesh," Tre'Hurr says softly, stunning me. *They know. They all know about Bo'Raku and what he did to me.*

"How...he had no right to share that information," I rasp, air punching out of me.

Va'El makes a face, something like a frown but it's filled with so genuine a sympathy, my anger falls away as quickly as it came. "It is important that this information is shared, so that the perpetrators may be condemned and so that your courage and resilience may be known. It is a brave female who continues to fight, as you do, after such a dishonor — his, certainly, not yours."

"It's...embarrassing," I wheeze.

I don't need to speak color to know that shock is the sentiment echoed around the room. "Embarrassing? Nox, my Xhea. Forgive us, but here on Nobu what you have faced only increases your honor and the respect we feel for you. To have a Xhea who has fought battles and survived horrors. It is truly an honor to welcome you, even if we do wish that these were battles you had never fought, and horrors you had never been through."

A memory comes on so hard and fast it gives me whiplash. *Malik and Everett smile at me as they pass by. Loudly enough for me to hear, Everett says, "She used to be so fuckable. Too bad that alien wrecked her." "Pussy's probably too loose to bother with now." They laugh until I advance on Malik and punch him square in the face. I fight the both of them and leave them with two bloody noses, one bloody lip, and three black eyes. The first moment I understood how good it felt to fight. And win.*

"It doesn't...make me seem dirty? Used?"

Surprise again. Tre'Hurr opens her mouth, but it's Ka'Okkari who speaks. He stands up, away from the wall where he'd been leaning. His tone is grim, expression set in a more severe mask than I've seen it thus far. "Has someone said as much to you?"

I shake my head. "Not here. On Nobu."

Red flashes in his forehead and I struggle to hold his gaze, but refuse to break it. I don't want to seem weak. I don't want to seem dirty. *Especially not to* him — *but he hasn't seen me in solars. Maybe he thinks the same thing colony kids do. Maybe he's done with me after the chaos I caused, the lives stolen too soon.*

"The answer to your question, Xhea, is nox." He says nothing more and I nod weakly even though I'm not sure I believe him.

Va'El makes a crude, angry sound before he rasps, "It honors us all to hear of the upcoming tsanui, in which the fallen Bo'Raku will be condemned. It is honorable that it was granted by the Raku."

The knot in my throat makes it hard for me to do anything, but I have to know. "What is that?"

"You forget, my Xiveri, she does not know our customs." Tre'Hurr gently lays her hand on her partner's arm before rearranging the furs covering him to the waist.

My heart squeezes. I remember... *The Okkari arches over my body, protecting me from the cold biting at my skin. He calls me warrior. Later, I look down on his head, that strip of white hair amidst so much black. I tell him I need him and it's the truest thing I've ever said aloud.*

"Excuse me, my Xhea," Va'El says, sitting up a little taller as his Xiveri mate places her arm on his shoulder. *He lives for her. What do I live for?* "The tsanui is the warrior's right to revenge. For his crimes, the one you know as Bo'Raku has been removed from his position. He is known now by his slave name, Peixal and is on trial for his betrayal of the Raku and the Voraxian people. He was involved in illegal trading with the King of Kor, as far as we were told, and was also complicit in the abduction of the Rakukanna and her advisor."

I clench at that, remembering how I'd felt hearing Miari and Svera's harrowing story when they were abducted by the Niahhorru king using an off-planet transport device never before heard of. If Svera's protector Krisxox hadn't been left alive, and he hadn't managed to plant a tracking device in Svera's communicator, they might never have been found.

"The trial was set to take place on Voraxia, however, our Okkari has requested that Peixal be brought here so that he may undergo the tsanui before his trial."

My whole body catches. I feel the sweat on my lip consume my whole face, my neck, my chest. I waver where I stand, reaching out to catch something *anything* before I fall. Suddenly, Tre'Hurr is standing in front of me, her arms on my arms. Touching me *kindly*. She's guiding me to a pillow and thrusting a cup of something warm into my hands.

"Be calm, my Xhea. You are safe. He can bring no harm to you. Never again."

"Bo'Raku is coming here?" I can't breathe. I've thought of seeing him dead in a million ways, but when he didn't appear on top of the mountain, I'd forgotten what it would be like to see him living. *What will that do to me?*

"Calm yourself, Xhea. You will not need to be near him, or even see him," she says as if reading my mind, "It would not dishonor you *not* to attend the tsanui."

"What happens during the tsanui?" I finally manage to choke out in between sips of this strange, earthy tea that smells of colony sand and a little of Okkari.

"The ceremony will constitute a fight between our Okkari and the exiled Bo'Raku, Peixal."

"A fight? A fair fight? But why? Why would he do that?" *Why would he do that* for me?

Color flashes for a moment in her brow and she bows slightly. "My apologies for the emotional display. I simply forget that humans are not fully aware of the power and effects of the Xanaxana. It would be impossible for me to explain other than to say, it is no question that the Okkari would do this for you. Exacting the tsanui against one who harmed his Xiveri mate would be instinctual for him."

"As it would be for me," Va'El adds. He takes Tre'Hurr's hand as she settles again at his side. He brings it to his chest where he holds it. I stare. I stare hard. My mouth dries and I cling to the warm drink in my hands, sipping gingerly as spicy aromas zap my taste buds. We don't have tea like this on the colony. Tea that's not tea, but thick and syrupy and spicy and calming all at once.

"But the Okkari could lose…"

"Nox." This time it's Ka'Okkari, standing a few paces away. His face is still so very stern. "The Okkari is the fiercest fighter Nobu has, and cannot be bested in a tsanui. It will be a fair fight, but you need not fear. Xaneru is with him."

"Then what happens?"

"Then the Okkari will exact whatever punishment he deems fit. He will likely exile Peixal to Nobu's endless ice ocean, though this he will need to agree upon with Raku, the Rakukanna, and the other xub'Raku. It is not known how far Peixal's influence with the outer planets extends and they will want to ensure that he cannot be a harm to Voraxians or humans wherever he is placed. You will never see him again."

"I meant…what happens to me? Will I be exiled with Bo'Raku?" My voice trembles. The idea terrifies me. Being trapped alone with him in an icefall I can't possibly survive by myself. Hunting and being hunted while I face off against khrui and hevarr and monsters unknown. Svera's Tri-God speaks of paradise. But it also speaks of hell. This would be mine. Alone with the tormentor who haunts my dreams in a cold white dungeon.

Tre'Hurr and Va'El share a look. She shakes her head. "But my Xhea, why would you be exiled?"

"Because I hid Mi…" I stop myself, remembering what Svera told me about names. They are a protected thing here, only shared among mates and close kin. To share Miari's now would be to disgrace her. "…the Rakukanna."

Everyone's ridges in the room light up in different colors. Tre'Hurr stutters as she speaks, "My Xhea, it is true that for keeping the Raku from his Xiveri mate, you and the human advisor *Svera* will be tried, however there is no chance that you would ever be *exiled*. The trials for you and the Svera will involve trials by combat. There will be no tsanui or anything of the like. You will have the opportunity then to choose your champion or your opponent. The Okkari will champion you and as Ka'Okkari well put, the Okkari is the greatest warrior Nobu has ever seen. He will not fail you."

He'll fight for me then too? I close my eyes and nod, trying not to think about how Kuaku lied to me and it was because of that lie that I ran off. I could have just talked to him. Been honest and open. Asked him to talk to Svera and Miari. Then all of this horribleness would have been avoided.

"Xhea," Tre'Hurr says, pulling my attention back to my tea-drink-thing.

She is particularly interested in the human colony and asks me polite questions. I can feel her desire to ask more, but she doesn't push. After a while, I notice Va'El's apparent fatigue. Wishing I'd noticed it earlier, I mumble an awkward goodbye, rise and leave. As I make it to the door Tre'Hurr thanks me for coming to see them and I somehow manage to apologize, and then thank them again.

Back in the cold white once more, I think to myself of how ashamed Jaxal would be of me, and how pleased my apology would make my mom. *When did I start looking up to him and stop looking up to her? And why can't it be both?*

The cold comes stronger now, and it only takes a few seconds for me to feel it on my face and in my lungs. I have to bite together to keep my teeth from shaking, and am grateful when Ka'Okkari finally leads me to another dwelling, this one in the middle of the valley and not sheltered at all by the mountain, but huddled along with other smaller, squat screa homes.

"This is the place of Re'Okkari," he says when we pass through a circular door — one he has to hunch to get through.

Again, I notice the stark contrast to the other two homes I've been in. Where Okkari's is all clean lines and efficiency and Tre'Hurr and Va'El's feels alive with their love, Re'Okkari's space is sparse. It doesn't betray much.

To one side, there's the same strange cooking apparatus and a dais that I *think* is either meant for storing food, or for chopping it. At the back of the space, there's a raised platform piled thickly with furs, though they don't sit in a curved bed like Okkari's do. There's a stone basin in the center of the space with ash in the middle, and thick, grey pillows scattered around that.

To my right, opposite the kitchen area, there's a low table on which I spy a half-finished game left for two or more players. My heart catches when I realize it'll never get finished.

Biting my teeth together, I say quickly, "He didn't have any family?"

"Nox, Xhea. He was unmated."

"But what about his parents?"

Ka'Okkari tilts his head at this. "The ones who sired him hail from another tribe. They relocated, seeking warmer climates once their kit was fledged warrior."

"They don't see each other anymore?"

"Nox, they do not. I see this troubles you, yet this is the way on Nobu. Across all of Voraxia, in fact."

I hug my opposite arms, thinking of what Kuaku said. *I'll never see them again.* Even if she lied about the other things, it seems that in this aspect she spoke truths. *I'll never go home. I'll never have a chance to tell my mom how sorry I am.*

Softly, I say, "In the human colony, we stay close to our parents until they pass."

"I take it you mean pass into the Great Ocean of the After."

I don't know what that is, but I get the gist and nod.

White flickers over his ridges and he smiles at me fondly and I feel strange, like I've known him for years instead of just a few moments. "Kits are carried forward by their sires until they reach adulthood and take on their new titles, divesting themselves of the names they kept as children."

Suddenly it makes sense why they do not share their names with one another. To do so would be sort of...intimate, representing a kinship it is not likely you'll share with many, especially not if the birthing rate is so low. It also makes me sad. *I want to know his name, but maybe that window is closed.*

Ka'Okkari says, "My Xhea, I will leave you now."

"What?"

"The Okkari has requested I leave you here."

"What for?"

He hesitates, flaring white. *White for surprise. Red for rage. Yellow for shame. Grey for grief. Blue for happiness. Purple for desire...* I may not speak color *fluently*, but I'm getting the hang of it little-by-little.

"He believed that you would be interested in maintaining your own residence apart from his."

My mouth opens. I can't speak. I feel hate and fear and terror and grief and bloodlust and savagery. *But only at the thought that he forsakes me.*

"If I may be so bold," Ka'Okkari says, filling the silence, "I believe it may be his intention to attempt to court you in the human fashion. The manual produced by the Svera clearly states that males and females — or two males or two females — live apart during the courtship process."

Svera and her Tri-God be damned. Leave it to a worshiper to write such a manual... I open my mouth to protest, but as I take a step, my foot falls onto one of the pillows by the fire. I stare down at the ashes, wondering when Re'Okkari's last meal was, what he ate, if the fire was roaring when he ate it.

"Would it not be a disgrace for me to stay here where Re'Okkari stayed even if I'm the reason he's dead?"

"My Xhea, no one thinks this."

I don't meet his gaze. I don't need his sympathy. I was there. I saw the hevarr upchuck its acid spit all over him. Meanwhile, I left the battle without fighting, with just a few flesh wounds. *Disgrace him? Hah. I've already done that.*

Finally, he says, "Nox. On the contrary. You honor him greatly by tending his nest."

"Then I'll do it. I'll stay here."

"Xhivey. I will inform the Okkari and the hasheba who will help ready the nest for you."

I don't know what to say next, and shift my weight uncomfortably between my feet. "Thank you."

"Of course, Xhea. I shall leave you." He turns from me to the door and I feel a strange sadness at his departure, similar to the one I felt when we left Tre'Hurr. She had been real...sweet. The kind of person — being — I could like. Maybe even be friends with, if I have to stay here. *No one said I'm not allowed to go back...why do I keep saying if?* I clamp down on the thought because the answer makes my whole body hurt with a dull ache, like I've been beat up over and over and over and the bruises left behind will never fade. *I don't want to go back.*

Like the ice that sweeps in from the sky, blanketing everything, this weird ice world has given me a clean slate. A fresh start. *More than that.* Panicky thoughts of the Okkari slip into my thoughts and I shake my head to clear them.

"Wait," I call out just as he reaches the door. He glances over his shoulder at me. "Will you thank him for me? This is…it's a good idea." *Time alone with only myself for company? What could possibly go wrong?*

"I will do just that," he says, lips quirking again.

The doors whoosh open in front of him and close at his back, leaving me in the dim world that was once Re'Okkari's. Alone, for the first time in *solars*, I take a turn of my surroundings. I take a seat at the place where the game is still laid out without touching anything. I'm cold and huddle down in my fur suit as I try to make sense of the curved board and its many black and white pieces. Distantly, I wonder how I should get food, but I'm not left long to debate when the door to Re'Okkari's home suddenly slices open.

Thinking for a second it might be Ka'Okkari again, I'm not prepared for the sight that greets me — not Ka'Okkari but Okkari himself. His black hair flicks in the wind, his brutal gaze pinned to mine. Framed by the white world behind him, he looks imposing and masculine and the golden thread in my chest is set alight. *Not a thread. A fuse.*

The space slicks between my legs as if daring me to stand, but before I can, he holds up both hands and takes a small step into the single room. The doors close behind him and without the strange slithery wall lights, I'm left to rely on the skylights that let in white light. It falls on his shoulders softly, making him glow.

He doesn't speak. My fingers clench and unclench. I turn away from the game and even though my insides are screaming to fight, to lunge for him, to take him down to the furs and wrestle him out of his suit, to claim him — I still manage to blurt, "I'm sorry. I shouldn't have been out there. I shouldn't have…"

He holds up his right hand again and I'm startled quiet by how quickly he gestures. He moves like a specter, coming three paces closer, presenting an occultation of the room behind him, making the whole world darker and more menacing and still, I'm not afraid — or rather, I'm terrified, but I'm not afraid of *him*. I'm afraid of me. Just like I have been this whole time.

From my low seat, my gaze licks up his body. He's got on fur-lined pants and a pelt wrapped around his shoulders and nothing else but I can still smell the oasis that follows him everywhere, that engulfing heat. His shoulders heave and when he glances down at my face, I notice surprising signs of fatigue — his eyes are a duller purple than they were, and his hair is greasy at the roots. In fact, I think he's wearing the same pants he was the last time I saw him fighting, though I can't know for sure.

My jaw works, searching for something else to say, something to ask him, but he breaks the quiet abruptly, in a hard way that makes me jump. Makes my insides rearrange themselves. Makes my heart thrum with the force of an ion round against Droherium.

"I have spoken to the Rakukanna, to our Raku, to Svera. I have read the compatibility manual Svera and Lemoria are drafting, all of Svera's notes, and every report ever drafted by your human Antikythera Council and its chieftain, Mathilda, and the human chieftain who came before her."

"You...how? All...in just...two solars?"

He doesn't reply. He instead edges another half step forward. I waver where I sit, but he still makes no move to touch me or grab me and throw me down onto the furs. *How disappointing.*

Instead he clenches his jaw. A muscle spasms in his neck. His voice is hoarse when he says, "I have come with only one request."

"I…" I cough into my fist. My face flushes. My toes tap out an incessant pattern against the worn rug. "Whatever it is, whatever I can do, I'll do it. I've made so many mistakes."

He hisses, effectively shutting me up. "As have I. I stole you from your home world. I savaged you on the mountain. I denied you answers that I already knew and thought you would not need. I treated you just as I would have a Voraxian. The list goes on, but it is not relevant here. You have spoken to Svera, as have I. From what you know now of Voraxian culture, and from what I know of human history, all mistakes are with explanation. Everything can be understood, even if the way forward remains unclear."

I swallow hard, wondering where he's going with this. If this is the moment where he tells me I'm nothing. Where he reduces me to ash in a way Bo'Raku never could.

"You will tell me if this is an accurate assessment."

I nod and, remembering the way he coaxed me into holding his gaze, I continue to maintain it. Even as his chest inflates on his inhale. Even as his pants tent over the crotch and my insides flutter painfully.

"It is accurate. But what do we do now? What's your request?" I wet my lips as I speak. I can't even say I do it unintentionally, but I like the reaction it elicits.

His foot jolts forward just a half a step, he growls in the back of his throat and then exhales gruffly, nostrils flaring. "I have claimed you in the ancient ways of Nobu, but I would like to claim you as a human would. I would like to…" He breaks off and clears his throat so loudly I flinch in my seat.

I lean back and when my hand comes down onto a smooth stone surface, I disrupt one of the game pieces. I wince away from that too, not willing to mess up any others and quickly stand. I hug my arms around myself, feeling so much shorter and smaller than him without a weapon. Not that that matters much. I've seen him fight. And it was beautiful.

"I will ask you a question, even though this is not customary for any Okkari or xub'Raku."

"Okay."

He inhales and exhales a steady breath. "Kiki, will you let me woo you?"

He is the oasis, and I'm swept away in the tide. Time passes. An indefinite amount of it. I don't speak and he doesn't move. There is no ceding on either side. And in the end, there's only one thing I can say as my insides war with one another and my brain shuts down one cell after the next. Only one thing I can even hope to do.

"I'll try." My fist unclenches. My shoulders relax. *I can do this. I can try.*

He nods at me once. "That is all I ask of you."

13
Kiki

"Gabel," I say and Kuana places the odd, square-shaped fruit back in the bowl with a soft trill, just as she does every time. The star-shaped fruit comes next followed by the entire bowl, fruit and all. "Splintar and hibo?"

Smiling, she shakes her head. "Almost. Heeh-*zoh*," she corrects, placing emphasis on the second syllable.

"Hizo," I say and I'm rewarded by another one of her trills.

I bite the inside of my cheek to keep a straight face and roll my eyes, determined not to give in to the temptation to smile though, at this point, I don't even know why. It's been two solars since I last saw Okkari, since I moved into Re'Okkari's house and since Kuana moved in with me.

When Kuana first showed up with supplies — pelts, furs, firestarters, chopped wood, skins of water and foods of all kinds, as well as a small device for me to contact Miari and Svera — I thought she was making a delivery. But when she started laying out a smaller pile of furs on the opposite side of the fire from the larger pile, I knew that was a fool's hope.

My first instinct was to kick her out...but I couldn't. Since I came into her life she's been hunted, rejected, locked up, ridiculed, and hated. She's my hasheba now — *my* hasheba — and though I don't know much of their culture, I know I can't dismiss her without bringing her great shame. *And I've done enough of that.*

So for the first half solar we operated around each other in an uncomfortable silence, each doing our own work to make the place livable. We hardly spoke. It seemed like we both tried to find excuses to be outside of the house as often as possible — much to the regret of my angry, wind-chapped skin.

The cold started to bear down on us in earnest and by the second half of that first solar, I knew we'd be cooped up together *inside* until the lunar came. Finally, I couldn't take it anymore — sitting in silence with my anger and no outlet — and I knew that she couldn't take it anymore — sitting in silence without fulfilling her role, being hated for no reasons she could possibly know or understand.

I don't know how it happened, or who made the first move, but eventually, we did the unthinkable — we started to work together.

We built a fire together. She showed me how to light the pink stones using a torch found in one of the sliding trays in the area I can only call *kitchen* by force. It's really just a series of sliding drawers, all polished black rock and filled with objects I can't name.

I asked Kuana what a few of them were called only to discover that those objects were actually articles of food. She found my reaction funny and released her first trill. One solar later and she's still helping me define the things that make up this strange new world around me.

I'm terrible at remembering what she tells me, but I have gotten a few words down.

"Banaba," I say, holding up a cup of the delicious thick tea first offered to me by Tre'Hurr.

She shakes her head. "Bakaba."

"Bakaba."

"Nox. Ba-*ka*-ba."

"Augh." I tilt my head back in frustration and toss my hands into the air. "I'm never going to get this."

"You have your translation mites. They will help you."

"Mites? You don't mean insects, do you?"

She trills again, face flowering with color. This time blue. She takes my wooden plate to one of the drawers which she slides open and shut. A funny rumbling sound begins and I can sense that there's energy at work inside the drawer but I don't know what kind, or what the effect will be. But I'm curious. *Curious isn't pleased. But it isn't hate either.*

Kuana nods. "Hexa, I do. They are very expensive. Not all here on Nobu have them. I was only given mites when I was named hasheba."

"So you couldn't understand me on the mountain?"

"Nox. Hurr translated most of what you said to me."

"Hurr?"

"She leads the other xub'Hurr. They are responsible for preparing the kills caught by the warriors and trackers. She was with us when we ran into the mire."

"Ah. And her name is just Hurr? Who is xub'Hurr?"

"The xub'Hurr are all those who work with her in preparing the meats for the village. She gives the orders and is responsible for training the others. Just as the Okkari is responsible for training and commanding the other warriors and hunters, the xub'Okkari."

I nod, wheels ticking along and slowly locking into place. "Like Re'Okkari and Ka'Okkari."

"Hexa, my Xh...I mean, human." She cringes at the use of the word, yet uses it faithfully. *Human. Is that who I am? All I want to be?* "The only ones who have no xub' titles are us hasheba, those who lead a discipline like Okkari and Hurr, and the Xhea or the Xhera — the male or female mate of the Okkari, though we have only had one female Okkari in the past and this was in the ancient days, before the breeding problem began to affect us."

"Svera told me a little about it when I spoke to her. She said that the Xanaxana thing shines to help Voraxians find partners since there aren't as many females as males and getting pregnant is so difficult."

"It is true. Only one in fifteen females is so fortunate to be able to produce kits. That's why the whole of Voraxia is excited to have discovered your human moon, full of so many fertile females. I have even read in the reports that your females are capable of producing more than one kit in a lifetime," she says, voice lilting up in question.

I nod. "Yes. I mean, hexa. That's true."

Kuana trills, either at my response or at my use of her Voraxian word, or both. "Incredible. I hope only that you and the Okkari will be so fortunate." I choke on my tea — my *bakaba* — and Kuana frets around me while I cough to clear my throat. "I apologize, my...human. I should not have suggested..."

"No. Just stop, okay. It's fine." She doesn't listen to me though, and keeps on trying to bring me new liquids in new cups. Soon I've got half a dozen cups spread out on the small eating table in front of me and I can't help it. I laugh.

The sound comes out of me weird and mangled and small, but it's there, real and audible and I can't stop it. And I'm laughing still when I hear the sound of a firm knock on my front door.

"Kuana," I choke, swallow, cough, choke again, "can you get that?"

Brilliant white flashes across her face — as it did the last time I asked her to do something for me — followed by a deep orange. "Of course, my Xhea. Of course." She bows to me twice, and then a third time, in quick succession and then jumps up to standing. She pulls a white fur pelt around her shoulders and hustles to the door and when she opens it by placing her palm to the reader just beside it, I'm still choking and laughing on the same breath.

The Okkari appears in the doorway, wreathed in white, and when he looks straight past Kuana at me and a symphony of color lights his body, I freeze. My laughter dies. Need becomes me and heat surges through my gut, so strong and intense that I feel sick with it. I quickly choke down more of whatever cool tang Kuana has placed closest to me and try to meet his gaze... but I fail.

"Is she ill?" Okkari asks.

His deep voice makes me shiver. *Makes me fucking melt.* "No," I say at the same time Kuana says, "Nox."

"Just went down the wrong pipe."

"Pipe," Okkari replies, a treble of concern on his tongue — *his ridged tongue.* He steps into the place I've called a home and the room that seemed so huge before shrinks rapidly around him. The doors zip shut at his back and everything becomes quiet. "There are no pipes in Nobu's dwellings. The temperatures do not allow for them. We use a system of aquifers built of screa and re'ien farrn."

"That's obviously not what I meant. It's just an expression." A gust of laughter puffs out of me and Okkari lights up again. Even his eyes widen. The muscles in his neck stand out like live wires.

I quiet, lick my lips and wait for him to say something. But he just stares unflinchingly at my face and my embarrassment swells. *I'm laughing in front of them and with no provocation. I'm laughing like I used to...*

I look away, then back and when I do, I blurt out, "Did you need something?"

The vulnerable shock he wore vanishes as his emotions shutter. *I'm almost sorry to see them go.* "Hexa. I came to see if you had interest in joining me for a *date*." He says the word in our human brogue and the shock of it feels like a palm to the cheek — *the ass cheek.* I shiver.

"A date? Like a date date?"

"I fail to distinguish a *date* from a *date date,* however the intercultural guide to human and Voraxian interactions produced by Svera and her team of experts detail the act of this *date* in great depth. It is an act of courtship, usually initiated by the male. I am here to initiate such a courtship and ask you to participate in this date ritual with me."

I feel air whistling into my open mouth past my teeth. *Slack-jawed idiot.* "I um...you want to go on a date now? Isn't the icefall coming down?"

"Hexa, but it is thin enough to walk through and we will be taking our date in the screa caves that line the mountain."

"Oh. I..." I want to say no. I really want to say no. In truth it's not got anything to do with hate either — the hate I carry for myself or the plaguing hatred I have for the memory of Bo'Raku and everything and anything that reminds me of him. I want to say no because he intimidates the shit out of me.

I open my mouth but a memory pinches my lips shut. *I'll try. That's what I told him.* Rejecting his first attempt to *woo* me as he put it, isn't trying. I lick my lips and pull my heavy braid over my shoulder. He inhales a little bit deeper — I can see it in the way the pelts strapped across his chest in intricate ties and buckles stretch over his pectorals. My gaze drops. *Is he hard again?* Oh stars...

Struggling to get my mind out of the gutter, I sputter, "What should I wear?"

Okkari exhales just a little and he glances to Kuana. I wonder if he's as grateful as I am not to be looking at me anymore. "Provide the status of her okami, Kuana."

Kuana scuttles to a supply pile not dismantled quite yet and pulls out a carefully wrapped package from among the rest. "Her okami is ready, Okkari. Gi hand-stitched it herself over the previous solar."

"Xhivey." He turns to me. "Kuana will provide adequate clothing for you and you will inform her if it requires any adjustments."

"Oh...kay."

"Xhivey. I will leave you now to change, then you will meet me just outside of this home."

"Wait — the date starts now? Right now?"

He meets my gaze and I brace myself against its impact, more startling than any icefall and made more startling by the fact that, without colors rising in his ridged forehead, I have no idea what he's thinking. *Is he happy? Sad? In any way pleased by this?*

"Hexa. The date begins now." He makes it sound so ominous that, when he leaves, I find myself standing up slowly. I'm full of regret. *Why did I tell him I'd try? I should have told the condescending brute to fuck off.*

"Don't worry, my Xhea, I'm sure the Okkari has prepared something to your liking."

I grunt noncommittally as she helps me out of the lightweight, fur-lined tunic and trousers I'd been wearing and into something much, much stranger.

"What is this?" I ask as she pushes identical cuffs onto each of my arms. The first two cover me from shoulder to elbow, the next two from elbow to wrist. She attaches another strip of fur over my back, and a form-fitting, fur-lined breastplate to my front. Equally strange pieces fasten over my legs and hips and ass and the whole strange contraption is finally tied together with an elaborate series of buckles, similar to the ones worn by Okkari.

"This is your okami," she says as she works. She has a little smile on her face.

My eyes narrow. "You know where he's taking me, don't you?"

"Nox. I have not been informed about this *date*," she says, mispronouncing it just as badly as the Okkari did.

I tut. "Dates are weird. I never liked going on them on the human colony. Dresses and little useless presents and all that. Sharing a meal together and making awkward conversation. The boys on the colony used to try with me, but I never enjoyed it, so the Okkari shouldn't get his hopes up. You shouldn't either," I pout petulantly, threats as grand as they are empty.

"Nox. I have not been told anything of your *date*, but I do know what an okami is and there is only one use for it and if I am correct, then I do believe you will find this date to your liking."

"What is an okami?" I ask when she doesn't say more. "Hmm?"

"I...do not wish to interfere with the Okkari's plans." She chooses her words very carefully as she speaks and I know her sense of honor is strong, something to be abused — *but only if I were capable of it.* I'm suddenly acutely aware that I could do Kuana no harm.

"I could order you to tell me, couldn't I?"

She nods. "Certainly. You would not need to order. If you would truly like to know, I *can* tell you...but I would prefer to allow the Okkari such an honor, since it is his date that he has planned to honor you."

I huff audibly — *theatrically.* "Fine. Is this enough?" I ask when she steps back to observe her work.

"The okami allows for maximum flexibility in these low temperatures, but to arrive at the caves, you will perhaps need an additional fur." She releases hers and tosses it around me, tying it securely in place with a knot at the center of my chest, somewhere in the space over my madly thumping heart.

Something about the act touches me on a deep, fundamental level as I watch her green features scrunch up in concentration. *She's giving me her clothes so that I'll be warm.* I look away just as she finishes and step up to the door, pulling a pair of thin, untanned leather gloves onto my hands.

Just before I leave, I mutter, "Thank you, Kuana."

I don't look back. I don't need to look back to know her forehead is orange again. *Pride. She deserves every ounce of it.* "You're welcome, Xhea."

And as I brace for the cold world outside of the doorway, it occurs to me that I forgot to correct her when she called me Xhea...

The Okkari tilts his head while a fierce wind whips between us. Flurries of cold white scar my cheeks with heat while a fresh heat scars my insides. I swallow hard, pulling Kuana's fur up higher around my face and head. Okkari has no such cover, so the cold white just sticks to his dark hair, which spins around him, threads in the wind, begging to be touched. *To be pulled.*

"It is only a few dozen paces from here to the cave. You will tell me if the okami prepared for you is adequate."

"It is," I say automatically, though I won't know until we start walking and the cold sinks in — that is, if the cold manages to permeate my wildly climbing body temperature.

"Xhivey. Then we go now. You will follow me and stay close."

His ridges change color ever so slightly, becoming a sickly green. *Is he remembering what happened last time I was out on my own in the cold white? Why wouldn't he be? Nothing has changed between us. I have given him no reasons to trust me.* But I can try.

Without breaking his gaze, I take in air. A lot of it. I let the cold fill my lungs, let its white flakes swirl through me. I don't break his gaze. "I'm with you," I say, firmly and evenly, hoping that he knows these words for what they are: true.

His ridges radiate color again, just a splash colored orange. "Xhivey." I smile at his back as he turns away.

Down the path from his house and around the rim of the valley, I realize that there are actual doorways leading directly into the stone. Sitting up a few steep steps, most are marked by crude stone awnings that keep the cold from totally claiming the space. A few of them open when we pass by and males and females bow to us from the entrances. One male is holding what looks like a pot, one female an ion tong.

In another open doorway a very old male stands slightly hunched and a *child* hides behind his legs. I only get the quickest glimpse of the small being, so quick I can't tell if it's a boy or a girl. Still, when we step past, I realize I've got one hand in the air. I'm waving.

At the place where the valley wall begins to curve in towards its center, there's another entrance. Low, but broad, I can already see that lights glow along all the walls of the huge space, swirling and pulsing like currents in a river. And I can hear the sounds echoing within, even through the cold white. They are fighting sounds.

"Is this..." I'm totally shocked. I don't know what to say.

The cavern is immense, easily large enough to dock a dozen intra-quadrant transporters. Passing underneath the awning and fully entering the massive space, the Okkari stands to the side. I can sense he's judging my reaction and he must be pleased with what he sees because he's smiling ever so slightly.

I turn to face him. "This is our date?"

"Though I am not overly familiar with humans or your customs, the examples given of *date* outlined in the manual were...insufficient, in my novice opinion. The manual spoke of evening soirées filled with meals and childish games. I thought that perhaps this may be more suitable for a female of your calibre."

"I..." I glance around, raking it all in. There are fifty warriors in here, maybe more, organized into five different groups. The closest group is headed by a male shouting orders while the rest of the fighters assume different formations.

Two groups slightly further away are made up of pairs squaring off against one another and fighting in choreographed movements. In the next group, pairs fight in free form while the last group closest to the cave's curved heart has formed a few small clusters. In each, a single fighter faces off against multiple opponents.

And the weapons. By *comets*, the weaponry. The armory lines one whole wall, though it looks like most fighters are using swords, from where I'm standing. A couple use spears that I find familiar, while a few in the farthest groups use weapons I've never even imagined — things that look like chains with large, spikey balls on either end; knives with multiple blade ends that whip and whirl around the one who wields them; large nets that, as I watch, are used to bring the largest fighters to the ground.

If I felt intimidated before, I don't know what I feel now. On the colony, all we have are crude spears made of wood and sometimes, if you're lucky, metal. Nothing like this. Nothing that's mounted to rock walls, gleaming black and white and chrome in stacks that span beyond my eyes' peripheries. Something must be powering at least a few of the weapons, because from where I stand I can feel their electric charge splitting the air, making it sing.

"Kiki," Okkari says in a low voice.

I start. "What did you say?"

"I said that I hope that this alternative for a date pleases you." He's asking a question again without asking.

It annoys me that he doesn't, but I also find it a little funny. Cocky. And cocky is something I find familiar. I feel the tension in my mouth relax just a little as I answer, "Hexa. It does. It's really cool, I mean. A good idea. Am I going to get a tour or just watch the training or..."

"Nox. It was my intention to have you train with me."

"You brought me on a date to fight me?" I say and when he doesn't answer, I laugh. It bursts out of me a little wobbly, a little tortured, but it unsheathes itself all the same. I laugh so hard my stomach hurts. I laugh so hard I see several fighting warriors turn. Ridges fire with color, but none so bright as the Okkari's. His face is bejeweled again.

I clap my hand over my mouth, sure that at least one of those colors is mortification. I'm laughing like a fucking lunatic. Not in a pretty way. And that's what all men want, isn't it? A woman who's pretty? *Men who want pretty women don't ask them on dates to fight them.*

His colors die, but there's a downturn to his mouth that wasn't there before. "If this is unacceptable, then..."

"No. No. I mean nox. It isn't," I cut in, feeling renewed flames alight inside my belly, more powerful than the cold that drifts into this cavernous space. "I love it. I mean, it pleases me greatly. This is a great idea. I'd love to fight you…I guess."

I bite the inside of my cheek to keep a straight face. In all my many dates of little colony boys, not one of them thought to do something like this. *And he's an alien.* And that fact is starting to distract me less and less.

"Xhivey." He exhales gruffly, turning to face the wall of weapons. "Then you will select your weapon, unless you would like to fight me barehanded as you did during the Mountain Run."

There's something seductive and teasing about what he says and the way he says it and I feel myself flush. Memories revisit me in living color. *His body on top of mine, pumping, pushing. My thighs clenched around his hips, holding, pulling.*

"A weapon would be most appreciated," I say, but my voice breaks.

He smiles very softly. "Very well." He takes me to the wall mounted with poles and pikes and metal swords with multiple blade ends, large squares with strange handholds, huge flails that look like it'd take seven hands just to wield one of them, huge discs that brim with electricity and look something like shields, and throwers and launchers and axes and hammers and thin little arrows that are covered in thorns that glow in the dark.

Walking the full length of the wall takes forever. *Or maybe it only feels that way because we're walking side-by-side.* I can feel the brush of his outer arm against the fur I'm wearing every fifth step. It's so consistent, I start to look forward to it. *I shouldn't. But fuck it.* I walk a little closer to him and wonder if he notices. There's no subtle rumbling, no comment, no colors from him. *Does he like it? Does he hate it? What is he thinking?*

It takes me a moment to realize we've walked the full length of the wall and have arrived at the very last weapon — some sort of curved bow with a blade on either end and no string connecting them. It dangles on its own hook.

"We call this a dagger bow, though it is neither. A hybrid sword-staff, it is very effective for hunting large game, particularly those that roam in packs, or when up against more than one opponent."

"Impressive." I pull my hand back and clear my throat, trying to sound confident. "You have an impressive selection here in general."

"I feel it is important that my xub'Okkari learn to train with every weapon they may use in battle, or when hunting — as well as defend against them. Here are samples of every type of weapon found on Voraxia."

As we turn back, my fingers reach out and stroke the length of a curved object, shaped like a bowl with one serrated edge. I can't even figure out how you'd hold it.

"These are just the training weapons?" I say quietly.

"Hexa."

"Oh."

"I see this troubles you. You should know that this selection, of course, does not include firing weapons. These are only for hand-to-hand combat."

"No, that's not...wait. These are just non-firing sample weapons? You have more?"

"Of course. All of my warriors learn to train with each of these weapons until they find their specialty. You will tell me if yours is absent here and I will have it constructed. The Rakukanna, in particular, can assist in the creation of more human-adapted weaponry."

Frustration mounts. A slight tickling of that anger that knows me. "No. I'm sure you have something I can use," I snap.

I force myself to move forward, blocking out the feeling of him lining my side, mismatching my steps so we don't touch anymore. I scan the weapons, the discomfiting feeling inside spreading until it blots out everything else. *That's called anxiety. That's called stress.* Nothing is recognizable to me at all.

"Don't you have any spears?"

"Of course."

Okkari stops, turns around and places his hand on a staff that I missed. Instead of handing it to me, he pulls and the staff comes free, opening a drawer with it. Inside, there are a dozen more staffs, each in a different style. Some have curved ends, others serrated, some that look charged with *something*, others white and slippery. Nothing that resembles the simple wood I trained with, or the grabar Miari made for me that I used to fight off the khrui.

"I just...all of these...there are so many," I mutter quietly to myself.

We have so little. And they have so much. What was I thinking *ever*? That I could fight off a warrior who's been training with these weapons his entire life? With every weapon in Voraxia? What would I do with my tiny fucking spear? A spear so small by comparison he could probably pick his teeth with it. I thought this would be fun. Get a chance to exercise a skill I've been working on for so long with Jaxal. Get a chance to make him proud. Make myself proud. Make *him* proud. And here I am, inundated and overwhelmed and shamed.

I'm a heartbeat away from calling this whole date business off and going back to my little den with Kuana when Okkari says, "May I make a suggestion?"

I look up at him, hesitant and guarded, but I don't say no. How can I, when he's asked me a question?

Without hesitation, he pulls a white slippery-looking staff from the row. "Helos," he says, handing it to me. "One of the hardest stones, it will abrade your skin if you wield it without gloves, but it is light and lethal. Even the lightest stroke to your opponent will break the skin. A harder hit will tear through the plates of a seasoned warrior. This is a training staff, so it is dulled, but given that human skin is more delicate than ours, I encourage you to keep your gloves on and your hands on the holds."

He hands me the staff and I'm surprised that it doesn't weigh me down *too* much. It's still heavier than my old grabar and just about as heavy as the clunky training staffs Jaxal trained me with. I look at it closer and see that it's not smooth, but striated with something pebbly and dark, like microscopic droplets of black water, or crusted in flakes of black onyx. I pull off one of my gloves with my teeth and press just my middle finger to it. Sure enough, I pull back and my finger is dotted with little droplets of blood.

I feel myself smiling as I look up into Okkari's frown. "It looks good." I clear my throat. "I mean, I'm not used to it, but it'll be fine." I pull back on my glove and stand back with the weapon, tilting it from side to side, testing its weight. *It fits me perfectly. And he* knew. *I was drowning and once again, he threw me a lifeline.*

Okkari takes a staff of his own, this one as black as the walls around us and longer than mine by several feet. He leads me away from the wall, away from the other warriors and where they're practicing. But not too far away. Not far enough for them not to watch us — and many of them are watching us. I can see their surreptitious glances tossed not so surreptitiously our way. I ignore them, keeping my chin up. *I've practiced for this. I've trained. I know what I'm doing. They're not better than me.*

"Have we started?" I say.

"Hexa." He comes to a stop and turns to me, weapon held aloft. "You will attack first."

I make a show of struggling to untie the pelt Kuana secured around my shoulders as I murmur my assent. My heart is beating fast, my stomach is a kettle of beetles writhing, and still all I can think about is the last training session I had. The last session I remember. *Jaxal coming at me with everything he had. Me beating him back. Me winning.* I'd never felt better than I did in that moment, and if I ever did, I don't remember it. I felt invincible.

I can do this. I've practiced. I won't humiliate myself. "I will offer you assistance," he says, right on cue. He starts forward and when he gets within striking distance, I let go of my pelt, wrench up with the staff and let it fly.

The weight of the staff is new and disrupts my center of gravity. I'm slightly off as a result, and don't strike where I mean to. I hit him in the chest, right where his thick plates are, and I can feel their resistance at the same time that I hear their soft crunch.

He looks down. I look down at the space between our bodies. About two feet. Close enough to feel the pall of his heat roll over me like the sun obliterating the shade. He glances up at me and is wearing another one of his small pleased expressions, droplets of blue swimming across the space above his eyes.

"Xhivey," he says quietly. "Give nothing to me."

With one swift pull, he dislodges my staff and tosses it back so hard I have to take three steps to find my balance again. He wipes one hand across the leather on his chest and I'm pleased to see that it's torn just a little over the left breast.

"I won't." I start to circle him, eyeing his movements, checking for weaknesses. "And what do I get if I don't?"

"You will explain yourself."

"If I win this fight, what do I get?" He still seems deeply confused by my request, so I elaborate. "My trainer on the human colony and I would make bets like this all the time. It made it more fun."

He doesn't answer immediately, but when I suddenly switch directions, he does too, so quickly it's as if he'd anticipated it. *I must have tells. I must be giving away something. No one's just that good.*

"You will tell me what it is you would like."

It hits me all at once and I slow, lowering my weapon just a hair. "Your name."

"Verax," he says and I can tell he means for me to repeat the question even though the word itself doesn't translate.

"Your real name. Not Okkari. Not Va'Raku. The name your mother gave you."

His ridges flash. He nods slightly. "I accept."

"And what do you want, if you win?"

He slows, but only for a beat, then his pace picks back up again to match my own. "I will take no prize. The date is prize enough."

I roll my eyes. "You're so lame."

He comes to a complete stop at that, holds out both arms, looks down at his legs. "Lame. You can see perfectly well that I am not."

I snort unattractively and resume circling him. "Yes, I can see that. But it's just another expression. It means you're boring. Pick a prize. It can be anything you want from me. I don't have much to give but I'll give it gladly — *if* you win," I offer, hoping to high hell he'll pick the thing I hope he does. *And that I'll lose.*

He circles me a beat more, feet moving seamlessly right over left, right over left. He moves like a sand cat, deadly and huge. My stomach lurches. My heart beats harder and faster. I inhale strength — the strength that he leeches — and exhale nerves and fear — those that I felt before at the prospect of ever fighting any alien. *But I've done this before and when we fought then, it felt incredible.*

"I would like to experience a kiss with you." The request is so unexpected I trip — actually trip. I haven't tripped in combat since my first training sessions with Jaxal.

"You want to kiss me?"

"I have read about this kiss in Svera's manual. According to this manual, the kiss should come before the act of mating in human culture. Xiveri mating took precedence in our case, but I would not like to deprive you of this ritual all the same. Deprive either of us."

I lick my lips automatically and the rumbling I'm familiar with oozes from him to infect the air. "I accept. But only *if* you win."

"Of course," he says, and even though I don't know him that well, I know he isn't condescending me. He speaks to me as if I haven't already seen him fight, as if I wasn't already prepared to give up something I knew I might lose, as if my winning is a distinct possibility.

And because *he* believes it, I believe it. And I fight like it too.

I cross the space in a few long strides, legs eating up the distance. He is utterly sure of my movements, I can see that, so I know that I need to do something to catch him off guard. I transfer my spear to my left hand and feint right, waiting until he follows before I kick.

I aim for his thigh, and as he uses his own to swipe my foot aside one elegant sweep, I bring my helos down hard. As I move, I catch sight of white in the ridges dotting his wide forehead. Though the slope of his high cheeks remain unmoved, his wideset nostrils flare and his jaw clenches. He still manages to block with his forearm, but that's to be expected of any halfway decent warrior and he's far more than halfway decent.

I hit the ground and spin, the staff's weight throwing me off but I quickly make the necessary corrections and when I turn to face him, I hit him in the thigh, stroke meeting another one of the thick patches that he's got growing all over him. I grunt in frustration.

Stupid plates. I accounted for the ones on his chest and forearms, but I forgot the legs. Ribs then, neck, shoulders — groin if I have to. With a quick flick of his staff, he pushes mine away. I spin out of his range, but he isn't fighting back. Not yet. He's giving me time to adjust to the weapon. To adjust to fighting him.

I thrust forward. He blocks with his staff, the two distinct pieces of metal and stone coming together with a loud, unceremonious clack. There's a moment of silence. *Grace.* His scent swirls around me, making it hard to think. *I'm in the oasis. What am I doing fighting here?* I shake my head and shrug my shoulders and dive in again. Another effortless block, perfectly timed.

We dance like this for some time, staffs thwacking against one another. Every time I start to find a rhythm, he forces me to break it again and again, until finally, after my dozenth attack, *he* initiates.

He charges forward, swinging his staff over his head in a wide arc as he moves. It leaves his chest exposed and I dive for it, but he moves faster than I anticipated and brings his weapon around to tag my left side. Blunt though it is, it's still hard enough to knock the wind clean out of me. *Swallowing asteroid gunk would be easier than taking another hit from him.* I bounce back on the balls of my feet, struggling to stay light and agile as I avoid the next blow. But it doesn't land.

He freezes, falling out of position. "Did I hurt you?" He says in a low, demonic cadence before he starts circling me again.

I shake my head. "Not a chance."

"Xhivey."

"Was that all you've got?"

He snarls or smiles or both when I reposition my feet into a fighting stance. Hip-distance apart. Right foot in front of the left. Body angled to present a smaller target. Hands positioned just wider than shoulder-width apart on the staff to give me better control as I learn this new weapon. It's incredible. Like wielding a blade made of water. My thoughts flick back to the wall of wonders and fleetingly I imagine that he just might let me try them all, even the dagger bow.

I charge and we spar, beating one another forward and back. "Again," he barks when I finally manage to connect my spear end with his shoulder. "Faster."

I try again, unsuccessful in hitting him this time, but I do manage to block him three times more and stop him from striking me in the stomach, back, arms and thighs — all places that on the coming solar are sure to be bruised and sore.

"Xhivey," he says. Then, "Pick up your feet."

I didn't realize I'd been letting my arches fall flat and quickly correct the stance. *He's training me. He's training me and he's an alien.*

And we're on a date.

We keep going. I fight harder and faster, wanting to prove to him that I'm something of worth. Wanting to prove it to myself too.

My arms are heavy and I'm sweating even though he doesn't look like he's winded in the slightest. We've been at this for eons and that little tear on his vest is all he has to show for it.

"Kiki," he says quietly in between two resounding *thwacks*. "We should stop. Training is winding down. Soon the warriors will tire from simply watching us."

I can see a dozen or so warriors milling about in my peripheries. Done with their own training, they drink from water skins and flasks and speak out of earshot with one another. *About me. They're all watching. Wondering if I'm just the pathetic girl who couldn't beat Bo'Raku, who cost them the life of one of their own, who thinks she's fit to lead.* I'll prove it to them. Prove to them who I am. That I'm a warrior. That I'm capable of anything. That I'm not lesser because I'm human. That I'm not weak.

I spin and swing and Okkari is forced a half-step back. He pushes me away from him, spear-on-spear, and I can't stand up against the alarming pressure. He's too strong. Much stronger than I am. I stumble and have to use my spear to stop myself from falling. I hear Jaxal's voice in my head screaming, *Don't ever let your sword touch the ground!* I wince and lurch upright. I attack again and again and again.

"Humans require sustenance three times a solar," he says between grunts and lithe spins, liquid movements that make him look more like a dancer than a warrior. "You need your final meal…"

"If *you* don't tire, then *I* don't tire."

"This is not your last opportunity to train. Do not fight like this is your final battle." *But that's what it feels like, doesn't it?*

I swing harder the next time and he edges back, pulling me in a circle, forcing me to give chase. I spin and kick up pebbles and earth from the packed ground, thinking to use the same distraction I did the first time, but as I'm learning, so is he. He isn't fazed by the pebbles and when I bring my staff down, too late I realize that he's just standing there waiting.

He maneuvers his staff in a figure eight and it's like he's turned the piece of metal to rope, knotting it around mine. When he pulls, my spear flies. *Never drop your weapon!* Jaxal's voice in my head rages like an angry tide.

I lunge for my helos staff, diving to the ground where I land hard on my knees. I grab it, but a heavy, booted foot is there already, kicking it out of my reach. The spear skates over the floor, landing next to two males clustered, talking *probably about me and how I lost. How humans could never fight against aliens. How I could never outrun Bo'Raku. How I could never hope to win against the Okkari.*

I'm panting now and it has nothing at all to do with the fight, well fought and well lost and everything to do with the voice in my head spitting vitriol and poisoning the well that my encounter with the hevarr and Re'Okkari's death purified.

I clutch my chest. The Okkari is a beast above me. *He can sense how weak I am. Hide it! Just hide…* I try to pull back, but all at once, he drops to one knee, falling damn near right on top of me as his entire body curves over mine, hiding me. Protecting me, even if only from myself. *But I don't need protection!*

I lurch up, but one gigantic hand slides around the back of my head as he arches over my body and presses his forehead to my forehead.

"Enough," he says and there is so much in that one word that it hollows out my insides. I close my eyes. I follow his deep, even breath with my breath. "He cannot harm you. Nothing can."

I nod, unable to speak. The rumbling gets louder, forming a shield around me.

"You do not fight for survival, not anymore. You are a warrior now and you fight for the tribe, for the hunt." His breath smells like anise and an ocean breeze.

I nod again and when I exhale, I shake just a little bit.

His hand on the back of my hair kneads the nape of my neck. "My warriors know better than to overtax themselves in a training. To be overeager is to be reckless and reckless warriors do not join the first hunt after the thaw. I will take no exception to you simply because you are Xhea. I am Okkari, responsible for all warriors, and if

I feel you will not be able to adequately defend yourself and your fellow warriors, then you may train with them but I will not allow you to hunt with them until you have mastered this anger."

I'm not allowed to go out with the hunters on the human colony. I train with them, but all our hunters are men. I've never even been considered. "You…you want me to go with you on a hunt?" I squeeze out the words.

He blinks, eyelids gliding over the round orbs of his eyes. He blinks from the side, reminding me of his alienness in a way I'd forgotten during our fight. "Of course. You are our warrior Xhea. If not fighting at my side, then you will tell me now where else you would rather be."

Where else would I rather be? Among all the places I've been and all the ones I have only imagined, I cannot think of one.

I pull back just enough to see him. To really *see* him. Purple skin. Black hair streaked with just one flash of white, a tease of years to come. Stoic and regal and utterly unlike anyone I've ever come across. And maybe the first being to truly *see* me in return.

I lurch up — not to fight — but to crush his mouth to mine. I pull at his lips with my teeth, suckling them one at a time. They're hard, much harder than a human man's, but they're smooth, like polished stone. I lick a line across their seam, feeling powerful as he sucks in an inhale, gasping at the promise of me. Of more.

His hand tenses around the back of my head while his other comes between us. He wrenches forward on the buckle across my chest and my whole body tumbles against his until we are pressed together, chest-to-chest, my thighs straddling his hips, my knees punching into the hard ground below. My fingers spear his hair and when he finally reacts to kiss me back — lips parting, tongue meeting mine hesitantly, teeth nipping at my lips hard enough it hurts just a little bit — I moan.

The sound echoes through the front half of the cave and even I can hear the sudden splash of noise that his warriors make in response. Okkari pulls away from me suddenly and wrenches us both to our feet. My body is limp until he kicks my feet apart, forcing me to plant them. Still, I hold onto his arms to keep myself steady.

He leans down and whispers gruffly against my mouth, as if wanting more, but denying himself — or as he put it, depriving us both. "I cannot share you with my warriors. Not even your moans. And I cannot let them see what you do to me. I am unraveled." I glance up and see his forehead full of light, but it's nothing I haven't seen before. Maybe more color. More purples. Brighter.

I reach a hand up, ignoring how it shakes. Or trying to. But this is uncharted territory. I've never done this before. I've kissed boys, sure. I even had sex with a couple before the Hunt, before, when I thought that sex meant a few passionate seconds in a field or some dark closet with a cute colony boy who traded whatever pennies he had for a few extra rations so he could treat me to real meat in the hopes that this would happen. They were nice, those times, quick and quickly forgotten. But this is new.

I've never touched a man before with intent, with promises unspoken. Never suspended my fingers and traced his face, started at his temple, dragged that touch across his raised ridges and then down the bridge of his nose. Watched him close his eyes and lose the strength in his torso, smiled a little as he gently swayed. Watched his lips open and his ridged tongue slide between them. Pressed my fingertips to his tongue, feeling its warmth and wet roughness, watched him inhale and exhale my name...

"Kiki." His eyes open and I pull away. Closing my hand, I can feel electricity fire through it and I know that even if I were never to see him again from this moment forward, I'm sure that the touch of his skin would be branded to mine for life.

"You got your kiss," I say, clearing my throat into my fist to clear the desire from my warbling tone. "So I guess I'll have to wait for our next fight to continue unraveling you."

He makes a small, choked sound in the back of his throat and takes a step away from me. I don't have any trouble seeing what the effect of my words are on his body. His pants are tented around the crotch. I try to cage my smile with little effect. I look away instead, grateful that he can't see my mirrored response.

"You speak as if you have forgotten your own prize or no longer want it."

"I do want it."

"Then you speak as if you do not intend to win."

I look away, but he slides his finger under my chin, just as he's done so many other times. "On the coming solar, you will come here to train with the warriors after your second meal. You will join the group led by Ka'Okkari."

Shock. "I'm joining a group? Training with the other warriors?"

"Hexa. You have sufficient foundation, but you need refinement, control, and an introduction to our hunting formations and our weapons. I will join you after your training to provide you with additional instruction."

"You will?"

He growls, "As Okkari I am not accustomed to repeating myself. If you demand this of me again, then I will punish you."

I swallow. "Punish how?"

He gives me a scorching look and all thoughts of rebellion die. Being punished by him is suddenly all I want in this world. I bite my bottom lip. Even without irises, I can see how he focuses on it, mouth parting in response.

"During your training, of course."

"Of course," I say quickly, and then I follow him out into the cold.

He walks me to Re'Okkari's home and waits for me until I step inside. I pretend I'm not disappointed that he doesn't follow, almost forgetting for a second that Kuana's still here, dutifully cleaning the same spot she's probably already cleaned a dozen times.

"Thank you, Okkari," I tell him before the doors glide shut. "For including me, even after everything."

"You are welcome, Kiki."

I nod, searching for something else to say. Some way to keep him here. "It was a really good date."

"I am pleased."

"And I will have your name, Okkari. Eventually."

"Do not make me wait. I wish to hear it on your tongue," he says, breath forming clouds in the cold. "And I do not wish to wait long."

14
Kiki

He's a crueler trainer than Jaxal, but he's a good one — even I can admit that. He pushes me hard — but not too hard — and it hurts — but not enough to stop me from training with him the next solar and the next solar and the next.

My whole body is sore and achy but the stinging pain doesn't last. I start to firm up. To remember what it was like to do hard work every day. To go beyond that and push myself, using new weapons and machines and stances and techniques I've never seen before, honing new muscles that I never even knew I possessed.

Kuana tries to gently coerce me into letting her repair the tear in my okami, but I'm obstinate and fuss over it myself until two males enter our space carrying four huge metal pails between them. Steam whicks off of their glimmering surfaces and I'm transfixed by the sight, as I am every time. Kuana directs them to a deep basin built into the ground by the kitchen area and even though I try to get Kuana to wash first, she's possibly as stubborn as I am and refuses.

I sink into the hot water, letting my aches and pains become one with it. I close my eyes. It's been sixteen solars. Sixteen solars living with aliens and already it's hard for me to remember any other life.

"Xhea?" She asks, hesitation in her tone. Even though I asked her not to call me Xhea, I don't hate that she does. What I hate is her reticence to ask. It's been too many solars living together now for her to still be afraid of me. For me to still be a bitch to her. *I'm no better than Kuaku. Except Kuaku was only being an ass hole to* me *and I'm already an ass hole. Now I'm being an ass hole to Kuana and she's nothing but nice. I'm worse than Kuaku by three and Kuana is paying the price.*

"Yes?" I try to say it nice and even look over my shoulder at her while my hands continue scrubbing at my skin in efficient strokes.

Naturally, she's in the kitchen busy scrubbing something that is undoubtedly already clean since cleaning is all she's done since she arrived. It makes me wonder what she did before. I want to ask her, but I… I've never asked her anything personal before.

"I would be pleased to lend you my assistance."

"In the bath?" I balk, "I'm okay, thanks."

Her forehead sizzles yellow — a color I know by now is something like shame. And the only reason I know that is because she's perpetually yellow in the face around me. "I would offer assistance only to help you since you seem to have strained many muscles these past solars training with the xub'Okkari. That is all."

Stars. She's got a point. "I've got it. All good."

She turns back to the clean surface and takes her rag to it again while I finish up, wondering what mama would think if she could hear me and see me now. *Wouldn't know a kind word if it slapped you,* she'd say. And she'd be absolutely right.

I finish quickly and let Kuana do the same. She finishes combing through her hair — an act that takes her about two seconds — and while I continue working madly to detangle the smallest lock of my hair, she goes back to cleaning that same imaginary mess again.

I laugh humorlessly and actually slap my palm to my face. "Kuana," I snap, harsher than I mean to.

She straightens like I've stuck her with a pin and meets my gaze in the mirror I'm seated in front of. It's a well-polished piece of black stone, very unlike the silver mirrors we use back home. Because of that, the color of my hair and skin blend in with it and my hair floats around my head now like a mane with a will and mind of its own — a thicket impossible to get all the way through…without help.

"Hexa, my Xhea. I am here."

"We both know you're not cleaning anything."

She sets down the gamma radiator and the wipe she's been using and turns to face me fully. "Nox," she sighs, "I am not."

"Well stop it then."

"What else would you have me do?"

"Come help me with my hair." If there was ever a point at which I wanted all aliens to suffer, it's time to backtrack now, because she *is* suffering and in the greatest feat of irony the universe has ever delivered me, I'm suffering too because of it.

Brilliant white and blue flutter across her forehead and down the center of her nose. She trills, "I am pleased to do this for you. Do you need help with combing it?"

"Yes…hexa," I say and her face lights up even more, bringing heat to my own. *I should give her more tasks and more regularly. I'm responsible for her.* "And braiding it."

"Braid? I do not know this word."

"It's fine then, I…" I'm just about to tell her I've got it when the colors in her face change again, shifting back to that grotesque and tormented yellow. I catch my own tongue — something I've never been very skilled at before — and offer her a weird smile of my own. "I'll teach you. I know my hair is very different from yours but it would be a huge help to have someone help me braid it…"

Surprise. "I would be *honored* to learn." She bows deeply and I feel myself flush all over again.

"Oh quit it, would you? Just come over here. None of that bowing crap."

A smile still on her face, Kuana takes a pillow and plops it down beside me and together we comb through my hair and separate the mass into smaller chunks. I show her the movements with my fingers and am not surprised at all that she makes a quick study of it. With just a few practice braids that she afterwards undoes, she's already better at it than I am.

I sigh, relaxed in ways I haven't been in so long. I'm warm and dry and the soothing touch of her fingers against my scalp, pulling ever so gently as she makes box braids appear one after the other, is enough to make me forget that I'm living with aliens — or maybe even, to help me realize just how nice living with aliens can be.

"Xhea?" She says softly.

"Hexa?"

Behind me, I can feel her cool breath on my neck when she exhales just a little. "Is it acceptable for me to ask you a question?"

In the mirror's gaze, I stare into hers, watching as her alien eyes blink. I tell her something I should have told her solars ago, the day that we met. A small crack of truth in the veneer of my hate, paper thin yet capable of unraveling the entirety of it. "You are my equal. You don't ever have to ask."

"It's just that...you don't often seem like you *want* to talk to me."

I cringe outwardly and even though it feels strange — alien in itself — I take her hand. It's dry and rough in places I don't expect for someone so delicate and soft. *She works hard.* Even in the little time I've known her, I've seen the evidence of that. "I know and I'm sorry. But I also know that you've seen the report from the Okkari about me and the human colony. A bad Voraxian hurt me very badly and I thought you were all like that. I know that's not true now, I just...I need your patience."

She bows to me slightly and her ridges flare blue again in pleasure. I turn to face forward and when she picks back up her braiding, she surprises me. "Who did these *braids* for you on your home colony?"

I smile and this time the expression comes to me effortlessly. "My mother."

I take in a breath and with my eyes closed I'm back there, on the colony. *Sand swirls softly around my ankles. My head tilts to the side onto mama's thigh. I'd fall asleep if she wasn't tugging on my hair something fierce. But every time she calls me brave, I'm reminded that I am and don't cry.*

I could stop there, but I don't. Urged on by something I can't give name to because I don't understand it myself, I let her in. I tell her, "It was hot on our colony so a lot of the time, she'd braid my hair outside. It would take so much of the solar, but I was never bored. Jaxal would come by and we would play stones, or Miar…I mean, the Rakukanna would show me one of her newest inventions. At just two or three rotations old, I remember she once showed me this trap she built for sand rats. We were hungry, even back then, and later managed to even catch one but…we couldn't do it. We couldn't kill it. So we let it go." I exhale and with her fingers on my scalp, pulling and teasing out the knots, I'm a child once again, safe sitting in between my mother's knees where nothing can hurt me.

"You miss this moon colony," she says and it's not a question, it's a fact.

"Hexa, I do."

"Will you…return?"

Vocabulary fails me, which is a bit sad since I only know the one *so far,* but I'm trying. All I can do is try.

I'm not sure what to say — not because I don't know, but because I can't decide what to tell her. I can't tell her that I was hurt there once and that the memory of Bo'Raku haunts me and I never want to see the colony again because of it — not because it didn't happen, but because it would be a lie.

The truth is that I don't want to go back because when I was sparring with a warrior called Tra'Okkari the solar before, we ended up deadlocked — neither of us gaining any ground until eventually Ka'Okkari came by and broke us up. *I'll be pleased to have you watching my back on the first hunt of the season,* Tra'Okkari said to me. I'd been too speechless to answer, but when he signaled me in a warrior's greeting — both arms crossed over his chest at the wrists — I'd been proud.

The truth is that I don't want to go back because on the colony, I lived in fear of the day they'd come back. But here, there is no fear because here, I am powerful.

"I don't think I will."

"You are pleased to be with us in the village?"

I swallow hard. "Hexa. I think so."

She trills and exhales, her fingers working quickly now. So pleasant, the sensation, I give up on my own braid and just...sit. "Xhivey. This is good to hear. Some were worried that you would not wish to remain with us."

"Some? What does that mean?"

Her fingers don't pause, but keep moving surely. I wonder if she can feel the sudden tension in my neck and back — or if she can even read my emotions at all given that I don't have the colors in my face that she does. "Hexa. When collecting supplies over the past solars, I have been approached by many of the females, curious about you and your humans in general. Some of them expressed concern that you are living in a separate residence as this is not common for Xiveri mates."

"Comets on a cracker. What did you say?"

"I explained to them that this is not your culture."

"And what did they say?"

"Most understood as everyone has read the guide provided by Svera, the advisor." She keeps braiding in silence, as if that's *not* an entirely unfinished sentence.

I scooch an inch to the left so I can see her in the mirror more clearly. "*And?*"

"Verax," she says that untranslatable word again, which means that she needs further explanation.

I huff. "You said most. Most is not all. So what did the others say that didn't understand?"

"My Xhea, it is not important what a few think…"

"Of course it is. What did they say?"

She waits, then confesses. "They think you shame him."

I inhale as if struck. That's not what I expected. I expected all manner of foul thing to come out of their mouths about *me* — a foreign female who's taken their leader for herself, who tried to run and caused the death of a warrior, who trains with the xub'Okkari and thinks she's one herself. I glance away from the reflective surface and focus on that stupid spot in the kitchen that Kuana cleaned to death. At this point, I don't really feel like looking at myself.

"And what did you say?"

"I said that they were wrong and that any business that affects your relationship with the Okkari is between the two of you alone."

"Thank you, but you know they're not wrong." I groan. "And that *sucks*."

"Sucks? How can something suck if it is only what was said? A sentence has no mouth."

I chuckle inadvertently, rolling my eyes and nudging her with my elbow, like we're old friends. "That's obviously not what I meant. It's just a human expression. I'm just embarrassed — not even on my own behalf, but for the Okkari and he hasn't even done anything wrong."

She doesn't answer right away which just makes me feel worse. "It is not known for us, to have Xiveri mates separated, or to have our Xhea try to run away… But neither is a warrior Xhea who fights her Okkari or who trains with the xub'Okkari. You are new for us. There will always be those who doubt."

"But they shouldn't doubt *him*. He didn't do anything wrong. I just...need time to figure this all out. This is new for me too."

"The Okkari knows this. I'm sure."

That doesn't make me feel better. "He doesn't." I finger one of the braids she made, hanging down near my breasts, which are exposed. It's a perfect braid, evenly weighted, not a frayed strand. Just as perfect as my mom would have done. Maybe even better, though she'd tut at that. *Scowling down at me with her hands on her hips, towel perpetually hanging from the apron at her waist — not that she cooks. It's where she carries her army of hair supplies. "Kiki, that is a sloppy braid. If only you could braid as well as you could hit."*

"Then you must make him. You are our warrior Xhea."

I don't feel like it. I shake my head.

Kuana pauses again, this time with a slight jerk, like she's restraining herself from saying something more.

"What is it, Kuana?"

"May I offer a suggestion?"

"Please," I grumble, only half sarcastically.

Luckily, she doesn't seem to notice. "It is important for the Xhea to honor her tribe. You honor the tribe, you honor the Okkari."

"How do I honor the tribe?"

She gives me a small smile. "You are our warrior Xhea. I leave this up to you, for anything I could suggest would be inferior, I'm sure."

She finishes the last braid and heats water on my instruction. We dip the ends of my hair into the hot water, sealing them, and she gushes over me. "Beautiful."

"What's beautiful is your work. My mom was always chastising me because I could never braid as well as she could. I think you might even make her jealous with what you've done." I shake out my hair, letting the weight of the braids and their tight roots remind me of her and home and a happy childhood. "Thank you, Kuana. For everything."

Deep blue again, against her bright green skin, the color looks alarming, but I'm getting used to it. In fact, it's only when her colors are truly startling that I even notice the color of her skin anymore. I wonder if she notices mine anymore either.

She opens her mouth to answer, but as she does, there's a knock on our door. A *knock. And that can only mean one thing.* Only one person here knocks while the rest hail on my or Kuana's personal communicator and then just enter.

Kuana quickly throws a pelt over my shoulders, one that drops all the way to my calves. She fixes it with a stone clasp and I amble awkwardly beneath it, heading to the door.

"Come in," I shout, but when nothing happens, I press my palm to the vein reader and the door whooshes open.

Air blasts into the space so cold I have to close my eyes against it. Even in the pelt I've donned, I can feel the icy sting against my feet and shins, whooshing up to touch my core. My lips pulse and heat and, like I do every time, I try to ignore it and can't. Seeing him, knowing that we've been so close these past solars when we've been sparring — but haven't touched — makes me restless. More restless than ever. Each solar is worse than the last.

His jaw clenches, his purple skin looking cool and grey beneath the clouds, which hang low. He clears his throat and there's no mistaking the voice that speaks. *It haunts me, but not like Bo'Raku, not in my dreams... this voice haunts me through the solar. It's taken the place of my inner diatribe...*

"Xhea, Kuana, pardon my entry. There is a break in the frost. We will honor Re'Okarru now with the chamar."

"Now?"

His ridges flash a dark and sinister indigo. "Are you giving me cause to repeat myself, Xhea?"

I bite my lips together and clench my knees to keep my legs from wobbling. "No. I heard you. The chamar. I'll get ready right away." I'm nervous to look at him. The promise of punishment has my body rippling, tingling, pulsing. I can feel heavy weights in my breasts, the peaking of my nipples. This enormous pelt shrouding me feels like nothing at all.

Meanwhile, he is entirely devoid of expression. It irks me. "Do I have time to change?" I say when he doesn't move.

"Hexa."

I pause, thinking of the human tradition of wearing black to show mourning. I don't have any black though. I only have the fur-lined suits Kuana brings me. "What should I wear?"

He doesn't respond. At *all*. His silence is a little shocking. He just stares at me with his huge eyes, dark and glossy enough I can see my reflection suspended in them. I can also see other patterns swirling through their endlessness. It hurts to try to follow them, but I can't look away. I don't want to look away.

Behind me, Kuana perks up. "Forgive my interruption, but I can assist you with this, if it please you, Xhea."

"That would be great. Thank you, Kuana."

Though the air is thicker now and harder to move through. It's *hard* to turn from him. I don't understand it. Everything was *okay* before — not fine, but alright — but now it hurts again. The *want* I've felt these past solars has returned tenfold.

I go to Kuana in the back of the dome who holds up another fur suit and lays it gently on top of the closed chest she removed it from. When I reach her, her fingers deftly untie the clasp at my front and without warning, she pulls the pelt away from me, stripping me bare.

"Woah, woah," I whisper, catching the pelt as it falls. I glance over my shoulder and see that Okkari is watching me with brutal intensity. He hasn't turned away and it sends shivers racing through my bones and goosebumps rippling across my flesh. Unwanted wetness surges between my legs. I squeeze them together as tight as I can and it doesn't help at all.

"Oh!" Kuana's forehead is bright blue with little slivers of white and gold and silver. To make matters worse, she flutters, "I can leave you and the Okkari, if you'd like privacy to consummate your Xiveri bond…"

"No! Oh my stars, comets and curses, nox. No, Kuana. That's so…awkward." I flush so hard I'm sure I'll burst into actual flames. And behind me Okkari isn't saying anything. But that doesn't mean he's silent. No. He's *rumbling. I need Svera. I need her to tell me what this is because the painful sensation below my waist is anything but human.* A hoarse moan chokes in my mouth and I quickly grab the fur-lined suit off the chest.

"Kuana, just hold up the pelt so I can change, please."

"Nox," comes the visceral rebuke from behind me. I glance back. He's an even deeper purple and one foot is a little further forward than the other like he wants to come forward but is held in place by an invisible barrier. I meet his gaze and he shakes his head. Slowly. "Nox."

I shiver and try to ignore him as Kuana helps me into the furs she's laid out for me. These form sort of a pant with a skirt wrapped around them. Another fur engulfs my torso and finally, Kuana pulls a heavy shawl over my head that covers everything. I feel like a paper lamp shade, but when I turn towards the Okkari, he looks at me like I'm a moon — no, like I'm *the* moon in a strange and distant universe where there is only one.

Kuana yanks a fur hat on over my braids. The ends flow free, draping over my suit down to my breasts and slightly past them. When I turn and approach Okkari, I see him staring at those tips murderously and I wonder what they've done to offend him.

I open my mouth, but I can't seem to find any words to ask. "I'm ready for the chamar now, Okkari," I say instead.

He nods once and together we step outside and wait the moments it takes for Kuana to ready herself. "During the chamar, you will stand at my side," he says and I don't understand why he's telling me this.

"Where else would I be?"

He exhales, shoulders dropping slightly as if in relief and I cringe. *He still doesn't trust me. I still haven't proven myself to him.*

"I will stand at your side."

I don't miss the way his left hand twitches towards me as I step up to his side. "Xhivey. Then we will go now."

The wind is calm, but the white that falls does so in big pieces, the size of my whole chest. I have a hard time walking through them, but eventually we work our way around the valley floor past the homes, past the training arena, past the place where the Hurr work, past the caves where the trackers practice their craft, past the medics and the granary, past several other doorways and entrances containing facilities I have yet to explore.

Walking becomes easier as we start an incline. The sounds become less muted and I slowly realize that we aren't alone. A shadow appears up ahead through the enormous, airy sheets of white that fall, and then another. And then I start to make out the sound of footsteps behind us and slightly to the left. Many footsteps. The valley winds dramatically through the craggy, black screa hills, twisting this way and that, so it's hard to see others for more than a few moments before they disappear behind the next bend, or we do.

Eventually though, an eerie hush settles over us and as we follow the next curve, the valley comes to its finish. There's an entrance where the two hillsides meet, a great hole in the side of the rock where the white cannot reach it. People — I mean beings — nox, the *tribe*, the community — draw nearer to it. It's the first time I've seen so many gathered.

Old and young, some with black hair, others with white, others like the Okkari's and something in between. Skin in all emerald shades, from violet to lime to rust, but most prevalently their faces beam from above their fur-suits in shades of cobalt and charcoal. The

Okkari's shade is rather unique among them. I look up at him now, having to crane my neck to see his face. When I do, I'm shocked to see him already looking at me.

"I have been informed that Kuana briefly instructed you on the procedure for the chamar," he says, "You will tell me if this is correct."

"Hexa, she has. She's been doing a great job. I only hope that I can remember everything and honor the tribe."

He blinks twice in quick succession. "You will."

"I don't know about that." I remember Kuana's words and the dishonor I have caused him and exhale in a rush, "So I pass the torch that's handed to me and once the body is lowered into the grave, I place my stone after Kuana does. Then you."

"Hexa."

"Where do I find the stone?"

"You will follow my lead. All will be clear. I will not allow you to dishonor yourself."

Too late for that, I think, but I don't voice it. I don't say anything. Because all this time I thought Jaxal was teaching me how to be strong, and though my body might be stronger, my heart is weaker than it ever has been. *They call me their warrior Xhea, but I'm a coward. Kuaku was right all along — they deserve better.*

"Thank you, Okkari," I whisper.

The lip of the cave entrance has risen up over us now, towering high overhead. So vast it makes me feel like an insect staring up and imagining the cosmos. My gloved hand flexes towards the Okkari's, wanting to hold onto something to anchor myself, but I restrain myself at the last moment.

Instead, I make sure to walk at his side as we approach the gathering crowd. Packed in under the awning of the cave entrance, even though they face away from us, their shoulders angle our way and they watch us as we walk. They're staring at me harder even than they're staring at him. I'm not surprised. After all, I'm the reason they're all here. Re'Okkari would still be alive if I hadn't been so vindictive.

Self-hatred hits hard and all I can do is roll my shoulders back and stare straight ahead, trying my best to mimic the Okkari's stance and attitude. Before us, the silent crowd parts. Their shuffling feet and rustling fur suits are the only sounds besides the fire crackling in huge screa basins carved directly into the stone walls. It gets warmer the further we walk. Never quite reaching a state of real heat, it's definitely not cold by the time we reach the front of the congregation. There, a long stretch of dirt extends to the back of the cave, which is trapped by shadows too dense for light to penetrate. And between us and that darkness are dozens of mounds. Maybe hundreds of them. Maybe thousands.

Stacked stones form cairns that remind me of graves on the human colony, but only when they're fresh. The sand comes strong, burying the graves by the end of the solar they were laid. Here, the graves are permanent, immortalized. Each mound representing someone who will never be forgotten by the passage of time because their stones remain. Their stones prove they existed.

The power of this place rushes over me like a wave, so hard I can't stand. I reach out, scrambling to grab hold of something. Finding his arm, my fingers snake down past his wrist and take his hand. He doesn't react, or if he does, I don't see it. I'm staring straight ahead at the patch of dirt that has been dug up. Lying there, as if in sleep, is Re'Okkari.

He lies face up, his eyes covered with two small, flat stones that frighten me. *Why does he travel to the Great Ocean of the After blind?* I can feel Kuana's presence as she steps in place beside me, but I still feel panic when Okkari surges ahead. He breaks the contact of our hand long enough to retrieve two stones from a collection near Re'Okkari's grave. He hands me one of them. Removing my gloves as he has, I take it, and with my free hand, I take his.

This time, I feel him jolt beside me as I lace my fingers with his, but he doesn't move or look at me or break the connection. Instead, he keeps his face forward and we watch as villagers approach the grave one-by-one to lay their stones on Re'Okkari's body. Time passes slowly, but eventually the cairn grows taller, forming a clipped peak awaiting its apex. It stands just as proud and jutting as the others.

My heart summersaults in my chest when Tre'Hurr and Va'El make their way to the cairn. Va'El is no longer limping, which is a relief, and when I manage to catch his gaze, he gives me a very subtle nod. I return it along with a half-smile before casting that same humbled, torn expression at Tre'Hurr next. She smiles back at me sadly before the pair folds into the crowd. Before long, Kuana, the Okkari and I are the last ones left.

Kuana returns from placing her stone and a reverent hush settles over the crowd. All is still. I inhale quietly. *Steady...steady...* I wait, but the Okkari seems to hesitate, and I realize quickly it's likely because our hands are still linked and I don't want to release him. *I'm scared. Petrified.* So when I move forward, I tug him with me. He pauses on the first step, then joins me, falling into line at my side.

The cairn is high now — up to his chest and my forehead. My shawl stretches as I place my stone beside his. Our fingers glance as I do. I look up at him and he is looking down at me and all I want him to know in that moment is that I'm sorry, so sorry for everything. *I thought I was here to kill aliens, but the death of one feels like death to me too.*

The Okkari jerks, his ridges hinting at color before he stiffens and the color dies. He turns from me then to face the village stretched out before us in a mass of stoic mourning. Though they may not be an expressive people, I can still feel the desolation of this place. The bitterness. The love.

"Re'Okkari was a brave warrior." The Okkari's voice is deep and more melodic than it has a right to be. He speaks loudly, but without shouting, and it sends splashes of ice rattling down my spine, followed almost immediately by a warmth that makes it possible to overcome.

"He fought honorably until the end in defense of our Xhea, and in defense of our home. His sacrifice will not be forgotten. Not only does our Xhea live, but the hevarr will provide sustenance to the entire village through the coming icefalls and make it possible for us to thrive through the storms. May the Xaneru within Re'Okkari go now to reunite with the Xana of the universe. We will raise our torches now to help light his path…"

"Wait." The word punches out of me on a breath. I can feel a fresh tension thrumming through the throngs, though it's nothing in comparison to the tension of Okkari beside me. I look up into his gaze pleadingly, and when he blinks that's the only concession I know I'll get. I take it. *What am I doing?* Something. Anything I can.

I take a step forward, releasing the Okkari's hand so that he and Re'Okarri's cairn are behind me while I face the village. The entire village. *What am I doing?* I look to Kuana and even though she is utterly expressionless, as they all are, the sight of her bolsters my confidence.

I inhale deep into my belly and say, "Kuana, would you translate for me?"

She blinks with her too wide eyes and a breath of color crosses her forehead before it fades. After a split instant's hesitation, she approaches me and bows at the waist. "It is an honor, my Xhea."

"Thank you, Kuana." I turn then and my bones feel like glass as I lift my voice and do the unthinkable — I address all of the aliens at the same time and with the express purpose of honoring one of them. Maybe all of them.

Words burn as they spill out of me. Raw and shameless, I confess, "I built a cairn for my best friend's mother. She died giving birth to a hybrid human-Drakesh child. That child is now the Rakukanna."

Kuana inhales so deeply I can feel the air shift between us. She raises her voice loud and it wobbles only once. The crowd is silent, but I haven't been stopped or dismissed. I keep going. "It was the first cairn I ever helped build. I've built many more since. We humans have known much suffering. For a long time I have blamed the whole of Voraxia for that suffering, including you here on Nobu.

"But to have condemned the whole because of the actions of a few is wrong. And to have brought any amount of reciprocal suffering onto you, is even more so. I am honored by the actions of Re'Okkari, Va'El, Ka'Okkari, the other hunters and trackers who took down the hevarr, fighting like beasts themselves. And I am deeply, deeply honored by our Okkari who delivered the fatal blow." I swallow hard and wait for Kuana to catch up to me. As I do, I dare a glance over my shoulder to see the Okkari standing there with his hands at his sides. He's stiff. Blank as a void.

"This fatal blow was made, in part, by Re'Okkari's sacrifice and his honor to the tribe. To the Okkari and to me. I know I don't know your culture and customs *yet*, but I am learning. In the meantime, it is my wish now to honor Re'Okkari in the only way I know how.

"I never sang the mourning song — Svera, the advisor to the Rakukanna always did the honor. But I will try for you now. I will try for Re'Okkari so that he may know he was cherished as he finds his way to the Great Ocean of the After, where he will find his peace."

Kuana finishes and I gently tap her arm. She need not translate this. I close my eyes and think of my mother, my father, Svera, Miari, Jaxal, Kuana, the Okkari. I let everything else fall away. Every fear, every hope, every hate. And I sing.

15

Kinan

Her voice carries through the cavern, haunting in its melody and utterly captivating. I am still, emotions locked down so that my ridges remain colorless though the same cannot be said for so many with us here. This is a somber, stoic place and yet I see ridges now in almost every shade. Many greys represent their grief, but also very many more blues. It pleases the people to hear her sing. Slightly off-key though she may be, the depth of her intention is known as she sings of loss and salvation, redemption and grace.

As her song concludes, ridged foreheads tip forward slightly, and then bow a little deeper. She returns to my side and laces her five fingers with my six. I hold her hand firmly, not wishing to disrupt the honor my people give her, but wishing that she knows just what an honor it is. *Is this acceptance? Not just the tribe's acceptance of her, but her acceptance of the tribe? Is this too much to hope for?*

I do not know, but catch sight of Va'El and Tre'Hurr beaming at their Xhea now. Hurr and several of the other females who participated in the Run on the Mountain are nearby and wear similar expressions of joy. I feel dangerously moved by what is unfolding before me. So many breaks in tradition all at once, yet we are somehow all here together, worshipping at the same altar, honoring the same warrior, and we are one.

There is no human and Voraxian. There is only honor and grace. As my warrior Xhea turns to look at me, I can see in her eyes the guidance she seeks, but I can also see the water rivulets dotting the hairs on her lower eyelids. They land with fat explosions on the crests of her cheeks, looking just like rain. *She may not wear grey, but her grief for Re'Okkari's death is clear all the same.*

Before I can stop myself, I too bow to her. Tilting my head forward in an utterly indecent display by an Okkari before his people, I show my tribe just what it is that I think of what she has done here on this day and I show her that I accept what she has done — the inadvertent consequence of her actions, poorly planned — and in exchange for the honor she gives, I offer her forgiveness. A chance to find and create her own form of redemption.

Continuing with the chamar, I take the torch that is brought to me and ensure that my Xhea does the same. Together, we step forward and light the unlit staffs of those before us. She begins with Kuana while I light the torches of Hurr and her mate. The twin flames of our torches soon spawn a kingdom of light, the staffs of all hundreds of members of the tribe soon creating a new world, illuminated in color. The cairns come to life, looking like cities built by shadow dwellers who worship and collect fallen moons. Just built, Re'Okkari's stands the highest among them.

I douse my flame in the earth beneath my feet and when I raise it again, the ember glows. The act is mimicked first by my Xhea and then by the rest of the tribe until finally the only light that exists is the light of our embers, representing starlight.

I stand stoic for the full length of the time it takes for the ember to sizzle out, becoming smoke. I then make my way forward, Kiki's hand still trapped in my own in a strange fashion I read about in Svera's human manual called *hand holding*. I have never had my hand held before, but I understand the sense of comfort it brings and that the manual describes so well. But the manual does not describe the accompanying knot of pain.

My Xanaxana has been compliant with me these past solars, allowing me space to breathe even as I touch her skin, or feel her hair against my hands. But not now. This solar has been *difficult,* and now her song has broken something open inside of me and I cannot close it, like trying to rebuild the fragmented shards of a glass tower.

We step out into the snowy world and we walk in silence — the only sound being that of our footsteps crunching over the snow, along with the footsteps of those whose embers have also died. They flank us now, some outpacing us and traveling into the center of the valley, or around its opposite rim, as they return to their homes. Meanwhile, my own corresponding steps have begun to slow. *I do not wish to return her to Re'Okkari's home. I want her with me in mine where I can ravage her and be ravaged by her in return.*

She balls her hand up into a fist in mine, seeking warmth and I quickly unknot the front buckle of my okami and slide her hand inside. She makes a small sound and I come to a complete stop as her cold fingers burn me. I have tried not to look at her — not to stare — for too long and I turn to face her now.

She meets my gaze, her eyes round and wet. Licking her full lips, she says, "Did I dishonor you or the tribe?"

My response is nearly bellowed. "Nox. Quite the opposite."

Her forehead wrinkles and the tresses of her hair flap in the wind. *Lovely.* I have never seen anything like them and long to inspect each and every one. They look so intricate. Spectacular. Again, I am overwhelmed by the grace of the goddess Xana. I was given a warrior for my mate, and of all the females in the universe, I was also given the most beautiful.

"Then why are you so still? You seem upset."

I shake my head and close the distance between us by half. Dropping my face until our mouths are mere breaths apart, I say, "I am. I will have to give you up to Re'Okkari's home."

She shakes her head. "If it's an option, I'd like to go back with you. And not just tonight. Every night. I can't handle this anymore. The space between us is too much. I want to live with you...if that's something you also want."

Surprise peels the skin from my bones. My hearts begin to quicken their pace. I wonder if, against her hand, she can feel them. "It is of course an option, but the human manual states..."

"Fuck the human manual. I love Svera to death but by comets, she's a prude. I can't go on like this. I need to fuck you. I need to kiss you. Please." She exhales, both laughter on her tongue as well as a hint of desperation. A large flake of snow comes down between us, and with my arm I clear it. "Don't make me beg."

I growl and close the distance between us entirely. With a fist, I snatch up the back of her suit and with my other hand, I tangle my fingers into her hair, securing her against me. She inhales sharply, her fingers against my chest curling, nails scoring the hardened plate of my pectoral.

Against her mouth, I whisper cruelly, "That is exactly what I will do."

I kiss her hard, searingly, hoping that I have mastered the technique I only experienced once with her after our first training, and that she feels the same pleasure now that I do. Because that is all that I feel. Her mouth is truly like two pillows, decadently soft and warm and firm in its caress.

I melt into her, coming to the awareness that my people can see us here, but her tongue is a distraction that I cannot ignore. Not on this solar. I meet it with my own and she releases a soft sound that thrills me. I clutch her harder to my chest and am surprised when she jumps up and latches her arms and legs around me. Her body undulates against mine and she fights against me desperately, as if she intends to rut me here in the cold in front of all of our people.

With great pain, I pry her legs apart and lower her to the ground. She fists the front of my suit and tries to drag me closer. I block her arm. She lifts her knee into my upper thigh, sending a spasm rippling through my entire leg. And then in my fleeting state of weakness, she does the incredible — she *punches* me. Her fist finds purchase in the soft section of my abdomen between my plates, just as I taught her. My next breath rushes out of me and I stagger a half step back, but she has anticipated this and comes at me again, kicking out my leg and pushing on my shoulders, trying to drive me to the ground.

I cannot help but release pleasure sounds into the snowy world, my mouth open, my throat contracting, my face twisting as my chest rises and falls. "Will you hunt me now, Xhea?"

Her mouth pulls into an expression of exquisite pleasure that renders me just as weak as the punch she leveled to my ribs. "It seems only fair."

"It does, most certainly. But it would equally be fair that I receive a head start."

"Not a chance."

She dives for me immediately, without giving me any quarter or time to prepare myself. *Xhivey. As she shouldn't.* Her fists connect with my chest as she tries to pull the loosened buckle open, which she does — but not enough to free it fully — before I spin from her grip and dance over the snow, away from her.

The snow comes up to my shins and above her knees, but we have been practicing in the snow over the past several rotations and she is quicker now than she used to be.

She removes the skirt around her hips so that, in only hide pants, she can move forward faster. When she reaches me, she lunges for my left arm and latches onto it. She spins herself against my body and I am distracted by the pressure of her ass against my crotch for a moment too long, and that moment is all that she needs.

She thrusts her elbow into my abdomen in the same place she struck before. I bowl over, stepping back quickly and pulling her with me by the shawl she wears.

She lets out a chirp as I drag her to the ground, but she rolls backwards over her own head and as she stands, she's free of the shawl once again.

I dance out of her grip, luring her further away from the center of the valley as I chart a path towards my home. Our home. I weave between the valley floor homes, hoping to confuse her and slow her down so that I have time to reach my home and prepare myself for her before she catches me, but as I run, I realize she has fallen too far behind.

I stop and turn, following the destructive path I've created through the snow while ignoring the stares of the ones who pass me, watching me — their Okkari — with hints of curiosity and amusement in their ridges. To see their Okkari *playing* in the snow with his Xiveri mate is atypical, untraditional, some might even say wrong. *Let them say it. Tradition be damned. Because, for perhaps the first time in all my rotations, I'm having fun.*

"Xhea," I call as I round the next bend and see the path I took, uninterrupted. At the pace she set, she should have caught up to me by now. "Xhea…"

And then it hits me — *she* hits me. Not from above, but from *below*. Dense enough to hide beneath, my Xhea has chosen a hiding place just off of the path of our feet *beneath* the top layer of snow. She is so small, it is not impossible for her to fit here, but it is impossible for me to see her and as I pass, she sweeps my feet with one of her own.

I fall and as I land on my back, Kiki throws one leg over me, straddling my chest between her thighs. Her core sits right over my sternum and the smell of her arousal renders me utterly blind. Her knees spear my biceps and her hands find my wrists. She grabs them and pulls them over my head, locking them there with all of her strength.

"I win," she says as she arches over me, her mouth coming so close to mine I think she will kiss me. I hope.

I feel my face form the pleasure expression and watch a mirrored pleasure light up her cheeks. My hearts thrum out of time. "Is this what you think?"

"Hexa. You're mine for the taking, Okkari."

"In this, you are not wrong." Overpowering her is not difficult. Despite her ingenuity and her speed, she is still much too small to match me in hand-to-hand combat. I lift up and dislodge her knees and she yelps as I roll over her, reversing our position.

"Uff! You brute! That's so unfair." She pushes on my shoulder and I allow her to roll me onto my back, before quickly resuming power and pulling her under my body. We repeat this many times until soon my pleasure threatens my determination and I begin to make the pleasure sound and then *she* begins to make the pleasure sound and now we are simply an Okkari and his Xhea rolling through the snow like children. *Nox. We are not leaders, not right now. Right now, we are merely Kiki and Kinan.*

"You are clever, I will give you that, but if you are to truly win against me, you cannot afford to be overconfident. You will never win strength-against-strength. You will need to read your opponent, analyze them, find their weaknesses."

Her gaze is hooded, eyes half-moons and glossed with what I know to be her desire. I can feel her Xanaxana *everywhere.* "And what is your weakness, Okkari?"

We fall still, her underneath me, my body pressing hers into the cold, hard ground. My pelvis thrusts into hers and she spreads her legs wide for me. I grind against her and choke out, "I should have thought it obvious."

She blinks quickly, eyes rolling back as I continue to hump her like this. I'm going to spill seed and I haven't even rutted her yet. "Comets, fuck me Okkari," she says, pleasure sound giving way to soft, whimpering groans. She arches up and tries to rub her core against my length, but I press into her, forcing her still.

With one hand, I cradle the side of her face. "Nox." I bend low and place this kiss on just the tip of her nose.

Stunned or confused by it, she stops fighting me for a moment. "Why not?"

"Because I will never fuck you. You are too precious for that. Tonight I will breed you and I will do it as Kinan for this is my slave name and I am nothing if not a slave to you."

Understanding dawns in her eyes and the pleasure expression sweeps her. "Kinan. Your name is Kinan?"

Hearing it on her tongue brings me new pleasures, before unknown. "Hexa."

"I'm honored that you're telling me."

"You have earned it." I wrap my arms around her fully, feeling like a madman as I attempt to rut her fully dressed out in the snow. "I will take you now back to our nest."

"Kinan?"

I could hear her say my name again a thousand times more and never fail to be surprised and pleased by it. "Hexa, my Kiki."

"I want to have sex with you...but I don't want to get pregnant. Not yet, I mean. I'd still like to learn more about being a warrior first and fulfilling my role as Xhea."

The disappointment I expect to feel at her proclamation does not come. Instead, I make the pleased expression and reach down the length of her body to cup her core through her pants. I long to shred them.

"An honorable desire, Xhea. Your request will be fulfilled."

"How?"

"There is a plant-based herb commonly used by males to prevent the ejaculation of kit-bearing seed. I have some of this herb and will take it now before I rut you."

"And why exactly do you have this herb?" Her eyes narrow and though she does not flash copper, I am still elated and thrilled by her jealousy. I massage her core through her pants with the heel of my palm. She clenches her teeth, fighting for control, but it is a losing battle. She whimpers when I release her.

"Krisxox was my guest the last time he visited Nobu. He left much of this herb behind."

"Stars," she moans, "thank the comets for that man slut."

I make the pleasure sound and scoop her quickly up off of the snow-covered ground, surprised to see the faces of many Voraxians standing nearby, spying on us. I make the pleasure expression at them and release pleased sounds into the world at the veiled embarrassment echoed by all. They have not seen their Okkari like this *ever*. Not even when I was Kinan.

"We go now."

She releases a squeal as I take off at a run, and clutches my neck in a vice grip. I feel the scrape of her teeth against the smooth, plateless section below my ear.

She whispers, "Since I was in the merillian, does this mean I'm a virgin again?"

"Hexa. Does this frighten you?"

"Nox. It pleases me." I do not understand her answer and request explanation, to which she says, "When I got to start over last time, I ruined it by running. This time, when we start over it will be good for both of us. I won't ruin it. It will be perfect."

We arrive at our home and I bound up the stairs, open the front door and enter the overlook room. I throw her down roughly onto a mound of white Edena pelts and pillows and she squeals and laughs as she rolls across them.

Quickly sourcing Krisxox's stone herb from my cooking area and taking it, I unbind the clasps keeping me caged and when I return to the overlook room, watch as she struggles to do the same. I drop onto my knees between her thighs and rip the rest of her clothes away, then cover her body with my own. I position my xora at her entrance and press forward without warning, spearing her until I feel the barrier within her pinch around me to the point of pain.

She screams and arches her back, hands reaching for furs to fist. I wait until she tilts her chin up to look at me. The black wall of my hair creates a curtain around us. I am nothing but fire, an unsetting sun. Through clenched teeth, I tell her, "It is always good for me when I am with you. Every moment."

Her face is pinched in concentration and pain and her hips are revolving beneath me, eager for reprieve or release or both. She grips my shoulder with one hand and with the other, grabs hold of my hair at the root. She pulls until I feel sharp pain too. "Same. But right now I need you to fuck me, Kinan."

I growl. Her core is dripping wet and pulsing around me. Every emotion rips me apart. Just as she promised, I am unraveled. Through clenched teeth I spit, "It is almost as if you desire to be punished."

"Hexa," she says impishly, torturous pleasure on her tongue, "I do."

I square my hips and the most fleeting fear crosses her face. In its presence, I slow. I hold her cheek, smooth her hair behind her ear. I kiss her deeply.

Her miaba mouth is divine, distracting me for the moments I need to be able to regain some modicum of control. "Kiki," I whisper between her mouth pillows.

"Kinan," she responds.

"I will break it now." And I remember when I said these words to her before. Then, white light of the mountaintop made her look like some ethereal being. Now, light of the ioni makes her look like ioni itself, seconds before it implodes. Though if she does, then she will only succeed in taking me with her.

Her core is clenching in little pulses around my xora, gripping it like a fist. Hot and wet, I feel myself slip into insanity. The things I would do for this female. The things I will do to this female…

"Wait," she whispers.

I fight to focus on my gaze on her face, hoping to relay to her that I understand her apprehension and will do my best to make this painless for her. But instead of seeing fear in her eyes, she cradles the side of my face.

"Xivoora Xiveri," she whispers, and then the ancient words tumble from her lips. "I cover your flesh with my flesh. I cover your heart with my hearts. I am claiming you. You are my servant, you are my king, you are my blade. And I am your Xiveri, Xhea to your people, future mother to your kits. With this union, I promise to be your shield. I promise to honor you. Forever."

"Kiki..." I cannot believe she says these things to me, now and like this. I have no reply. None whatsoever.

She beams up at me, all radiant light. She would make Voraxia's suns jealous. "Now I'm ready..."

I nod, mute, feeling every bit a boy. Feeling every bit a king. I brace my forearms on her either side and I press my hips forward. She tries to keep her eyes focused on me, but the pain becomes too much for her as I finally meet the last of her virgin body's resistance.

I push and slide home and we bellow out our mirrored agonies to the room. I do not allow her the reprieve she may need however, but continue to rut her, all the while peppering many of these kisses across her face and holding steady until her pain passes and gives way to pleasure.

As it does, I roll forward, coming as close to her as I can while still being able to move. Our mouths are fused, our tongues are tangled, sweat ripples across my skin.

"Xivoora Xiveri," I tell her in the heat of our passion, instances before my first release rolls over me and seed shoots out of my xora and into her womb. Though it will not take yet, I know that it will on a solar when we are both ready and when it does, I will fill the world with more warriors just like her. Just as savage as they are beautiful.

She closes her eyes as she screams her own pleasure to the room. Her impossibly tight core clenches even tighter around me, milking me for everything I have. And when she breaks my gaze, I cannot help but make the pleasure expression down at her. Her eyelids flutter. She knows what this means.

"You have broken my gaze. Now, my Xiveri, ready yourself for punishment."

"Please," she says, her arms splayed to reveal her full, soft chest mounds.

I dart forward, moving quickly enough to make her jolt, and latch onto one of those darkened peaks. I suck on it hard and when I bite gently on the side of her breast she releases a soft scream.

My xora is firm and ready inside of her yet once again. I hold her hands down at the wrist and prop up her hips so that she has no control and beneath me, is entirely vulnerable. *Mine. To hold, to worship, to do with as I please.*

"Don't hold back," she says, full of trust that I cannot believe I deserve.

"I will not, Kiki." And I do not for the full length of the lunar.

16
Kinan

The early light of the solar filters into the overlook room. I ignore it and the tasks and responsibilities it brings and instead, pull the tattered furs up higher over us. Kiki stirs but only slightly, shifting onto her side and throwing her arm carelessly across my stomach. I smirk and trace the line of her shape with one finger, letting it roam absently over her perfect skin, taut and unblemished, before finally exploring her hair and its many tresses.

"What do you call this style of your hair?"

She makes the pleasure expression without opening her eyes and my two hearts beat firmly beneath my chest plates. "My braids?"

"Braids." I exhale. "I like these braids very much."

"Thank you. Kuana braided them. I taught her how."

"You honor her."

"That's what she said," Kiki sighs. Her tongue flashes between her teeth and though I want to press my own mouth to her delicious, spicy, shorba mouth and taste that tongue once more, I see that she is slightly swollen there. *I was too hard with her.* She encouraged the roughness, but I will need to be more careful with her in the future. That thought thrills me. *There will be a future between us.* A bright one.

"I like your hair too."

Surprised, I blink. "Thank you," I say in her human language, for we do not have these words.

"You're welcome," she sighs. I think she will sleep again when she says softly, "Why is there a strip of white?"

I hesitate, warring with myself on whether or not to tell her — but I realize quickly that not to tell her the truth, would be to lie. "It might surprise you to know that eons earlier, our ancestors here on Nobu looked much like today's Drakesh. Their hair was the color of snow, skin red. Many generations later, once inter-planetary travel had been discovered, a portion of Nobu's ancient population sought to leave.

"They wanted to find more fertile lands with less harsh conditions. They took off and, thinking they were heading towards the capital planet of our federation, Voraxia — the same place where Raku and Rakukanna are now seated in our capital — they made a mistake in their navigation. It led them to Cxrian. The native tribes they found there were either assimilated or decimated and several hundred rotations later, the planet established itself as an independent planet from the Voraxian federation. Their race they called the Drakesh.

"Voraxia was at peace with Cxrian until, not many rotations ago, the Drakesh population stopped producing kits altogether. In an effort to rekindle their diminishing numbers, they sought new females to breed.

"The Drakesh are a proud race, most unwilling to mate with any outside of their race. However, a militant group believed that Nobu, having shared ancestry with Drakesh ancestors, might be acceptable as an alternative. They invaded this tribe. My Okkari before me was felled and as his second, I championed our warriors to victory. But not without loss. Two females were killed that day, along with twenty-three warriors. One of the females was with kit."

Images of that battle revisit me. *The smell of blood. The taste of smoke.* I was hardly more than a kit myself when Drakesh invaders arrived on our planet, hungry for females. They succeeded, but only for instances before the battle hunger and fierce need to revenge came over me. In my tribe they called it tsanui and it is a sacred rite. I killed twelve fully grown Drakesh warriors that day, but I could not stop just one of them from taking her life. The life of a female *with kit.* Not my own, but all kits and all females are sacred. That Drakesh male died in pain, but it was not enough.

"What happened next?"

Blinking myself into the present, I quickly clear my throat and return my gaze to the brown face pressed against my chest, shining up at me. Purple against brown. Our colors look as if they were selected specifically to match. They look beautiful together. *I wonder what our kits will look like.*

"The Drakesh planet was folded into the Voraxian federation. So as not to disgrace them, we agreed that the Bo'Raku would remain equal to the other xub'Raku, rather than treated as a protectorate, much as your human moon is regarded currently. I was named Okkari that day by my people and elevated to Va'Raku by the Raku of the time. The Bo'Raku of the time was exiled and the next, now fallen Bo'Raku took his place."

Her body tenses in my arms, fingers tracing small patterns over my plates. I take that hand and bring it to my mouth, then kiss my way down her palm to the inside of her wrist. "He will face his retribution in the tsanui where I will skin him alive, remove his plates, pluck out his eyes and his claws and his teeth and then leave him there to die."

She snorts, the sound one of pleasure and flicks her eyes up at me. "That might be the most romantic thing anybody's ever said to me."

"It is the truth. For harming you, tsanui is my right. I will be cruel."

"I know. I just...never mind."

"You will tell me what is on your mind, Kiki."

For a moment, I think she will not, then she says, "I'm just nervous to see him again."

"You have built him up into a monster in your mind. And while he is monstrous, he is no different than any other male. Than me. He is only flesh and blood. You will see just how much he can bleed."

She smirks again. "Xhivey." Her pronunciation is terrible, but I am pleased that she tries in Voraxian all the same. "You still didn't answer my question though."

"You are correct. My long explanation is merely a way to tell you that we were once Drakesh until Voraxia expanded from its current capital to other planets. They arrived on Nobu first. Blood mixed — back then the Xanaxana was strong, weaving many Xiveri mates. What you see now in this village and across the villages of Nobu are the product of those couplings, so many generations later. Some of us still have evidence of this." I pull the strands of white hair flowing from my scalp towards her, letting them drape across the back of her hand.

She watches them without speaking and I can read nothing in her expression.

Disgruntled, I say, "Do you hate us because we have Drakesh blood flowing through our veins?"

"Nox. I don't. I did, but really the person I hated most was me."

I feel anger at her words and it warps my speech. "Hating yourself for what another did to you is nonsensical."

"It might seem that way, but it's true. I don't even *really* hate Bo'Raku. I mean, I do. But what I hate more was the fact that I couldn't beat him."

"All warriors lose battles. We are not invincible…"

"It wasn't that I lost." There's a hiccup in her voice and when she pulls her gaze to meet mine this time, I understand that she's revealing something to me that is utterly and profoundly sacred. "It wasn't even that he raped me. I'd had sex before. I knew what it was like. My mom went through the Hunt and what she described wasn't terrible. She even said she felt pleasure. Svera's mom went through it too, and was able to communicate with her…with the guy. Like my mom, she was okay after. But Jaxal's mom? Miari's mom? They died.

"Mentally, I prepared for the Hunt. I knew that there were so many possibilities and I thought I accounted for them all. I knew my body would heal from whatever they did to me and it did, but…"

She bites her lips together. I do not speak. I wait for as long as it takes her, until finally she exhales, her breath fanning across my chest, making every place it touches tingle. "He laughed."

I do not speak. I cannot. By her small admission — two little words — I am gutted. Flayed. Massacred. Dishonored. I feel that to share the same blood that he does makes me nothing in this moment and suddenly I understand how Kiki must have felt. What drove her.

"It was the single most degrading and humiliating moment of my life. The pain I could have handled, but the laughter... I hear it all the time. When I'm asleep. When I'm awake."

"Do you hear it now?"

She pauses. "No.

"That is because Peixal is ruled by hate. Do not be like him. Not when there is something much more powerful that can drive you to becoming the greatest warrior Nobu has ever seen, for you are already the most fearsome Xhea we have ever witnessed."

She bites her bottom lip and looks up at me, terror in her gaze dimmed. She shines brighter now than she did, or perhaps I am only imagining things. "The Xanaxana, you mean?"

"I was going to say love."

She lifts a hand and gently brushes her fingers through my hair, paying particular attention to the strands in white. My scalp prickles as she scrapes her nails across it. "Peixal," she says. "Bo'Raku... I didn't think I could even say his name out loud."

"Names have power here. More than this pleasure sound you call laughter. Peixal's name has been revealed for all of Voraxia to hear. He sits in a well of shame he cannot crawl out of and as soon as the first icefall ends, he will stand trial for his crimes and I will exact tsanui in your honor." I press my mouth to the top of her head and inhale the scent of her hair. "He will either die or be exiled where the only beings alive to hear his laughter are the hevarr."

She snorts again, making the laughter sound. "I'd love to see him get eaten by a hevarr. That would be fun."

This time, *I* am the one to make this snorting laughter sound. "Then it is as you wish. And speaking of hevarr, you will need to meet with Hurr early on the coming solar. The hevarr has been successfully skinned. You will now help the xub'Hurr in the tanning and curing process."

She blinks up at me and I know this time her expression is one of shock. "I'm not training anymore?"

"You are. You will do this in the latter half of the solar. All warriors have multiple positions. We cannot simply play with swords while the rest of the tribe does all of the work. I have been too lenient with you thus far."

She gapes. "Are you calling me *lazy?*" She lands a punch playfully on my chest.

"Perhaps I am. How will you retaliate?"

She sits up quickly and throws a leg over my chest only to wince and clutch her thigh. Dramatically — near comically — she lilts to the side, collapsing onto a pile of pillows. "Cramp!" She shouts.

I cannot contain laughing sounds as I come to cover her. "If you think I will not rut you simply because of a cramp, then you are wrong. You have much more work to do, my Xhea."

I impale her with my length without warning and she moans deeply from the back of her throat. Her eyes roll and she struggles to meet my gaze as I pound into her. "More work," she moans, "You're going to be the death of me…"

"Nox." I capture her lips with my own and between pants and kisses, grunt, "But I will kill for you."

Forty-eight solars later…

17

Kiki

Tre'Hurr laughs uproariously and I can only assume it's because of my expression. "What is this?" Bile pitches in my stomach and climbs threateningly up my throat as I maneuver my paintbrush up and down the stretch of hide in front of me.

Other females stand in even intervals to my left and right in the huge screa chamber. One of the biggest in-built caves I've seen in the village so far, it's second only to the Okkari's training pitch, though this one is broken down into many antechambers — so many, I haven't even explored them all.

In this cavern are a little more than thirty of us working, but some filter in and out. All are busy with different hides, carrying them from one antechamber to another for skinning, tanning, stretching and airing.

For the past however many solars, I've been helping carry newly skinned pelts from one place to another — all of them white Edena hides — and stretch them across wooden frames of varying sizes. Thinking back to all the manual labor I did on the colony, I thought this would be a breeze, completely underestimating how hard the work would be. Still, I find myself smiling as I notice a few faces shining in my and Tre'Hurr's direction. They're smiling too.

"Don't act so surprised. This is dolloram, what we've been using to cure the hides."

"But it's never smelled so bad before — I mean, it's smelled bad, but this is a whole other level. Like a bowl of rotten fruit was beaten to death with a fish."

"Colorful, I'll grant you that, but you should know better than anyone what this is."

I stand back from it for a moment, head cocked to the side. Dread fills my belly. "Is this the hevarr?"

"It is."

"It reeks."

She laughs. "That it does. It's an incredibly dense piece of material. We thought for your first time, it would be easier to start you with Edena."

"And now what — I'm one of the team?" I smirk.

She looks at me, pausing mid-stroke and smiles up at me guilelessly, "Hexa." She resumes working without saying anything else. As if that single word didn't mean something special to me. As if it were totally obvious. "You have improved considerably over the past solars. You are almost as adept at this as nearly matured kits."

"*Wow,*" I say, elongating the word, "You are throwing major shade right now."

"Throwing shade?" She tuts under her breath in a way that's become familiar over these past solars working alongside her in this muggy cave. "That is not possible. Another one of your human expressions, I must assume."

"Indeed." I laugh lightly under my breath and pick back up my brush, moving it over the horrifying-smelling hide in even strokes, just as Hurr and Tre'Hurr taught me. "We did something similar on the human colony, but we didn't have dolloram, or any particularly effective tanning solutions for that matter."

"What did you use then?"

I shrug. "We mostly just mixed sand with acolic acid and did the process once instead of soaking the hides after and applying salt. We didn't have enough salt to spare. Or acolic acid. In fact, the only thing we can spare is sand. If y'all ever need any, you know where to go."

She smiles at me slightly, her laughter ceasing as she turns back to the skin with her brush. She dips the frazzled hairy brush tip into the thick, grey goop and applies a layer onto the pale grey underside of the pelt. "Your colony will not have these worries again. I am sure."

Something irks me then, a recurring thought I've had, one that I finally have the courage to voice. "Do Voraxian females resent human ones?"

Tre'Hurr's ridges flash white with surprise. She opens her mouth to respond, but just then there is a commotion at my back, towards the entrance of the cavern. I turn and am surprised, just as I am every time, when Reema enters the cave. Currently auditioning for different roles, she's begun helping the xub'Hurr these past few solars and sometimes we are stationed close enough to one another to speak. I've learned a lot about her.

Her mother is a xub'Xhen — what I've gathered to be some sort of scientist who studies organic matter — and her father is Garon, the weapons keeper. She doesn't like skinning or tanning, but she likes the brining process because she gets to paint. She likes painting. They don't have artists here on Nobu, so she hopes that in the coming solars, when she vies for a title of her own, she'll become the xub'Garon, apprentice to the weapons keeper — she wants to take after her daddy. She doesn't think she'll have a chance for the post however, because there is only one xub'Garon and no female has ever vied for it before. But she still hopes. She also likes sweet shorba fruit and nut bread pudding — we both do.

"Surprised again, my Xhea," Tre'Hurr says with a chuckle. "I would have thought seeing Reema would be a common sight for you. Especially after all I've heard of this human moon and its fertileness. You must have babes suckling on breasts and little kits running rampant."

Reema is looking for something — someone — and when her gaze meets mine she smiles sheepishly and waves in the human greeting custom I taught her. I wave back and watch her until she is directed by Hurr into the antechamber where hides are soaked. Lifting my paintbrush back to the hevarr skin, I tell Tre'Hurr, "It's just crazy to me how *few* like Reema I've seen — and she's not even that young. I mean she's obviously younger than we are, but I don't know if I've seen any babies at all since I've been here."

Tre'Hurr nods and a skein of grey grief winds across her forehead.

Stupid mouth. "I'm sorry. I didn't mean…"

"Nox, my Xhea, you are correct. The Okkari's village is the largest on Nobu. We are just over three thousand. Of that, we have only two hundred and ninety who do not yet have titles and, of those, only thirty two kits. No babies have been born in the past four rotations."

I curse. "Comets, that's terrible. And even for kits, that isn't very many."

"It is not. It makes it hard to picture this human colony you speak of. The thought of kits and their games, suckling babes and the guileless laughter of youth helping to carry us through these long ice storms is truly a wonderful thing to imagine. But so distant. Like trying to snatch ice from the air before it lands without it melting."

"I've tried that. It didn't work."

She laughs lightly, but it does not reach her ridges. "We all have. So for now we are content to treasure our little ones. The few that we have. It is a wonder we have any sane adults at all with how badly we spoil our kits."

I smile and we lapse into a pleasant silence. Around me I hear other females talking, renewed laughter and the occasional high trill of a much younger voice giggling among them. Distracted by thoughts of children, I drop my brush and when I turn to retrieve it, kick the bucket of dolloram accidentally — the *screa* bucket.

Needles shoot up my leg and I curse a thousand times before grumbling, "If only every blasted thing on this planet wasn't made out of screa."

Tre'Hurr laughs and tries to cage it behind her hand. "Deepest apologies, Xhea."

"Xhea?" The word I hear everyday spoken in a voice I know only from another lifetime rattles me to my core. I turn and see a ghost and grin.

"I must be dreaming," I say. In my peripheries I see that everyone has stopped working and is focused on me and the female standing near the entrance. Nothing but packed earth and pebbles separate us. I take a step forward and she grins when I do, her red face reflecting a heritage that I could never begrudge her, just as I can't begrudge any of them, no matter how badly I've tried to. We can't help the skin we're born in.

Her hands move instinctively to cover her stomach, which bulges noticeably despite the many fur layers she's wrapped in. Foreheads beaming with color tip forward as she waddles and wobbles further into the cavern.

I burst out laughing. "Oh my stars, I can't believe it's you!" I rush forward, dropping my paintbrush and throwing my arms around her shoulders. Half-Drakesh, she's taller than I am and when I step back, I have to look up at her.

"What are you doing here?"

She laughs and there is a glaze to her eyes that she wipes at. "Oh stars, Kiki, you don't know how good it is to see you." She brings me back in for another hug and when she turns this time, she drags me with her. "I wanted to surprise you."

"Well you definitely have. I didn't know it was safe to travel yet." My stomach is in knots. My tasks forgotten. I can't believe it. *She's here.*

A flash of a memory. Another life. *Miari squats inside of the cave, knees tucked under her chin, chewing on a piece of fruit leather and loaf of sand bread. Her eyes are wide and scared and still she's smiling at me at something stupid she's said or that I wrote down. I wasn't speaking then, but when the khrui came for us, I stood up and held my grabar out in front of me. Of one thing I was certain, if it came to me and the khrui or Miari, I was prepared to die. She means so much to me.*

Her belly presses against my belly in a way I find just a little unsettling. I make a face and hold her back and she laughs. "I know. I'm still not used to it myself. But to answer your question, the first icefall has passed and the next won't start up again for another thirty solars or so, giving us just enough time."

"Enough time for what?"

"To catch up."

"I thought that's what we've been doing on our calls these past solars."

"I didn't mean with me." She pulls me to the entrance of the cave and when she steps out of the way, my jaw drops and I'm rendered completely speechless. Miari laughs, "So how about now? Are you still surprised?"

I must be hallucinating. Maybe the fumes from the dolloram really did kill me. Because standing ankle-deep in the snow close enough to touch are my favorite people in the world. All of them. Svera, Jaxal and my mom. And of course, just behind them, Kinan. He stands beside Miari's Raku and a small contingent of warriors, looking on.

I shriek like a little girl and storm forward, embracing my mom first. "Oh my," she says as she takes my weight. She's shorter than I am and she seems much older than she had the last time I saw her. *But she still smells the same. Like sand and earth and lavender-scented root butter, the kind she uses in her hair.*

"It's so good to see you. I can't believe you're here," I exhale into her shoulder. Her braids twine with mine and when I pull back, she looks even more surprised than I feel.

Her mouth works. Finally, she says, "Well, it's not like they could have kept me away. When Svera announced that a group of us would be allowed to travel to a far and distant planet to visit Kiki, you can bet your bottom dollar that I was the first one in line. Even had to ruffle Mathilda's feathers since she and Deena thought they should be the first ones on board, but of the twelve of us here, they weren't even selected. Svera saw to that."

Svera cuts in, her face turning a brilliant scarlet everywhere except for the silver scar cast high on her cheek — a product of her abduction by the pirate king of Kor. "It's not that I wanted to exclude them, but the rules state that priority be given to females and families of females who have been through the Hunt. Mathilda and Deena haven't."

"Oh honey, we understand the rules," my mom says, throwing Svera a carnivorous wink that has Miari and I howling — even Jaxal cracks at that. I turn to him next and step forward to hug him, but he jerks away from me awkwardly, his dark cheeks flushing and his gaze flicking back over his shoulder.

"Not allowed to hug you," he grunts out through gritted teeth before refocusing on me. "But it's good to see you though. You look...different."

I feel myself warm, embarrassment making me shift my weight from hip-to-hip. It's hard to meet his gaze. For too long we've fed off of each other's hatred. Now that mine's gone, I don't know what to say. "I feel different," I try.

"You look healthy."

"You sound surprised."

"I am." His tone is flat and bleak. His hair, which falls in locks to his shoulder blades, is tied back from his face with a band. He looks so out of place here wrapped in furs, the white cold they called snow falling so softly around him. So gently. Meanwhile, he looks like he's ready to lift both fists and shred apart the world around him. *Is this what I looked like?* My spine prickles. My teeth ache.

I step forward despite what he says — the order he's been given — and wrap both arms around him. I close my eyes and breathe in his scent. *Minted steel, dry wood, arid desert winds promising nothing but thirst.* It reminds me of so much pain. His. Mine. The whole damn colony's.

I squeeze him tight and as his arms tentatively come around my shoulders, I whisper against his chest, "I don't know who I am anymore. But whoever I am, I like her better than who I was after the Hunt. I just..." I exhale. "Thank you for helping me through the darkness. I wouldn't be here now if it weren't for you."

Behind me, a dark voice calls my name — my title. "Xhea." It's a threat, loosely veiled and leveled straight at Jaxal's heart.

Releasing Jaxal and whatever burden of guilt I felt at him seeing me here, now, like this, without hate coloring my every inch, I turn and smile at the Okkari. His forehead is a blank slate except for a single escaped note of copper. I've seen this color a few times before when I spar with some of his soldiers. I know what it means — that acute jealousy — because I've felt it too whenever he speaks with the tribe's females. Even Kuana who tends our home isn't immune.

I step up to him and take his arm, bringing him forward. "Okkari, I want you to meet my family. My mom, my brother and my sisters."

"I have made a brief introduction, but I am pleased to be reintroduced." He steps forward to my mom first and extends his hand.

My mom looks at it, then looks at me, unsure. Her brown eyes are full of questions and hesitation and indecision, but the laughing lines around her mouth and that crease the corners of her eyes remind me that there isn't a hateful bone in her body — not even the Hunt could change her.

Women on the colony, as a rule, don't speak of the Hunt, but I wonder now as I watch her watch me standing next to an alien male I've claimed in body and devoured in soul, if maybe I shouldn't have. If I still should. Because I never believed her when she said her time in the Hunt wasn't bad…that it was even *good*.

"Mom, this is Okkari. He's my man."

Infectious laughter pours out of her, even though she has tears in her eyes, which she quickly rubs away with her thumbs. "Oh is he now?"

"He is."

"Well then, I suppose that makes you family now too." She bats his hand away and hugs Kinan, her short arms hardly fitting all the way around his chest. "If you're family, then I'll be calling you son."

As Kinan smiles down at her, his hand takes mine and brings it to his lips. He kisses the back of my palm and very quietly, so only the three of us can hear, he says, "You may call me son. But you may also call me Kinan. This is my given name."

The surprise in my mom's expression lets me know that Svera has clued her into what a big deal this is. I feel shocked too, but more than that, deeply grateful. "You may call me by my given name, Mirella, or you can just call me mom."

Kinan grins and my mom shines back and for a moment we all just stand there stupidly smiling at one another until Miari laughs. She waddles back over to Raku's side and he kisses the top of her head in a gesture that surprises me in how human it is.

"The other humans have been called now to join us. We wanted to give you a chance to meet with your family privately before we give them all a tour of the village."

"Thank you," I tell her. She just shrugs and waves a hand dismissively. I turn to Kinan. "And I'm guessing you had quite a lot to do with this shindig."

"I would not be Okkari if I did not."

I grin. "Cocky brute."

"Hexa," is all he says.

I laugh and look up at him and meet his gaze head on and in a way I never ever want to break from. "Thank you."

"No thanks is required. It pleases me to please you."

Standing up on my tiptoes — and with him bending down — I manage to reach his ear with my lips. I kiss the lobe, nipping it with my teeth, and say, "Then perhaps I can thank you this lunar, in other more creative ways."

Kinan clears his throat gruffly and straightens, ridges flaring a dark and dusky purple, much deeper than the color of his skin. "That will be acceptable."

I laugh. "In the meantime, if it's a tour of the village they want, let's begin."

18
Kinan

I have not seen my Kiki so radiant as this. She flits through the village and with every word spoken to her humans, every introduction made to the Voraxians of our tribe, every explanation of the smallest thing and most subtle nuance I am reminded of a startling truth, one I never thought to hope for: Kiki has claimed this village for her own. *She wants to be here.* She returns always to my side, her eyes filled with warmth and satisfaction and hope. *She wants to be here with me.*

I encourage her as she shows Jaxal and one of the other males the armory in the training hall, even if every shared look and glance of their fingers as she hands him various weapons makes me want to skewer him with the helos spear she values so highly. *No, something duller. Then it will hurt more.* But begrudgingly, I trust her.

I believe her when she calls Jaxal her kin even if the concept of *brothers* and *sisters* does not exist here on Nobu — for females that are able to produce kits, there is only ever one — and even if they are not kin by blood. I believe her.

Raku, Krisxox and I hover near the rear of the group with the contingent of warriors that accompanies this human delegation. Of the twelve humans, eight are females and four are males and though I do not know if they are all considered exceptional beauties on their moon, I do know that they would all be held as rare and treasured prizes here on Nobu.

Despite the threat of the coming icefall, the village has never looked so full and bustling as it does today. Doors are wide open, faces of those old and young and everything in between peering out of them as villagers hope to be introduced or, at the very least, see the humans. My Kiki does her best to make introductions to each villager we come across, but they are too many and there will be other opportunities and the lunar approaches and on this lunar, more than most, Kiki will need her rest.

"Okay okay," she says as I remind her of this for the fourth time. "Just let me show them our place, okay?"

Floored by the way she says *our*, I nod my ascent. *A strong Okkari, Kinan is weak and can deny her nothing.* She nearly skips up the screa steps to our home, her humans following closely behind. I notice that, while most are curious, there is one female who seems quite frightened, and then there is Jaxal who views all he sees with disgust or revulsion. He makes no effort to hide it.

It is clear his reactions hurt Kiki, even if others may not see the slight tensing of her shoulders or the surreptitious way she watches this male she calls *brother* as we enter our home and she introduces him to her — to *our* — things. *I will need to speak with him if his attitude does not change. Or fight him. He calls himself a warrior, yet I do not doubt I would defeat him in combat in the span of a heartbeat.* The thought brings me pure delight. *I believe on this trip, I may be able to manufacture a way...*

"Oh my and who is this?" Kiki's mother, Mirella says as Kuana appears in the doorway of the overlook room.

"This is Kuana," Kiki answers when Kuana does not. "Kuana this is my mom, the Rakukanna, Svera, and other humans from our colony." She goes through them name-by-name, but Kuana seems distracted, her gaze unfocused, her ridges flashing white and then pink and then gold. "Kuana, are you okay? Is she okay?" She goes to Kuana and places a hand on her shoulder while I push my way to the front of the crowd.

There, Svera joins me, Krisxox stalking her like a shadow. "Alhamdullah," Svera coos in her light, strange hymn that could not be more opposite Kiki's deep snarl. Svera's gaze pans across the humans gathered in the overlook room and I believe we both make the same observation at the same time.

"Guards, please help Jacabo and bring him here," she says in nearly unaccented Voraxian. Krisxox nearly lunges to arrive at the male in question first. He grabs him gruffly by the collar just as the male buckles. He falls forward with a cry, but Krisxox does not show him reprieve, instead dragging him forward too roughly. Raku issues a stern warning while the Rakukanna orders space to clear.

The human called Jacabo is a burly male with medium brown skin, a broad chest, short-cropped hair on his head and a bewildered look on his face. He wrenches free of Krisxox's hold when Kiki, behind me, issues a startled curse, "Kuana...comets you're heavier than you look..." She sinks under Kuana's weight — Kuana whose colors have suddenly dimmed as her body collapses onto itself, like a dying star.

Miari reaches forward to help, but Raku, ignoring her protests, scoops her up and places them both out of the way in the rear of the room where she cannot be injured in the commotion. It is best, because then Jaxal tries to intercept the meatier human male, but is shoved off of his feet by a palm to the chest. The male continues forward and his stare shifts to me where it burns.

"Don't touch her," he snarls, and though I am the closest male to Kuana and my Xiveri mate requires assistance, I am not stupid.

"I will do no such thing, but you will calm yourself before you approach the females. In your haste, you may injure one of them or yourself. My Xiveri mate is a warrior and she will not hesitate to defend herself."

The thing that is broken in his brain clicks into place. He staggers in his next step and I watch as he slows his approach, my own feet rooted to the ground even though my muscles itch and twitch and flex and burn. The restraint may be the death of me, but I am Okkari and master of my own body. For Krisxox, the same cannot be said.

Impertinent and ever impetuous, he rushes forward. With a terse order to the warriors, I have him blocked so that there is only a wall of warriors on one side, Svera, Kiki and Kuana on the other, and myself and Jaxal flanking the male called Jacabo as he slowly advances. His eyes are wide, his expression tortured. *A sensation I know well because I have lived it.*

Calm now — at least outwardly — the male drops to one knee at her feet. He reaches out, his hand trembling, and touches the curved edge of her foot. On contact, she starts awake. Blinking, she looks up into

Kiki's face and though her mouth opens, she does not speak.

"You're okay," Kiki answers. "I think you just felt the first effect of the Xanaxana. Jacabo, do you feel a burning sensation? A desire to be with Kuana more than anything else in the world?"

The male in question nods, mute, before an expression of pain twists his features. Svera sits up straighter at Kuana's side, as if pricked by a pin. "So humans *can* feel the full effects of the Xanaxana right away. While Miari felt it's presence right away, the full effects only occurred for her after some solars."

Kiki responds, words instinctive and spoken with no great ceremony even though I am deeply humbled by each and every one. "I felt it right away. Took me just a few moments before I was like this. Or worse. We should get them out of here, back to Jacabo's place. He does have his own place, right?" Svera nods. Kiki grins impishly. "They're going to need some time alone."

Kuana looks up, dazed, and holds a hand to her ridges. Her pure white hair spills over her shoulders as she rights herself and finally sees the male she will be bound to for this lifetime *and the next — the male that she has always been bound to.* Color intensifies in her ridges, the full effects of the Xanaxana becoming apparent in a way that embarrasses all of the Voraxians in the room and visibly confuses the humans.

Jaxal, in particular, watches the pair on the floor with a contempt shared only by Krisxox who shines a bloody burgundy. With his red skin, white hair, and high breeding, Krisxox carries an even fiercer pride in his Drakesh heritage than most, and views inter-species mixing as an aberration. I feel momentary anger that either male was permitted to join this expedition, however, as neither Krisxox nor this human male who I glibly wish to gut dishonor themselves, I remain rooted and silent.

Kuana gasps, "Xivoora Xiveri." She blinks wildly, flashing white, as if surprised by the words she herself has said.

The human male grins, as if he understands her words for what they are. Perhaps, between his translator and Svera's manual, he does. Or perhaps he *knows* in the way we all *know* when we encounter our one true mate.

"Ziv-ooh-rah, Ziv-are-hee," he says, the words butchered as he attempts the Voraxian language.

Kuana does not seem to mind. She returns his pleasure expression in full. He extends his hand towards her very carefully, like a scientist attempting an experiment he must get just right. So slowly even time seems to wait, Kuana places her six-fingered hand in his five-fingered one. His hand is large. Despite the Voraxian's naturally larger physique, Kuana is small in stature and this male is quite the opposite. His palm dwarfs hers as he rubs his thumb across her skin.

"Stars," he hacks, each breath he takes sounding painful for him. "This can't be real." The Xanaxana in Kuana's chest begins to sound, a light purr rumbling throughout the room. Startled, the human looks at her chest where she wears only a light linen tunic and trousers beneath it. He licks his lips. Bites the lower. "You're so fucking beautiful."

Kuana's ridges intensify in color and she tenses. Less than a heartbeat later, I scent the sweet aroma of a female's arousal. The Voraxian males in the room stiffen and I clear my throat as we each shame ourselves by experiencing this collective sensation.

"Kiki, come to my side," I say, before turning my attention to the guards present in the room. "Xcleranx," I address them, "Please accompany the humans back to their quarters. Ensure that Kuana and Jacabo have the privacy and supplies they need for as long as they need them."

Embarrassment blasts over Kuana's ridges in near fluorescent yellow, however, her human merely laughs. "That sounds good. Really good. That sound good to you, Koo-ah-nah? Is that your name?"

She nods. "Hexa. I mean, yes. That does sound good to me. And my name...I will tell you later, when we are alone."

Jacabo smiles at her so tenderly, I feel a knot in my own chest I did not realize I carried, release. Kuana is an honorable female. It is an honor to us all that Xana has chosen a Xiveri mate for her. One who is honorable, for he would not be here as part of this congregation were he not.

"Then I don't want to wait. Can I carry you?" She nods and Jacabo lifts her in his arms. He turns to face the group of humans and protectors they arrived with. "What are we waiting for? My mate and I need some privacy."

The guard begin towards the door, but one of the human females — the frightened one — says, "So it's real? This instant bonding thing?"

Jacabo nods. "Yes. It's real." As he speaks, he does not look away from Kuana's face. "Very real."

"What does it feel like?" One of the males asks next.

Jacabo exhales, "Like I just met my wife."

The humans murmur amongst one another, but I do not look away from Kiki's face. She is smiling, so resplendent and genuinely happy I know I will commit this moment, this vision, to memory for the rest of my rotations. Her laughter breaks me out of my trance — something one of the humans must have said.

Raku, behind me, whispers in his Rakukanna's ear, informing her of the scent of Kuana's arousal growing more potent and the Rakukanna quickly issues orders for the humans to disperse, the guards with them, until eventually Kiki and I are alone in the overlook room. I remain frozen where I am. She remains frozen with a smile on her face.

"I can't believe it," she says at last. "Like really cannot believe it. Jacabo is a farmer back home. He hates it and is this ridiculous, sarcastic person. Kuana is so calm and gentle and straightforward and diligent in her duties. They make an unlikely pair."

"Don't we all."

Her gaze hits mine then and I feel appropriately struck by it. I release the hold I had on my ridges and my Xanaxana, allowing the room to fill with color and sound. Kiki's grin holds and she comes at me in a run. Thinking she means to fight me once more, I'm caught off guard when she jumps, clinging to my frame. I wrap my arms around her and take her down to the furs and we commit this love act to and with one another throughout the lunar and it is only in the aftermath, as we lay bound together in the quiet dark, that I remember what it was I intended to tell her the moment her humans landed on planet.

"Your humans," I whisper as the re'ien farrn fire glows softly, illuminating the gold notes in her skin. *Ioni so full of life.* "They did not come alone to Nobu." I hold, awaiting her reaction. For her to pull away from me, to fight. Awaiting her hate to resurface. *I would deserve no less. Svera and the Rakukanna's surprises be damned, I should have told her before this.*

But my Kiki only sighs, "I know."

I sit up so that I may look down at her. Her full lips and their scandalous shape are slack and begging to be suckled. I take her face in one hand and tilt her head back so that she sees me and knows the meaning of the words that I say next, "No harm will come to you while he is on planet."

"I'm not worried," she says and I am surprised.

"You…are not?"

She takes my hand and licks a line up the center of my palm in a way that I find disastrously erotic. I will soon have her beneath me again, but first I must know, "You are calm, my Xhea…an honorable reaction."

She laughs. "There's nothing honorable about it. I just realized that the only power he has anymore is the one I give him. He's a disgraced fool and he deserves nothing from me, least of all power."

The rattling in my chest blots out all noise. Blots out all thought. I bend over her and plant my kiss against the center of her forehead. "You are a wise female," I say. "The trial that will take place in two solars will be over quickly."

She smiles as she begins her own slow caress of my body, my neck, my abdomen, my ribs, and then lower. Her mouth follows her hands, moving over me in movements that are possessive and sure. The whole room smells of her. Dark and devouring smoke. And I am happily inundated.

"I hope it isn't," she says against my skin. "I want him to suffer."

19

Kiki

The wind whips around us, feeling a lot like the day I ran onto the tundra and met my first hevarr. It's cold, but I'm used to it, and the white isn't as thick as it has been, falling in star-shaped clumps that are only the size of my hand, all fingers splayed. Letting the cold white fall onto my okami and melt, I inhale and exhale deeply. *Breathe...*

We stand in a lumpy circle, looking like an informal gathering about to start singing songs at a bonfire, except instead of a bonfire, we're standing around an empty pitch of frozen earth. The only thing that makes it look like a tribunal at all are the armed guards. They stand interspersed along the perimeter of the circle, the bulk of them positioned in diamond formation around a single male who gleams like a bloodstain against the white world behind him.

I can feel him watching me and I don't shrink from his gaze, but turn to meet it, betraying nothing. *Breathe. Just breathe.* Then I look away. Making eye contact for too long could be seen as a sign of respect in Voraxian culture, and if only one thing is certain in all of the universe's many galaxies, it's that I don't.

I can feel Kinan's tension to my right, bleeding out of him like pus from an infection. The whole arena is tense. The inner circle is formed only by a dozen or so of us, while slightly further back the entire village has come to witness what's about to happen. *Spectator sport, much?* I grin, emitting a half grunt-half laugh. *I love it. Let the carnage begin.*

A slight shift to my right draws my attention up. Kinan is looking at me and even though he is stoic as ever, ridges devoid of color, I know that he thinks I've lost it. Perhaps I have. This is the solar I live the nightmare that's haunted me for the past three rotations. *Breathe.* And then, in the face of my suppressed terror and rage, Kinan does the unthinkable. He winks at me.

Startled, I almost smile even though I'm on trial in front of an entire village of beings whose respect I fight — sometimes quite literally — to earn, and when I do receive it, cherish. Now I merely fight to keep my hands to myself even though I want nothing more than to take his arms and wrap them around my body like the blanket of security I know they are. But I am Xhea. Stoic and proud. At least, this is what I must appear to be as Raku steps into the circle and announces that the trial has finally found its start.

"We come together today to recognize a series of crimes perpetrated by and against the human colony residing on the eighteenth moon of Cxrian." His voice is booming and impressive, nearly jarring in its impact. Even the wind seems hushed by it. He's king for a reason, and in his tone, I'm reminded of it.

"Proven guilty, Peixal faces exile or death; *which* will be decided during his tsanui, a sacred rite performed by the Va'Raku of our federation. The tsanui will be carried out in response to acts of horror committed by Peixal against the Va'Rakukanna during an illegally sanctioned Hunt three rotations ago."

He gestures at Peixal with his hand — an act of dishonor — before lowering his arm and then nodding slightly to Svera and then to me. "On trial today is also the human advisor, Svera, and the Va'Rakukanna. They will be tried for their attempted abduction of the Rakukanna. A fourth and final trial will take place on this solar — that of Lisbel, former hasheba to the Va'Rakukanna, for her deception that led to the Va'Rakukanna's flight and resulted in the death of a warrior, Re'Okkari."

Surprised, I glance around until I spot Kuaku — *Lisbel* — at the far side of the circle from where I stand. She stares at the ground between her feet and I feel simultaneously furious and ashamed that she's even here when all she really tried to do was what I asked her — *well that* and *get me killed, but who's really counting?* I'm about to say something when Okkari reaches over and takes my arm in a gentle grip. I settle and manage to hold my tongue without interrupting.

"Given the nature of these crimes, Svera, the Va'Rakukanna, and Lisbel will be afforded the ability to appoint their own champions while Peixal will face tsanui at the hand of Va'Raku, as has already been decided."

He pivots to Svera who stands not too far down the row to my left, separated from me by the red male called Krisxox, who seems to hate humans as much as Jaxal hates Voraxians. He seemed a strange choice for her protector, but Svera already explained to me that even though she chose someone else, he refused to relinquish his position.

My gaze flashes once more to Bo'Raku, even though it's inadvertent. *I hate that I do that. I hate myself for it. I hate myself that I let him rule me.* Hush. *Breathe.* Calm. *Breathe.* Exhale. *Shut the fuck up and just breathe already!*

As the crowd settles, the only sounds gently falling white, Raku returns to his place along the perimeter of the circle where he stands beside his queen. Miari remains seated, a female healer called Lemoria at her shoulder. Despite being head of all healers and needed pretty much everywhere at once, Lemoria is overseeing Miari's pregnancy. Every second of it.

"Svera." Raku tilts his head towards the center of the circle. The arena. The pit. *The grave it will become even if the white cold doesn't know it yet.* "You may now choose your champion."

Svera steps forward slightly, but before she can so much as speak, a Voraxian guard steps forward. He has blue skin that's darker than Raku's and slightly bluer, where Raku is more grey. His hair falls in jet black strands around his shoulders but is plaited back from his face, almost identically to the way I wear mine and Jaxal wears his.

It's the way hunters on the colony with long hair keep it out of their face and out of reach of opponents. I wonder if Svera helped him. I remember her speaking highly of one of the guards. I wonder if this is him... The thought has the corners of my mouth twitching in the makings of a carefully repressed smile and just like that, hate slips so easily away. Love weighs so much less. *Nothing at all. It is pure buoyancy.*

"I am Tur'Roth, one of the xcleranx of Voraxia and one of the personal guards to advisor Svera. I would be honored to assume her place in this trial by taking up my axe against whichever opponent is deemed suitable and act as her champion." Facing Svera, he bows to her at the waist. "If it pleases you, advisor Svera."

I can see from where I stand that Svera is blushing, a small, not-quite-suppressed smile on her face. She opens her mouth, but before she can speak, Krisxox storms forward into the pit. In a complete break in decorum, he steps up to Tur'Roth, covers Tur'Roth's face with one enormous hand and shoves. Tur'Roth stumbles back, falling onto his ass in the now empty place next to Svera.

Svera gasps, taking hold of Tur'Roth's arm as he rises again to his feet, ridges a deep and unsettling red. "Krisxox, how dare you…"

"Punish me for it later," he barks savagely to the wind. It picks up in response, as cold as the breath of Xaneru himself. *Breathe. Svera is safe. Even if Krisxox is being an ass, at least she has two revered warriors vying to be her champion. Exile will not be her fate.* "No one else will champion for you on this solar."

"Krisxox, you dishonor advisor Svera. You dishonor a proud xcleranx. You dishonor yourself." Raku shakes his head slowly, sadly almost, like someone who has seen and condemned this behavior before and more than once. "You will accept one stroke of the lash."

"Accepted." His black eyes flash and he speaks through teeth that are clearly clenched, "But I will champion."

Raku glances to Miari. She bites her lower lip as she watches Svera's face, full of conflict. Svera is bright red again and looks near tears. Between disappointment, humiliation or frustration, I'd put money on the latter. She's prim and proper in everything she does. To be shamed in such a way and so publicly is a disgrace many others might be able to shrug off, though I know she can't.

Svera nods. Miari nods. Raku nods, short and sharp. "Then it will be delivered now."

"Fine," Krisxox snarls.

"By Tur'Roth."

Krisxox's forehead. A skein of black streaks through the bright red already present and his torso swells. He nods in silence and his upper lip pulls back to expose his teeth. He looks like violence made flesh.

"Tur'Roth," Raku says, inviting him into the arena with a wave of his arm. Understanding and evidently accepting Raku's edict, Tur'Roth goes to the Garon standing near Miari. Three males guard the weapons cache while an older male rifles through a large werro wood chest and withdraws a whip. Unlike the leather whips I've seen before, this one isn't *static*. Like the holoshields I've practiced with, it zaps to life when Tur'Roth takes the thick metal handle, activating it. Energy crackles and sizzles as Tur'Roth releases the tail end of the whip, allowing it to uncoil onto the snow below. It lands so softly it makes no sound.

Despite the temperature, Krisxox sheds his outer layer — first, the hide shell, then the chest and back pieces of the okami he wears. Clad in only hide pants and boots now, he turns his bare back to Tur'Roth and holds his arms out to the sides in a vulnerable display. Tur'Roth does not hesitate.

The slash of the whip against Krisxox's bare skin sputters and pops, energy meeting flesh. A blazing line of copper opens up from Krisxox's right shoulder to left hip. The force of the blow jolts him a half step forward, but he doesn't cry out. He hardly even flinches.

"One lash only," Raku says when Tur'Roth lifts the weapon a second time. Tur'Roth hesitates. *There's something here, beneath the surface. Something between them. None of it good.* "Krisxox, as Svera's champion, you will defend her honor now by fighting Tur'Roth and two warriors that Va'Raku nominates."

"Bre'Okkari and Naimi'Okkari," Okkari answers immediately and two warriors step into the arena across from Krisxox. They are joined by Tur'Roth and at the Raku's word, they select their weapons and tear into one another. I don't miss the fact that for his weapon, Krisxox selected the same one as Tur'Roth.

"Blooded warriors will be removed from the tribunal floor. Should Krisxox allow himself to be blooded before all three warriors have been removed from battle, then Svera's punishment will be fifteen solars in exile in Qath's outer lands."

Miari shoots Raku a death glare at that, one so aggressive he must feel it because he places his hand on Miari's shoulder. It might be an attempt to reassure her, but I know for a fact that if Krisxox loses this battle, it's Raku who will pay the price.

"Accepted," Krisxox says, followed by Tur'Roth and the other two warriors invited into the arena.

Krisxox lowers into a crouch, single axe dismantled to reveal smaller twin axes that he takes in each hand. He pivots slightly to the side while the other three warriors ready themselves. They all hover there on the cusp of action, waiting for something...

And then a restrained, muted word, spoken in a voice too gentle and light for this harsh, cold world says, "Accepted." Svera's single word falls harder than the stroke of any blade and it falls with impact. Without delay, the solar's first battle starts.

Impulsive and flat out nuts as he is, I'm surprised that Krisxox doesn't attack first. He hovers back, watching the three males circle him wielding axe, flail and sword — no holo weapons are allowed here, and no shields.

He skirts the first onslaught of the flail, spinning smoothly out of the way like a dancer would. Bre'Okkari darts forward, engaging with his sword while Tur'Roth moves around to Krisxox's bared and bloodied back. He raises his axe and for a moment I wonder if the battle won't be over this quickly.

And then chaos explodes over the battleground.

Krisxox explodes, erupting like a storm. He bats away Bre'Okkari's sword, hitting it so hard the sword flies from Bre'Okkari's fingers. Spinning the rest of the way around, he ducks out of Tur'Roth's path so that Tur'Roth's axe meets only air and the motion throws Tur'Roth wildly off balance.

Krisxox sidles up next to Tur'Roth and with one quick jerk, releases his elbow into Tur'Roth's face. When Tur'Roth canters back, Krisxox slashes downward with one axe. He would have removed Tur'Roth from the battle there — possibly removing his arm at the wrist as well — if Naimi'Okkari hadn't then intervened.

Krisxox grunts as he turns on the xub'Okkari, forcing them back and then back further and it occurs to me as Krisxox releases such gently caged fury that even though they are three on one, they don't stand a chance against him. None at all.

The battle is bleak and brutal. Watching Krisxox fight is unlike anything I've ever seen and for a moment, I forget where I am and succumb to my emotions — deep, deep envy. I thought Kinan was the most impressive fighter I'd come across — and to be honest, he might still be — but there's something almost poetic about the way Krisxox moves. He's not the largest male — though he's among them — but he moves like a specter, vanishing and reappearing again like the ghosts my mother is sure haunt the abandoned wreckage of the Antikythera satellite that the colony's first humans landed in.

Bre'Okkari steps left, but Krisxox was only feinting. I feel my front teeth clench together as I will Bre'Okkari to move left and out of the way, but he falls into the trap Krisxox set for him and when he dives forward, Krisxox pulls back and sends Bre'Okkari sprawling. He spins and kicks an advancing Tur'Roth in the chest, driving him back in the time it takes for him to return to Bre'Okkari, kick away his sword and draw a thin line of blood from the side of his neck — one of the only places the okami armor does not cover.

As Bre'Okkari is removed from the plain of battle, the flail spears the air to the left of Krisxox's head. He sweeps his axe up, flinging the flail out of his path as he charges forward, advancing brutally, but Tur'Roth meets him in the center of the arena first. Axe-on-axe, the duel is short and savage.

Krisxox's fighting style changes dramatically — no longer smoke, he's stone now, and uses raw strength to beat Tur'Roth to the ground. He falls and I feel myself wince. It's hard to watch, but I can't look away from the scene. Back shining slick with his own blood, Krisxox's muscles bunch and flex as he brings one small axe down onto Tur'Roth's weapon again and again.

Tur'Roth's arms shake as he falls first to one knee, then collapses onto his hip. His axe handle splinters and when Krisxox brings both of his own axes together around the handle, he splits it.

Krisxox kicks Tur'Roth onto his stomach and, pinning one shoulder underfoot, draws his axe blade from Tur'Roth's right shoulder to his left hip. The implication makes me cringe. *Resentful, bloodthirsty bastard.* It makes me suddenly nervous for a whole different set of reasons. He might be the most capable person of keeping Svera safe, but he's also a fucking lunatic. *As her protector, he needs to be replaced.*

With Tur'Roth off of the field, it still takes some time before the outcome of the battle is sure. Naimi'Okkari is a master of the flail and it is a tricky weapon to defend against. Krisxox may be belligerent and confident but he is not overconfident. He waits, drawing Naimi'Okkari around the arena until he makes his first mistake.

Not as surefooted in this new environment, Naimi'Okkari takes one step too quickly and slips, just a half foot, but it's enough for Krisxox to take advantage of. Spinning onto one knee, he ducks under the advancing flail and cuts a line across Naimi'Okkari's thigh before rising up to stand in one fluid movement.

And just like that, Svera's trial is ended.

Silence settles over the arena, broken up only when Krisxox tosses his axes down onto the packed white earth, leaving them there for another warrior to pick up and return to Garon. Despite an impressive victory, Krisxox doesn't look happy about it. He throws a pelt around his shoulders as he resumes his place to Svera's right, only this time, there's a bigger space between them than there had been before. Her arms are crossed over her chest, her stare fixed straight ahead and her face, the same brilliant red.

I might have found it funny — might have even laughed — if my blood hadn't started to push harder through my veins and sweat started to build between my shoulder blades and under my breasts. I lick my lips, tasting the cold on them despite their heat, and feel the craziest kinetic energy rattle through me as I stare at the droplets of copper blood on the arena floor, reminding me of what my reddish-brown blood had looked like staining the sands of our colony three rotations before. Sand whipped through the air then in place of snow and yet, I can't help feeling the same thing I felt then — not at the end of the day when I was ruined, but at its start.

Mama was so optimistic that the male who hunted me would be like the one who claimed her — even Jaxal had been begrudgingly hopeful — and for just a second as I knelt naked on the sands and watched the alien ship touch down onto our planet, I thought that nothing could hurt me. That I'd be forever invincible. *It's because I am. I'm still here, with none of the scars he gave me, and he's in chains.*

"The trial for advisor Svera is complete. Svera is absolved of her *crimes*," Miari sneers the word in a way that casts major shade Raku's way even though he doesn't let it rile him.

Instead, he steps forward slightly, into the circle. "We will now begin the second trial. Va'Rakukanna, step forward and name your champion."

The nape of my neck is slick beneath the intricately woven braids I wear, but my palms are totally dry. I flex my fingers, feeling the perfectly tailored hide stretch and flex around my joints. *Breathe.* I take a step into the arena, the pressure of many, many eyes on my body tracking each and every movement I make, none so aggressive or so distracting as the one behind me. Kinan's. Breathing becomes easier when I realize that I can still taste the oasis with every breath I take.

I inhale and when I speak, my voice is even, sure. "I nominate no champion."

There is a rumbling throughout the crowd as my edict is passed on to those who stand too far away to hear it, but Raku speaks over them. "As one who nominates no champion, you have the opportunity to choose your opponent. Your opponent may be selected of any warrior present here who has not yet been blooded."

I hesitate just a tenth of a breath before making my will known, "For my opponent I choose Peixal, the fallen Bo'Raku."

The murmuring grows louder, threatening my composure. *What am I doing? Am I going to get myself killed? Is it pride that will kill me? Hate? Both?* No. *Breathe. Remember…*

I picture familiar faces in my mind, all of them alien — Tre'Hurr, Hurr, Va'El, Ka'Okkari, Kuana and her new mate, the other humans, my mom — and I recall their strength and their love, but I don't look for them now. I let the murmurs fall away. I let Jaxal's very audible *fuck* glide right off of me. I turn and face — not the male I'm about to fight, but the one who's given me the confidence to fight.

His gaze is on me and I feel a nervous rush all the way to my toes. Behind me, I hear Bo'Raku — *Peixal's* — impish cackle, "Accepted." But all I see in front of me is Kinan, utterly impassive, but for a small twitch in his neck.

He tilts his head forward and comes to me. "You will need a weapon," he says.

I nod, mouth dry, feeling suddenly shaky. "I will go now to Garon."

"Hexa. Follow me."

As cold crunches under my feet, I can't help but feel the need to explain myself to the male I love most. "I hope you know that I don't mean to shame you. I know that the tsanui is your sacred rite and that you had every intention of acting as my champion, I just…"

"I was wrong." We reach Garon who nods at me stoically and makes the warrior's greeting. So distracted by such a sign of respect from him, it takes me a moment to realize he isn't opening the werro chest. Instead, he produces a long swatch of black cloth and hands it to Kinan.

Kinan unwraps one end and very carefully slides the sheathe off of the weapon, which he places in my hands. "I recognized the error of my thinking many solars ago. It was as I watched you fighting Ka'Okkari. It was your first time wielding an axe. It was much too large for you, but you were clever, skillfully finding ways to inflict damage without having to support the bulk of its weight, or even letting that weight work in your favor. It occurred to me then that I was a fool to dare dishonor you by taking your place in this trial. This trial is not mine, just as the right to tsanui against Bo'Raku is not mine. Both are your own."

I shake my head, staring down at the weapon now in my hands. Trying to make sense of this. "I remember that day and I remember that fight. But that was also a fight I lost."

Kinan's mouth quirks. His hands fold around my own and I can feel the cold of the helos through my gloves contrasted against the fire of his fingers as they hold mine so steadily, so sure. "Hexa. You have lost many fights and you will lose many more. But you will not lose this one."

Air fills me so fully, my toes hardly touch the ground. "You believe that," I say, voice in awe, half disbelieving. *His words cannot be real when I only half believe them myself.* But they are and suddenly that half that did not believe I would ever do this or could ever do this, is gone, wiped away cleanly.

"I would not allow this battle to proceed if I did not."

I exhale, fists firming around the staff. He reaches forward and grips my neck as mates sometimes do — one of the only Voraxian signs of affection shown in public. "This staff is the same size and weight as your other helos staff, so it will require no adjustments on your part, but for the one." He tilts the right end of the staff up and I blink, shocked, as I study the weapon carefully for the first time.

I grin. "Is it...it can't be..."

"Hexa. I supplied the Rakukanna with ideas and she came forward with designs of her own. Together, we made this for you."

"It's a grabar," I balk, "The same thing I used to fight the khrui, except it's made of helos."

"With the same cutting ends as your practice staff, in addition to the sharpened point of the grabar you already know."

"Did you make this specifically for me?"

"Hexa. Specifically for this purpose. For this trial."

"But when? How did you know I'd choose to fight myself and wouldn't ask you to be my champion?"

"This weapon I commissioned the day you fought Ka'Okkari with that axe. And I have always known." He leans in close and kisses my ear, then speaks directly against my cheek. "Now I want you to take this weapon and I want you to gut him with it." His lips leave fire every place they brush against me.

When Kinan pulls back, I search the expanse of his gaze while soft flakes flutter between us. There is nothing in the universe left but the two of us as he gives me this gift and issues both a permission and a warning. With his command, I understand clearly what's about to happen. This won't be a fight to first blood. This is a fight to last blood.

My fingers find the grips of my helos grabar and whirl it upright. Its weight is perfectly distributed, and perfect for me. "Hexa, my Okkari."

"Show him no quarter. Give him no ground. Do not forget that I am the reason the Bo'Raku before him was exiled. This was his sire. Between his lust for you and his hatred of me, he will show you no mercy."

"Hexa, my Okkari."

"He will attempt to humiliate you. Control your anger, bottle your pride, find his weakness, and when he laughs, remember the truth. That he is nothing."

"Hexa, Kinan."

He meets my gaze. "I will be watching."

"I'll make you proud."

"You do every day," he says, "Now bring me his plates. All of them."

We walk together into the arena, but only Kinan walks out of it. I remain planted near Miari and Svera, the other humans behind them, Kinan just a little further. Jaxal stands near him and is watching me now with a fiery look. His chin thrusts down and his jaw clenches. It's in his reaction alone that I know Bo'Raku has entered the arena with me. *Breathe.*

I turn forward to see Bo'Raku select what they call a throwing hammer from the chest of weapons provided to him. It's an effective weapon if you know how to wield it well, and even more effective when your opponent has no shield to defend against it. It looks like a chain, about half a foot around, and ends in a giant bolt the size of three fists. It's not anywhere near as effective for a battle like this where only a blooding is required, which just confirms what Kinan has told me. *Bo'Raku has nothing to lose. He isn't going to just cut me with that thing. He's going to try to bludgeon me to death with it.*

The arena clears so that it's just us. The red face I thought I'd memorized looks so much different. So... *normal.* He grins at me and his ridges flash a homicidal purple and black. The same colors that they were during the Hunt. I should be more afraid by them, but I'm not. *That was another male, another me, another history. This one I write myself.*

"The tribunal is until first blood. Should Peixal succeed, the Va'Rakukanna will be required to spend fifteen solars in Qath's endless ocean before resuming her post here as Xhea. The outcome of this trial, while it has no bearing on the tsanui or on Peixal's trial, may determine whether Peixal is shown leniency during his tsanui. My Rakukanna and I expect an honorable trial."

"Honorable..." I can see his lips mouth the word from where I stand, as if it's a joke. I can understand why he'd think that. Nothing honorable is going to take place here, on my part or his.

"Accepted," I say.

"Accepted," Bo'Raku echoes and I'm chilled once again by the sound of his voice. Though he may look different and I may feel different, that voice is just the same as the laughter that chimes in my thoughts.

He takes a step. I suck in a breath and hold it in my lungs. *Comets. Fuck! It's starting. It's really happening. I'm really here.* With the cold falling around me and skating beneath my feet, I take sure steps across it until I'm close enough to reach him with one end of my grabar. The pointy end. That also means that he's more than close enough to reach me.

He lifts his hammer and I'm prepared for the first swing, but not the second. It comes too quickly. I didn't anticipate he'd be able to recover from its momentum that fast, but he did and I'm left scrambling. I dart right, flipping onto my shoulder and rolling out of the path of the chain. It grazes the outside of my okami but not hard enough to penetrate it.

He howls, "You thought this was a game, human?" His laughter echoes through my bones and it *hurts*. It hurts more than it should.

I hold my staff with both hands, backing away from him as he comes towards me, chest exposed, taunting me, *humiliating me,* showing me just what I'm worth —

nothing. No. I wait for him to attack, needing more time to assess his fighting style, his speed, agility and strength.

He swings his hammer low, trying to disrupt my center of gravity, but I use the blunt*er* end of my grabar to propel his chain up and over my head. I don't try to stop it's advance. That would be the fastest way for him to take my weapon away from me and I'm not that stupid or arrogant. *Though I used to be. Back when he knew me. But he doesn't know who I am anymore. He doesn't know that when I leave this battlefield today, it will be with every plate covering his ugly red body.*

His grin doesn't fade as he attacks a few more times, trying to probe my own defenses and find his way in. I know what he wants. I can see it in his eyes. He doesn't want to beat me as he would any other opponent. He wants to make me bleed just like he did the first time. *He wants Kinan to watch.*

His hammer swings and misses when I deflect the stroke and the moment it sails over my head, coming close enough to graze the braids that are cornrowed so neatly by Kuana against my scalp, I charge. As silent and small as I am, he seems staggered for a moment with what to do with me. It leaves his chest exposed and I whip my spear up with my left hand, striking my mark and tearing a hole in his hide covering and exposing his plates. I shave the first layer off of them and as I whirl past him, I strike again, this time performing the same act against the plate high on his right thigh, only this time, it's with the grabar end.

While the plate prevents me from drawing blood from his flesh, a huge chunk of the thing comes off cleanly, like slicing into a red fruit with a deadly sharp knife. We only ever had one knife sharp enough to slice a red fruit on the colony and growing up, I cut myself on it a hundred times. His plate lands on the ground with a thunk, heavy like a massive, overgrown toenail.

That's when I hear it. The soft clapping of human hands. I know they are human because Voraxians don't clap. A voice chants my name, I'm not sure whose and I don't dare look.

"Fuck him up, Kiki!" Jaxal's that time, there's no mistaking it.

Peixal grins at me, like he's won some prize off me. "Kiki," he sneers.

"Hexa, I am Kiki." I grin at him and level my grabar, distributing its weight evenly between my hands. I am sure. I am me. *"Peixal,"* I sneer.

His smile wavers and I know I've struck something within him. Something deep. And that's when I remember every word and piece of advice Kinan ever gave me. He was giving me the answer all along. The hate I've carried was one Bo'Raku gave me, but that hate was never mine. *It was his.* And now I must return it. In kind.

"How does it feel, Peixal? Knowing that you're about to be killed by a human you once raped?"

He winces at the word, as all Voraxians do. It is dishonorable to rape in their culture. A dishonor he never saw, because he never viewed humans as equals. "This is a fight to first blood. And you are Va'Raku's mate. You're too xoking honorable for that."

"If that's what you think, your brain's as small as your cock is."

I run at him and he pivots to the side, letting me pass as I expected he would. He comes at me, trying to tag me in the back, but I swivel, skating over the ice like Ka'Okkari taught me to. I drop to one knee as I switch back around and when I do, I tear open his other pant leg and this time, when I sweep the grabar up, I take plate *and skin* with it.

A thin line of copper, sweet-smelling blood pours freely down his leg and the roaring chant of my name breaks through my concentration. I smile and stand, watching the surprise and horror that crosses his ridges in shades of white and red and pink.

I say, "Or maybe I *should* just let you live out your days in the tundra, where only the hevarr beasts of Nobu will know you were once Bo'Raku. Meanwhile, the rest of Voraxia will call you only by your true name. *Peixal*," I shout the word like a curse and feel it linger like a stain.

He growls through his teeth, the air wheezing in and out of him, and when he looks at me, he is the beast that I know him as. *But I've fought beasts before.* He roars out a battle cry and attacks with a violence that catches me off guard. I narrowly avoid collision with one of the bodies forming the perimeter of the pit — I don't know whose — before I manage to skip back into the clearing.

Raku is shouting for an intervention, but Kinan's voice rides over his. "Nox! Let her finish this."

I dodge and dodge again, bending backwards, ducking low, jumping when he goes for my legs. As he advances, I have no choice but to defend with everything I have. He outmuscles me by tons and he's not a *total* moron. He's not trying to hit me with the hammer, he's trying to use it to distract me. It's working. Because I don't realize how close his body has gotten to mine until he releases the chain end with one hand and lets his fist fly forward.

He hits me in the face and the pain is splintering. Blood fills my mouth, but I somehow manage to remain coherent enough to jump back. I don't jump far enough. He kicks and his foot meets my stomach which punches up into my lungs as I fly. I hit the ground hard, left wrist searing in agony as I land. My body travels, skating over the cold. I feel feet jump out of my way and know I've broken through the first ring of attendees and when I finally manage to blink my eyes open, I'm sure of it.

Somehow, the first face I see when I open my eyes is Reema's. It's the only face I see too. Suspended against so much white like an inverted teardrop, her face is full of emotion, a riotous display. Even her eyes are wide and huge. She's sniffling, body curled slightly into the one beside hers. I know this is her mother because her father is the Garon, and one day she wants to grow up to be just like him, but a female has never been weapons keeper before on Nobu and she's afraid. I know this. I know this like a truth branded onto my soul.

I shove my legs beneath me and as I stand, I flash her a smile. I can feel blood seep between my teeth and when she shrinks back even further, I offer her all I can in that moment. A shrug and a wink. *Fear is what hurts us. Blood is nothing.*

She gasps and that's all the warning I need. I can *feel* his energy behind me, burning into my spine. I spin to meet it with energy of my own. It's a manic energy — just as hard, just as crazed, but somehow in that madness, controlled. I know that he can't hurt me. Even if he cuts me down with his hammer, I might die, but he'll *never* recover from this.

He tries to grab me with one hand, but I move faster than he does and bring the blade of my grabar against his arm, severing muscle and the tendons beneath. He's bleeding profusely now and roars. He advances, swinging his chain this way and that. He manages to wrap it around my grabar and with one pull, I know he can take it from me. So I let him.

"Peixal," I shout when he turns to face me, a smile on his lips. *He thinks this is the end and that he's won.*

I wear a smile of my own and it must unsettle him because he hesitates when he could have killed me in one stroke. "Kiki…"

"Yes!" I roar, "That is my name and I own it. Kiki!" I scream to the wind, letting it ravage my voice. "But who are you? You are *Peixal*," I laugh. "My mate exiled your father and now I'll do the same to you. A disgraced family, dishonorable and shamed! Or would you rather die, Peixal? I'll cut you down and throw you into the water." I laugh and I laugh deep and from the belly. "Not even the hevarr will know your name!"

He comes at me and when he raises his weapon, I do something that should scare the piss out of me — I duck under the curtain of his arms and come up against his chest and deliver two swift punches to the places where I know plates don't cover him. *Wrestling with Kinan in the cold was hard. This is effortless.* He buckles, weapon drooping and I use that momentary lag to dive past him, rolling again and retrieving my grabar.

He's close behind. Too close for me to rise. Too close for me to avoid the path of his hammer this time. It impales my left shoulder, the okami providing cover, but not enough to stop the hammer from meeting skin, tearing through that, and then flesh, tearing through that too, before finally landing at bone.

I don't scream. I don't make a single noise. I take the pain as I lay there on the ground, face down, listening to Peixal come up behind me, laughter on his tongue. "You thought you were clever." *Breathe.* "You thought you mattered." *Wait.* "You are nothing but Va'Raku's whore." *Calm.* "You'll be mine again too before this is over." I can feel his heat against my back. I can hear Miari screaming, Svera now too. More voices join the chorus. Kinan's is not among them.

The thud of footsteps is loud now, right on me, but I wait for them to get even closer. So close that I can feel his heat, or at least, imagine it. Too close. Close enough that I should be afraid. But I'm not. Close enough that when I flip myself over, plant the butt end of my staff and lift the blade end and the big red bastard takes a step forward, he impales himself.

At first, only a little. But it's still enough to startle him. He looks down at the dagger-end of my weapon, watches it disappear beneath his hide covering, watches blood radiate out from around it, soaking through hide and fur.

I grab the helos staff by the rough leather holds and push. A punctuated grunt comes out of me, the first sound I've made since this battle began that wasn't an insult. Pain tickles my consciousness, but I ignore it. At least, for now. I shove harder, using my abdomen to lift my torso as I press my blade further into him.

He swipes at me and I can't move. Now that he's slumped forward, I'm carrying most of his weight and it's a *lot* of weight. Sharp, serrated claws find purchase in the okami covering my chest. They tear it open, scoring lines of heat across my sternum. But I don't give in. I don't give up. I want to finish this.

I lift a little more, pushing my grabar into his belly until I'm up to the first handhold. I glance around his body and can see bloodied helos pointing up towards the hidden suns. He moans horribly and paws at me with his claws, but his motions are slow, weak, defeated. He's slumped almost all the way forward and when he opens his mouth to issue another cry, copper droplets spill from his mouth onto my cheeks, like rain that tastes like metal and redemption.

I push even harder, until I can feel his hot blood seeping into my gloves, until we're eye-to-eye, face-to-face, cheek-to-cheek. He smells like sweat and metal, like sand and violence, history erased.

My lips move close enough to his skin to taste and I feel no fear as I whisper, "You are Peixal, the worthless. And that is all you will ever be known as to me. And you can be sure that I will be the last soul alive who remembers you. I will never speak of you to anyone and when I die, you will be forgotten. It will be like you never even lived."

His eyes blaze and his ridges shine, just once, and only fleetingly. They are a color I've never seen before, one that cannot be described in nature, but that is something like grey, only more profound. A color that speaks to unblemished agony.

And then the tension flees his body all at once and his torso releases. The pressure is surreal and I only barely manage to roll my spear to the left to avoid being crushed underneath his weight. He hits the ground with a thump, white flakes puffing up around him like dust, and for a moment, I just drink in the sight of his face. His eyes are wide open, lips slightly parted. He does not look at peace. He looks to have died how he lived — monstrously.

I place my hand against his face and use it to push myself onto my feet. Standing, I sway as I turn a full circle. The humans have gone berserk and most of the xleranx now are actively holding them back. My name is being shouted loud enough for the cosmos to hear. "Ki-ki! Ki-ki! Ki-ki!" Even the Voraxians, for all their honor and weirdness around names, have joined in.

But I don't care what they call me. They can call me human for all I care. My gaze switches across so many faces in so many colors, losing focus. I see my mom covering her face with her hands in horror and wonder if she watched any of the fight at all. Miari holds her wrist and tries to tug it down while Svera, on her other side, is jumping up and down, earlier battle forgotten.

I stagger, using my grabar to keep me upright when a sharp voice draws my attention left. "Xhea."

Kinan stands there and I notice something odd — four of his warriors, including Ka'Okkari have their hands on him. They hold his arms and legs and his body by the buckles of his okami. As if they are holding him back from something, restraining him from charging forward and making me wonder if that's what his intention had been.

He wears all his colors in his face, though this time, color even rolls down his neck, like some sort of strange party is being hosted underneath his skin. It makes me smile, and when I do, I feel hot, sticky blood dribble down my chin. But he still doesn't come to me. His body is flinching wildly, but he forcibly shrugs off those holding him and crosses his arms.

"You are not finished," he barks. "I demanded his plates and you are empty handed."

Nodding robotically, I return to Peixal's body, that red smear of a corpse, and one-by-one, I remove all thirty-two of his plates. I don't know how long it takes me. Moments. Half a solar. All I know is that the sky is at its brightest as I rise, gather all of Peixal's bloodied bits to my chest and drop them at Kinan's feet, where I too collapse.

Kinan dives at me. It comes as an attack, his lips on my lips. He kisses me feverishly despite the blood and in public view of everyone. His body rolls against mine and if I had more blood in my body and more space in my head to think, I might have done more than just lie there, waiting for whatever will happen next to happen.

He grabs my arm and I gasp, pain spearing me and waking me from the spell he has me under. "Xok," he curses — the first time I've ever heard a curse from him. "You did well, Kiki. You just rid this cosmos of a bad male. No one will ever suffer at his hands again." He grabs the tattered front of my suit and pulls me into a sitting position. "I will prepare a merillian bath for you."

"Nox." I shake my head and grab his wrists, smiling giddily as my face and shoulder begin to throb. "I think three times a virgin is enough."

Kinan smiles and I laugh. I laugh and he laughs and soon, Jaxal is at his shoulder and so is Miari and so is Svera and Tre'Hurr and Ka'Okkari and my mom. Even Krisxox makes an appearance as Kinan pulls me onto my feet.

"Not bad," Krisxox says, what sounds like begrudgingly, "for a human."

I lift my middle finger in his direction and I don't miss the way the corner of his mouth twitches, releasing a smile I'm guessing he wished he hadn't. "Alright," I say, panting now as I try to take my own weight and failing at it. "Let's go home."

I start to turn, but Raku's voice projects over the messy throngs. The outline of the arena is no longer visible. There are just beings and bodies and white and copper. "We are not finished yet with the trials. We still await the outcome of the trial of Lisbel, the former hasheba to the Va'Rakukanna."

I burst out laughing. "Fuck. I forgot about Kuaku."

"You do not need to remain for this. We should seek medical attention."

"Medical attention should come here. I'm not going anywhere," I pant.

Kinan curses again — *that's twice now* — and issues a few orders before taking a seat and settling me on his lap. Soon, I have a female I've never met before, but have heard lots about from Svera at my shoulder, holding up some kind of ray gun to the wound on my arm.

"I'm Lemoria," she says.

"I know," I answer. "I'm Kiki, Va'Rakukanna of the Voraxian Federation and the Xhea of Nobu."

She smiles. "I most certainly know, and will not ever forget."

Kinan's face is radiant light, having settled on a brilliant orange, where it's chosen to stay.

Meanwhile, a misshapen circle has reformed and Peixal's body has been dragged away somewhere where it will be buried in an unmarked grave and appropriately forgotten. The sight of his blood on the arena floor, and his dismembered plates laid out before me, coupled with the taste in my mouth makes me feel less like a human and more like a barbarian. But Kinan's forehead still shines and his arms continue to cradle me. *Proud. And that's what I feel now. Limitless, like the Xanaxana's unforgiving energy, coursing through my body. Pain is nothing to that.*

I struggle to focus as Lemoria calls over another Voraxian, someone called Ki'Lemoria, who rushes around and follows her commands, stitching and patching and spraying and raying. They have me seated on a chair now, Kinan's arms fixed around my frame.

"Why were there xub'Okkari holding you?" I ask as Kuaku shuffles into the arena, head bowed.

Kinan nuzzles my neck. Places his hand to my stomach. Pulls me up against his thighs. "It was all I could do not to storm into the tribunal after you. I know what I said, but my body fought me at every turn. Watching you was the most glorious torture."

I kiss him deeply, the taste of the oasis overwhelming me and blotting out the taste of my own blood — until I hear a cry. Alone now in the center of the arena, Kuaku stands with her hands pressed over her mouth, horror scrawled in violent colors in the ridges above her eyes.

Raku's booming voice carries as he says, "If none will step forward to act as Lisbel's champion, then she will be forced to take up a weapon herself. If there is one here who will accept to champion for her, then they must step forward now."

The pitch is silent. Lisbel is shaking. Our eyes meet briefly and I know that if I weren't so badly injured, I'd have accepted to champion for her. She doesn't deserve exile. She doesn't deserve a hevarr. Not even a bitch like her. Or even a bitch like me.

I open my mouth to say something — anything — to delay Raku's next words, when all of a sudden, a throaty groan rises up on my left. I glance past Lemoria's body to see Jaxal on one knee, both fists planted into the ground. He's shaking his head, eyes clenched tightly together, shoulders heaving.

"Fuck the sun," he damn near moans, and when he looks up — straight at Lisbel — he shouts, "I'll champion for her."

Lisbel is staring at him, eyes huge, forehead white. And then the other colors come. "Are you..." she starts, but for once it looks like she's at a loss for words.

Jaxal rises and though it looks like it pains him to say it, he grunts, "Yeah. I'm your Ziv-whatever. Your mate. You're not fighting today, and you're not going into exile."

I'm the first to react, and I do so with a laugh. It belts out of me carelessly, euphorically. *Whatever drugs Lemoria is feeding me in those ray guns...keep 'em coming.* "Comets and stardust," I say, "What a xoking time to be alive."

20
Kinan

I watch from the mouth of the training cavern as Kiki attempts to show Svera a few basic moves in hand-to-hand combat — moves any being, male or female, human or Voraxian, should be able to master in their own self-defense.

Even without being able to hear each word she utters, it is clear she is frustrated by Svera's lack of progress. It is not even that Svera is so uncoordinated — on the contrary, the female is one of the most graceful and elegant I have come across of any species — it is that simply, she does not want to fight anyone.

"Svera, plant your right foot and lift your right hand. The left one stays down. When I try to hit your face, you can bring your left hand up to block me. Okay?" Kiki's voice is not the loudest in the hall, but it is certainly the most aggravated.

It has been six solars since the other humans, including the Raku and Rakukanna, left to return to their colony — Lisbel among them. Jaxal, unfamiliar with his weapon and the terrain, was unable to best the xub'Okkari I pitted him against. However, instead of exile to the endless ice ocean, Lisbel was exiled to the human colony. A rather ingenious idea. One of Svera's.

"Like this?" The human female says.

"Hexa — I mean, yes, but you actually have to mean it." Kiki advances on her friend, lifting both arms as if she will punch Svera in the face.

Svera closes her eyes even as she brings her left forearm up, successfully blocking but only because there is no effort behind Kiki's thrust. Kiki rolls her eyes and stomps one of her feet. "This is so frustrating."

"Tell me about it." Krisxox does not often speak to the humans, but I have found that he makes an exception for Kiki. "She's like a holoscreen. There's nothing there to fight against."

He keeps his arms crossed and moves away from the pair towards the other fighters. He joins them at their request. It is not often they have occasion to be trained, or train against, Krisxox, who is known to accept only Voraxia's most honored fighters at his base in Qath.

Svera shouts at his back, "You know, you are very rude!"

Krisxox snorts, but does not rise to her attack. I chuckle to myself as I start forward. Kiki is still moving Svera's hands and feet into position, thus it is Svera who sees me first. Quickly straightening before dropping into a bow, her headscarf ripples in the wind as she ducks her head lower than she needs to.

"Okkari, it is lovely to see you on this solar," she says in high Voraxian.

"As it is every solar, to see you, advisor Svera. Particularly on the eve of such good news."

Svera beams and bows again. Her pride shows. "What good news?" Kiki asks.

"It seems that your friend Svera is responsible for the discovery of more humans."

"*More* humans? What are you talking about?"

Svera nods. "Yes. It looks like the Antikythera satellite was launched along with *two* other satellites. One of them appears to have been destined for a planet in an uncharted quadrant called Sasor, while the other one was meant to be orbiting a planet in quadrant five. Sasor will be too far to venture to, but the location specified in quadrant five is more than reachable. We're coming up with plans now to go after them."

"Why bother?" Comes Krisxox's murmured retort as he returns momentarily to retrieve a different weapon, this one a throwing net. "They're as good as dead."

"Krisxox," I snap.

He removes the net from the wall and turns to face us. "It's true. If they're in quadrant five it's likely that someone else will have picked them up by now. Rhorkanterannu of Kor is probably having a field day. And as for the ones on Sasor? They're as good as dead. Sasor is ruled by snakes who don't have any access to technology. They're animals there, barbarians."

"Ignore him," Kiki says before I can deliver a harsher reprimand.

Svera's face fires with color and so softly I do not know that she meant to speak the words aloud, she whispers, "I always do."

Kiki laughs at that while Svera reddens further. Krisxox frowns.

"Krisxox," I say in warning.

He meets my gaze and holds it before showing me his back and storming off. The insolent creature. I would ordinarily challenge him for less, but on this solar, my Xiveri mate takes precedence.

She says, "How'd you figure this out anyways?"

"It only took a thorough review of the archives the Antikythera Council keeps under lock and key. Because of my new…status, I've been given access."

"Good work."

"Excellent work," I concur.

"Thank you Xhea. Okkari." She burns a subtle pink that startles me, as it does each time. This is an anger color, but on humans it appears to be *either* an anger color, one of pride, shame, embarrassment, rage, bloodlust, guilt… the list goes on. I am grateful only that Kiki does not have such a distressing display that is so difficult to interpret.

The frustration on Kiki's face from her earlier fight — evidenced in her tightened lips, wrinkled forehead, and pinched chin — falls as she exhales. "What a time to be alive…" she says, repeating the words she said once before at the conclusion of her battle against Peixal. A memory I will never forget.

The way she moved, sharp and true, she was so self-possessed. And when she lured Peixal into lowering his guard and advancing on her while she was down…it had taken every inch of willpower not to end the battle then myself.

I'm glad I did not. When she rose, covered in her own blood, I had never seen anything more glorious. Or more deserving of glory. *Not often do we have a chance to slay our own demons.*

"So what are you doing here?" Kiki says to me. Her forward question and her lack of decorum are deserving of punishment.

277

Thoughts of her battered and battle-hardened body and Peixal's corpse forgotten, I feel my teeth clench and my groin tighten. Instead of rushing her back to our home and into our nest, I manage to compose myself just enough to press a single, punishing kiss to her mouth. My colors blaze and I do not care who sees them. To taste her will be enough, for now.

"You will tell me if I will require permission to come check on my Xiveri mate, or if I may do so at will, because you are mine." I grip the side of her neck, careful with her right arm. Though she refused merillian and Lemoria is the finest healer Voraxia has to offer, the wound is still less than twenty solars old, and still pains her from time to time.

And such a pain is all that is left of Peixal, the ruined.

I smile at the thought, and in response to her pleasure. "You don't require permission," she says mischievously, "but checking up on me in the middle of training may have consequences." She loops both arms around my neck and as I lean in to kiss her again, she kicks my feet into a stance too wide to assume comfortably and slips out from under my arm when I react to stablize myself.

"You are getting cocky, my queen," I growl, eager to fight now that she has presented challenge.

"Getting cocky?" She wags a single finger at me. "I've always been cocky."

"Your desire for punishment knows no bounds."

"Then come and punish me."

For a moment, I hallucinate the shape of her body melded to mine in the quiet light of the ioni of our nest. I take a step forward, and then I force myself to announce why I am here before I forget *again*. "This lunar, you will be punished. But for now, I have something else for you."

The fire in her eyes dims, but her smile still holds. She tilts her face to the side, full cheeks catching the light from the rock pits hanging high on the screa walls. "I'm ready for any task my Okkari needs fulfilling."

She pleases me to no end. I know that I am undeserving of her and, to use a human expression, I don't give a shit. "Xhivey." I cock my head to the mouth of the cave where Reema stands waiting. "Come forward."

"Reema," Kiki says, genuine pleasure in her tone, as the young female makes her way nervously forward. "Good to see you. What's going on?"

So human. So informal. Punishment this lunar will be slow. I clear my throat. "As you well know, Reema has come of age to select her position within the tribe."

Kiki nods. "I know. And I know you wanted to join your father. I'm sorry that Jacabo took the position of xub'Garon."

Reema looks to me quickly, as if seeking permission to speak. I nod, encouraging her. "Thank you for your wishes, my Xhea, but it's alright. I'm glad Jacabo will stay here with Zeina'Van. It's exciting to have humans around — I mean *more* humans."

Kiki smiles at that. "I'm glad he's staying too. Kuana..." She shakes her head, recalling Kuana's new title once more, "Zeina'Van and Jacabo are good people. They make an awesome pair. And besides, now that Jaxal took Lisbel back to the human colony, I think keeping another human here is only fair." She winks at Reema, who laughs lightly even though I can see that she attempts to be strong, to prepare herself.

"It is true," she says, "And I harbor him no ill will. My sire offered me the position, but I...I said no."

"You did? Why? It's not because you're afraid. You know that your gender doesn't stop you from doing or being anything you want to..."

"Nox. It is not this I..." Her ridges burn electric yellow. She looks down at her feet, but I say her name. She glances at me quickly, inhales, and then returns her gaze to my Xhea. Her Xhea. Xhea of our people. "I want to train as a warrior. I want...I want *you* to train me, if I may be so humble to ask and if you would consider honoring me in this way. I may not have trained with the other males growing up, but I can learn quickly. I...I spoke already with the Okkari, seeking his council before I approached you. I...am hopeful..." Her voice trails away, ridges brighter than ever.

Kiki meanwhile stares at her in an expression I know is one of profound shock. She does not speak. Reema glances to me and I hold up a hand, offering her assurance in the Voraxian way, before speaking to Kiki.

"Since it has become inappropriate for Kuana to tend to our nest as your hasheba now that she is mated, I have asked that Reema take up the position of Kuana with part of her time. The majority of her solar can be spent training with you, if you agree. Once she is proficient in her weapon and has undergone her first hunt, she may then take on her new title. She will become the first xub'Xhea."

Kiki's lips move with a will of their own. "The first xub'Xhea..."

"Hexa," I tell her. "And there will be many more, of this I am certain."

Still suspended on this rope, Reema begins to prattle. "I promise, I'll take care of all your needs as Kuana and I'll train even harder than the males. I want to be able to live up to you. I want to be like you. I want to fight, to hunt, to help my tribe, to feed it and and defend it if I ever need to. I'll…"

"Yes! Oh my stars, yes. Hexa, of course I'll train you. I'm sorry, I'm just…" Kiki waves her arms around, looking nothing like a Xhea at all until she catches my gaze. I shake my head just once, urging her calm, but the petulant female merely grins ravenously.

Throwing caution, and decorum, to the wind, she throws her arms around Reema's neck. "You are most welcome to train with me. I will teach you all that I know, and when that is not enough, I will learn more to teach you." She plants her kiss of affection in the center of Reema's forehead, startling the young female so much that she flares bright white and then blue.

When Kiki steps back, it is as a different woman. The depth of her joy so profound that I am made to feel as a mountain, so effortlessly moved. "We begin tomorrow, Kuana, though do not expect to hold that title for long. I fully intend to have you prepared to join on the hunt after next rotation's first thaw."

Joy radiates from Reema's gaze, and then from her ridges too before she is able to marshal them. "Hexa, my Xhea. I will be ready. It would bring me no greater pleasure than to wear an okami and fight just like you and alongside you."

Kiki nods and I see water well in her eyes, which she struggles not to clear with her hands. Instead, she blinks many times. She nods again. "Then for now, you are dismissed. Enjoy your last lunar of freedom. The coming lunars you will sleep well and you will sleep hard. It will not be easy and I will not go easy on you simply because I like you."

Reema bows. "Hexa, my Xhea. Stree'vay yah," she says, and then repeats very cautiously in human, "zay-enk yoo."

Kiki beams. "Thank *you*. You are dismissed."

Reema dashes off into the bright solar outside while Kiki holds both hands to her mouth and looks at me, Svera gushing at her side. "This is incredible! Can you not see the impact you're having? How incredible. I'll need to document this…"

"Can you see such an impact?" I echo.

Kiki shakes her head and covers her face fully with her hands. My warrior Xhea, for the first time, sheds happy tears. She laughs as she cries and as she cries, I fold her into my arms and hold her head to my chest.

"Shh," I tell her as she rocks, shoulder shaking with laughter as she finally releases that last and final burden of her grief. "You are here."

She nods and looks up at me, her chin resting on my chest. "I am here and the future is so bright."

I brush the backs of my fingers across her cheeks. Of the six, four form claws while two remain faithfully blunted. "Hexa. But it only shines because of your light. We only shine because of your light. And that is why I shine too."

"Then it will never be dark again."

"Nox," I say, allowing my ridges to unleash the full impact of the light that she brings out in me. I shake my head, kiss the tip of her nose. "It will not."

Thanks so much for joining Kiki and Kinan on Nobu! I hope you enjoyed their story! Reviews, even the one-liners, are very much appreciated on Amazon or Goodreads.

To get access to future books filled with hot, possessive alphas and the resilient, warrior women they worship _first_, not to mention freebies, exclusive previews and more, sign up to my mailing list at www.booksbyelizabeth.com/contact.

Until the next time,
Stay wild ¤°′`°¤,‚‚ø*

Elizabeth

Continue the journey and be…

Taken to Sasor

They came. They shifted. They conquered. Mian expected to be made a slave by the cocky shifter barbarian and, when a rival horde takes her, discarded. But what happens when he won't give her up?

Taken to Sasor: A SciFi Shifter Romance
Xiveri Mates Book 3 (Mian and Neheyuu)

Available in paperback anywhere online books are sold or on Amazon in ebook or hardback

1

Mian

My breath is hot against my fingers as I sit huddled, muscles straining, body clenched. My head is bowed over my knees. I try to block out the sounds of the other slaves panicking around me, but it slaps onto my skin like the sticky stain I spent all morning applying to the alehouse fence. Flimsy, weak little posts fixed together with braided reed stalks. It hadn't looked like much to begin with and the dark, oily stain hadn't helped. Now the fence is gone and all that's left of it is the black-brown ink still clinging to my arms and the fumes caught in my hair, smelling of chicory and fear.

A huge crash in the front room makes me wince. I'm dizzy with fear and hunger and thirst. *When was the last time I ate?* The fact that I can't remember does nothing but drive an agonized pang through my stomach. *Breathe. It won't matter soon. Maybe it will help. Maybe they won't want to eat skin and bones without the flesh.*

Cold seeps in through the packed dirt under my bottom. I inhale shallow breaths through my mouth, but I can still smell the other two dozen slaves' unwashed bodies beside me, even more powerful and cloying than the smell of the wood stain. More revolting. My fingers curl into the shirt sheathing me from neck to knees, the rough-spun fabric still scratchy despite having all but disintegrated. It clings to my shoulders with threads more than fabric and makes me wonder what they will take from us when they realize we have nothing to give.

Deep baritone laughter follows jests flung back and forth in a language I don't speak. The sounds, though distant *for now*, crash through my focus and behind me, one of the other slaves stifles a sob. I freeze, wondering if *they* heard it. From where I sit near the front of the group, that one little sob rings louder than the huge reed horns that trumpeted when they arrived at our gates. Gates that didn't even stand a full solar. They carved through those gates like knives through milk.

A mutinous thud slowly separates itself from the commotion in the front room. I jump, and then I jump again when it gets louder. *Footsteps? Or the panicked tattoo of my own heart?* I know what they do to the ones they find. Everyone knows the stories. *They eat humans. Flay us alive, then boil the flesh off our bones. They make great big soups out of us.*

"They're going to find us...they're going to find us!" The panicked voice at my back makes my heart clench in my throat. I glance over my shoulder and spot Sorsha over the tops of many crouched bodies trying to stand. Her brother Mika yanks her back down, but she's fighting him. Others are trying to shush them both now, and Sorsha's face is ghostly white, even in the dark. I try to swallow but my mouth is too dry and when my lips part, I inhale dust. I clap my hand over my lips, trying not to choke on it.

Mika's hand slips when Sorsha yanks again. She careens into one of the ceramic casks we stowed away in the hopes that if we did survive, one barrel of vinegar-preserved meat, a ceramic cask of bread flour, two satchels of dried fruit and three casks of water would be enough to keep us alive until we found another human settlement, or rebuilt this one. But now I see no chance of that.

As if in slow motion, Sorsha flails, hip bumping into the cask, hand flinging out to knock off the lid. It hits the packed earth with a dull clunk that rings like shattering glass.

My gaze connects with Mirabelle's, beside me. We were both sold in the last trade to this settlement. At our old settlement, we worked the grain mills together. She was really too old for that kind of work so I took on some of her chores. In exchange, she told me fantastic stories about satellites and ships and cities and great, big bodies of water from a planet once called *Earth*. Stories she says she inherited from her mother, and her mother's mother and her mother's mother's mother who actually lived on the satellite that brought us to this planet.

I don't know how much of what she says is real or not, but I always liked her. A kind woman, she doesn't deserve to die here. *Do any of us?* She reaches out and takes my hand, holding it so tight I can feel the bones through her thin skin like twigs aflame, right before they turn to dust. She smiles, her half-moon lids drooping over bright blue eyes. They frighten me, those eyes. They see everything.

Mika curses, "They heard us…"

"Can we escape?"

"Where would we go?"

"Does it matter?"

"*Is* there even a way out?"

"No, the only way out is through the alehouse."

Sweet silence settles over us. It tastes like death. My vision gets fuzzy. *Fear or hunger? Have I eaten in the last solar? The last two?* I can't remember and remind myself that it doesn't matter. *Skinny humans make for crappy stew.*

Footsteps have entered the distilling room. The weight of my own breath is heavy in my lungs. It's hard to breathe. They're going to find us and skin us and boil us. Even the kids. But maybe, just *maybe*, they won't eat any of us if the offering is poor enough, and there's no offering here more abysmal than my own...

I inhale. Exhale shakily. I squeeze Mirabelle's hand just once before letting it slip from mine. Cool air brushes against my damp rear as I rise to a crouch. My head spins. *Hunger or fear? Doesn't matter. Soon it'll all be over.*

"Mian, what are you doing?" Mirabelle rasps in a voice that's barely audible.

I don't have an answer for her as I step around the bodies in my path and reach the curtain, drawing just one little corner back. I don't look behind me as I step past it into the storage room, letting the only safety I had fall shut at my back.

Silence. No one tries to pull me back in. No one comes out to sacrifice themselves at my side. *Thud.* The quiet is punctuated by the boot. It has to be a boot because it's too heavy, too forceful, to be anything else. I've never seen one of the Sasor in real life, but I've heard stories of their size. People likening them to boulders and houses and hilltops.

The storeroom is ringed in ceramic casks. I take a seat between two grain tuns, press my forehead to the gritty, bowled ceramic surface in front of me and wait for the world to settle. Then I hold my breath as the storage room door is forced open with a short, contained crack. There's a precipitous hush at my spine, but the leaden gait of a Sasori barbarian ruins it. I clench. I focus. My head spins. I nearly pass out. *Fear or hunger?* He's right on me now.

The little hope I had, more delicate than a flower, slimmer than a knife's blade, recently whetted, is filched away from me when the heavy barrel in front of me is lifted and set to the side with surprising gentleness. Goosebumps break out over my arms as I look up into his face.

He blinks and when he does, his already dark irises darken further, becoming the shadowed side of a fray leaf, glittering mahogany, but sticky and thorned. I shudder as I quickly take in the rest of him.

He wears a leather cuirass over his right side only and has similar leather plating covering his legs, but beneath that, he is all corded muscle heaped onto an enormous frame. His skin is a lighter bronze than mine is, but his hair...his hair is shocking. It's *gold*. It drapes almost to his waist on the right side, while the left is cropped close to his scalp. Against the honey of his skin, it looks...it looks like he's a male fashioned by the sun in its own image. Pretty, even if nothing else about him is. He's far too brutal-looking for that.

He's got a scar that twists away from his cheekbone, disrupting his hairline to follow the serrated line of his ear. He doesn't have an earlobe. His jaw is hard. His eyes are mean.

Without warning, he bends down and slides a massive hand through my hair. A shocking surge of laughter rises in my chest that I do my best to choke down. He's a breath away from me now, completely bent over so that I can't see anything behind him. We're face-to-face, nearly nose-to-nose.

He smells like fresh cut grass and sweat. He smells like blood above all else. Human blood. *How many has he already eaten?* A very terrible part of me I haven't met before is pleased he smells like blood. After all, maybe that mean's he's full.

His hands comb across my scalp in a way that's nearly intimate, until the gesture changes, becoming feral as he yanks me to my feet by the hair. My boneless limbs wobble like a newborn's when he sets me down. Fear and hunger war with the adrenaline, which wins out. I plant my feet and inhale blood, wood, metal and leather and I don't exhale. Can't exhale. Not when I take in the size of the alien in front of me.

His shoulders span mine three times over and his chest is as deep as my shoulders are broad. He's three heads higher than I am, maybe more. All I know is that I have to crane my neck way back to hold his gaze. And I do hold his gaze. I hold his gaze like my life depends on it, watching as the color shifts again, darkening until it's so black I can see through it to the depths of the universe.

What a funny way to go. Shipped from settlement to settlement, never staying in one long enough to find friends or family or roots. About to be killed by an alien barbarian with the universe in his eyes because a woman was nice to me once and told me funny stories about the universe. I exhale, ready, and smile.

But when his face-sized palm charges towards me again, it isn't to reach out and snap my neck or sever my spine. The brute is reaching straight for...straight for my breast! Instincts kick in and I give the back of his hand a decisive swat.

Shock.

I jump three feet out of my skin. *I just swatted him. The cannibal barbarian alien.* I meet his gaze, hold fast and watch as the most terrifying thing of all happens. His lips...they curl up, parting to reveal a flash of perfectly white, square teeth. This cannibal barbarian alien is smiling at me.

I jerk back, stumbling into the tun. I reach out to catch it, but he's already there, one hand on its smooth side, the other holding the lid in place. He rights the ceramic slowly, without releasing me from his gaze. It tracks my hand when I touch my chest. My heart seems to be trying to make a break for it, despite the fact that the rest of me is rooted in place.

Cask settled, he reaches for my palm and, catching it, tosses it aside so forcefully, I stumble again. *What's he doing?* He's looking at my...buttons. They're giant mismatched buttons that look like the buttons on doll clothes — some that I think actually did come from the dolls' clothes of the highborn mistresses — and he's *inspecting* them with an expression that suggests they just insulted his dead mother. And then he lifts a single finger and I watch in fascination and horror as a sharp, serrated point *grows* from the tip of his nail.

A finger-long at its longest, he brings that freshly formed claw down in one swift motion and slices through the loose thread anchoring my top button. My shirt falls open to the navel, exposing my bony ribcage and small breasts. I tell my body to grab it and hold it closed — *for comets' sake!* — but my body does something else.

I slap him. *Again.*

I rocket four feet into the air instead of the puny three I shot up the first time. When I land, I forget about the shirt. My arms are frozen away from my body, waiting for him to slice me open as quickly and easily as he did that piece of thread.

I wait. And I'm left waiting.

Because he touches his cheek where I hit him, blinks many times in that strange alien way, then his lips peel back and he laughs. He laughs so full and from the belly it makes razorblades appear in mine. *I can't remember ever hearing anybody laugh like that.* And he's a barbarian cannibal alien.

I jump again, shocked, when his laughter dies and he fixes me with brown eyes that are both condescending and indulgent. He shakes his head, grabs my arm and starts dragging me towards the door.

He says something to me. It sounds playful, but he could just as easily be telling me that it's time to be disemboweled now.

"Okay," I answer, knowing that whatever he means, I don't exactly have a choice in it.

He grunts out another laughter-like snort, but just as we reach the door, I hear a light cough behind me. I freeze. He freezes. He looks over his shoulder and his eyes meet mine and when he shakes his head so slow like that, the long tresses of his wavy hair tickle my bare arm.

"Tokan, ya reesa, teka annak," he says, and though I don't know the words, all I can think in response is, *human stew, here we come...*

2
Neheyuu

"Tokan, ya reesa, teka annak," I tell her. *Close, but not enough.* I call her *ya reesa* — a title of honor when intended and, when sneered, a title of disrespect. Perhaps I use a little of both here when I call her brave. *Little brave one.* She *is* to defy me as she's done. I just didn't realize how brave until this moment.

How clever too.

She nearly succeeded in distracting me, and if not for the clumsiness of the humans behind the curtain, she would have.

I look upon the gaunt human faces in hiding. They are each as poorly clothed as she is, and so thin as to be considered starved by Sasor standards. Slaves. Reesa is certainly one, even if her coloring would be considered rare among the United Manerak Tribes.

Like raw bronze, she is both red and gold at the same time. She shines, even in this dim, dusky cellar, illuminated only by the outside light filtering in through uneven slats in the walls. Similar though our colors may be, that is where our likeness ends. She is a puny, runty little thing with bones like dried reeds and strange eyes that are dark and expressive. *Human.*

They are a species I have encountered before, though never as First of my tribe, and I feel a renewed rush of adrenaline and pleasure that my warriors and I have finally found and taken such a substantial number of them. It's considered a great success to come across a human tribe and decimate it.

Their females are compatible with our species and their males weak. I don't know if I've seen a human that was this pretty though, funny mannerisms and all. She hit me several times — a strange defense as she is without claws and likely a small fraction of my weight, with no warrior training at all — and now she just watches me, as if waiting for something.

Typically, I would have rutted her by now and there is no question — I *will* rut this little reesa. I reach out and touch her hair. I have never seen such a color before. As if it were stolen from the depths of an ocean, or stripped away from the stars. So black it's nearly blue. And even in filth, so *sviking* soft. I pull my hand back, wanting to touch it again — knowing that I *will* touch it again — but I allow her the chance to give to me what I seek. Because not even her matted hair, the stench of her unwashed and threadbare clothing, and the smudges of dirt and ash on her skin are enough to deter me.

"You want them to live, ya reesa?" I know she does not understand my words, so I show her what I mean. I lift a hand again for her breast but she angles away from me, shielding herself with that filthy rag I mean to tear from her body.

She says a word in a language she knows I do not speak. She shakes her head for added meaning.

"Tszk," I say, though why I tell her the word she needs to deny me, I have no idea.

Irritated with myself, I flit away her hand when she tries to block mine, and mold my palm to her chest, admiring the weight of her small tit as I hold it. It's larger than it should be given that I can see the bones of her chest through her skin, and the bones of her ribs. Her hip bones are likely to be just as prominent, and it doesn't matter. I want to see them too.

Her jaw sets, pupils contract. She pries my fingers away from her tunic and shakes her head just once, firmly. She says her strange alien word again.

"Yena," I answer. This is a better word. One she will get accustomed to saying to me, once she realizes who I am.

She does not break. I do not move. We stare one another down, silence stretched like a tanning line between us. I think it surprises her as much as me that I am the one to cede first. Irritated, I am ready to return to my warriors and enjoy the celebrations from battles easily won. I glance meaningfully at her people, huddling against one another, trying not to meet my gaze at all costs. Funny, that they cower when she does not.

Reaching among the mass of their bodies, I grab the first human I see. A female. I assume she is older given the shriveled way her skin clings to her frame. She has thick grey hair tied away from her face. Her lower lip quivers and she says something to the reesa that makes her wince.

Reesa looks from the woman to me. An expression of pain crosses her face. She takes a half-step towards me that surprises me again, then holds her wrists out between us, revealing their slightly paler insides. She is covered in black markings, sketches drawn all over her skin that will not fade.

We don't have this tradition in my tasmaran — no manerak tasmaran does — but on this little reesa, I find the markings beautiful. Though dozens of small patterns are scattered over her arms and shoulders, for now she focuses on thin, black rings just below her palms. The lines are straight, but incomplete. A small gap of clear skin tantalizes me, making me want to rub my thickest finger over it.

She speaks to me then in sentences. When I don't answer, she repeats what she has said, shaking her wrists slightly for emphasis. I don't understand her. Holding the older human by the upper arm, I again feel the front of reesa's chest, making it clear what I want. What is at stake should she refuse.

Her mouth turns down. She breaks my gaze and looks to the female. She is weighing her options. Deciding her price. And when, with the slight lowering of her chin, she agrees to pay it, I don't feel the satisfaction I thought I might. Her shoulders cave, making this already slight female seem almost insignificant. Swirling shadows, where before she was pure light.

I catch her wrist as she turns from me, my gaze roaming over the markings there and wondering about their significance. So many mysteries, beginning with why this little reesa denies me.

"Tszk," I tell her finally.

She blinks at me, her expression hollow. Lost. A deep chasm opens up at the sight of it, and I feel, for the span of a heartbeat, her mirrored emotions even though I have never felt them before. She is utterly transparent and through her, I can see and feel and experience everything. Beneath my true form skin, my manerak stirs slowly, as if waking up from a deep sleep.

I squeeze her breast roughly and say, "Tszk." I let her go immediately, dropping the other human female's arm as well. I push the older female slightly back and snap the curtain shut between us so that I can no longer see the human slaves, the alien barbarians.

Understanding flits across her face and she smiles at me just a little bit. Her teeth are white and straight in her small mouth, except for two on the bottom row which overlap. She doesn't have any fangs to speak of. Just reeds for bones and smiles in her eyes. Why does she smile at me when I have taken her kingdom? Mysteries. Interest. She has mine. And she has all of it.

Dangerous. My manerak is fully awake now, needling the underside of my skin. But I ignore it, just like I ignore any thoughts of danger in her presence. She's just a puny little human to be taken, rutted and forgotten. There's no danger here.

"Strena," I tell her. *Come.*

Her head tilts to the side, unwashed hair falling around her shoulders in matted locks. Her thin fingers still clutch her tunic together, but they no longer tremble. She glances to the heavy mud cloth hiding her humans from view.

"Tszk." I snatch up her wrist, which is thinner than the hilt of my sword and far easier to break, and lay her palm against my chest, where the leather does not bind it.

She shakes her head. I nod. Her eyes grow large in her face, making her look like she will soon transform. But humans do not have such an ability. Tszk, my little reesa is utterly transparent, totally defenseless, and mine for the taking.

I pull her roughly out of the smallest room, through the next room and finally into the main area of this shack. There, Dandena and Mor are busy brawling over a golden crown they found hidden in an ale cask. They tower over me in their manerak skins until, seeing me, they shed them and return to their true forms.

The human in my grip tugs pitifully on my arm, trying to free herself. I wonder if she's ever seen manerak before and if she hasn't, what level of terror she's currently feeling. I snort out a laugh at the thought and when I tug her forward, her heat crashes into me. *Warm. Feels nice.* I'd think her feverish if she showed any other signs of it.

She stands frozen on her feet, one hand locked in mine, the other clenched at the V of her throat. She's staring straight ahead and I follow her gaze to Mor. He licks his lips and takes a step towards us, his focus locked on her in a way that makes my skin prickle. My gaze narrows on him, sharpening, becoming lethal. *Becoming manerak.*

"What do you have there?" He says with a cocky sway of his hips. The crown forgotten, he takes a step forward. His gold hair, stained red, flutters in his wake.

"Found her hiding," I answer with a grin. Anticipation rears its restless head. My manerak opens up inside of me like a mouth.

"Was she alone?"

"Yena," I lie for reasons unknown. My fingers twitch.

"Then there is only one to be had."

"Yena."

He wipes the back of his hand across his mouth, smearing the blood of dead humans across his face. "I'd like to have her."

I laugh. "Come on then."

Mor's thick eyebrows fade back into his skin the moment the challenge is accepted. The corners of his mouth stretch back towards his hairline and I feel my pulse hammer, manerak unreasonably thrilled as it expands and elongates in response.

The little reesa jolts beside me when my shoulders begin to swell and my thighs thicken and lengthen. Already hunched over her, soon I tower. The uncomfortable wooden roof is no match for my manerak's size. It brushes the top of my head and then my shoulders, forcing me to either stoop or tear straight through it. *Do it.* But then the roof might cave, crushing her beneath it. The thought nags, and then disappears like vapor.

My manerak sizzles beneath my skin, aching with a tension that feels distinct from the way it usually does, though I'm damned to put my finger on it. *Eager.* I feel my brow bone flatten, my eyes expand, my pupils slit. My fangs come down to shield my teeth and I only release reesa when I feel claws claim my all ten of my fingertips. From between my forked tongues, I issue a hiss.

Mor charges and though he is one of my better fighters, he is still no match for me. I am First of my tribe for a reason. I wonder if his heightened bloodlust is the reason that he issues this challenge — one we both know he's going to lose — or if it has something to do with the slave beside me. Can he also see her radiance? The thought grates. My manerak seethes and spits.

She jerks wildly now, back slamming into the nearest wall. My forked tongues loll out of my mouth, tasting the air she creates. Something sour and sticky, like the tart rathra leaves used by our woodsmiths, and beneath it something sweet that makes the first wave of bitterness possible to overcome. *Blossoms. The nectar of the carnivorous egra flowers. Beautiful. Dangerous.* I release her fully and with a gentle push against her thin chest, guide her behind me so that I can have both hands free when I meet Mor in a clash of thunder.

There are no weapons in a challenge, so he swipes for me with his claws. He is a smaller male, both in his true form and in his manerak, but his strength lies in his speed. He spins away from me as I block and comes in below my arm, attempting to switch around me and bring himself closer to reesa.

My manerak call reverberates deep in my chest, causing my whole body to tremble with its might. I bring my foot down on his thigh, stopping his path. I swing my fist around to meet his cheek, drawing blood. He rises with a hiss, claw raking my ribs as he spins out of my grasp.

My manerak skin stretches, becoming broader with the tangy scent of his blood — and mine. The other warriors back to the very edges of the room, dragging casks — mostly ale — that they want to preserve with them. I attack first this time, moving straight through a flimsy piece of wood these humans once used for a table.

My shoulder connects with Mor's sternum. He tries to absorb the blow, which is his second mistake — after issuing challenge in the first place. I take him down and together we fly through the nearest wall. We land on the sand outside and before he has a chance to blink, I score his chest twice more.

"That's three times to blood, brother," I rattle, my voice distorted as I am still manerak. I push myself off of him with a grin.

He punches the packed sand angrily but still takes my hand when offered. "Challenge is to you, warrior," he says.

I yank him to his feet and feel my manerak begin to settle — at least, until I return to the shattered shed and see Dandena, Rehet and Ock closing in on my prize. I open my mouth and my manerak hiss is so deafening that I can't speak through it.

They turn, surprise etched onto their true form faces. Dandena breaks the quiet. "One blooding to three, in favor of First?"

I nod once. Dandena applauds and holds out her hand to take her winnings from the other two, who curse. I don't care for their bets, and break through the semi-circle they've made surrounding reesa. She stands with her spine still welded to one of the flimsy wooden walls. She's managed to find a knife and holds it out in front of her with two hands. She clearly has no idea how to use it, but it does look sharp. Very sharp. And it has an emerald jewel in the hilt.

"That isn't *your* blade is it, Rehet?" I balk, laughing hard enough to make my belly ache.

The others laugh too, while Rehet at least has the decency to grumble softly in shame, "She is quicker than she looks."

I inhale pride, and exhale relief when I push the males and Dandena away and see that reesa is unharmed. Her wide eyes turn up at me and I glance at the blade in her fist, shaking my head. Misunderstanding my reaction, she jumps in the air, unfurls her fingers and holds the knife out to me. She is shaking. Afraid. *She is unused to manerak.* I hiss as I feel the bones in my body contract and scale, my fangs retracting, my face slimming, my rattle dying, my shoulders narrowing, until I am finally in my true form once again.

Settled, I reach for her hand, hesitating a breath away from her fingers when she jumps, this time half a head into the air. I grin and she seems to like this because half of her mouth quirks. She still offers the knife between us but I wrap my fingers around her fingers.

"Tszk," I tell her. She won it off of Rehet. She has earned this. I press the blade back to the center of her chest and turn to the others, eager to get out of here — eager to get *her* out of here, away from the males and into my own private dolsk. "We ride now."

———————————

Continue reading in ebook or hardback on Amazon and in paperback anywhere online books are sold

All Books by Elizabeth

Xiveri Mates: SciFi Alien and Shifter Romance
Taken to Voraxia, Book 1 (Miari and Raku)
Taken to Nobu, Book 2 (Kiki and Va'Raku)
Taken to Sasor, Book 3 (Mian and Neheyuu) *standalone
Taken to Heimo, Book 4 (Svera and Krisxox)
Taken to Kor, Book 5 (Deena and Rhork)
Taken to Lemora, Book 6 (Essmira and Raingar)
Taken by the Pikosa Warlord, Book 7 (Halima and Ero)
*standalone
Taken to Evernor, Book 8 (Nalia and Herannathon)
Taken to Sky, Book 9 (Ashmara and Jerrock)
Taken to Revatu, A Xiveri Mates Novella (Latanya and
Grizz)

Population: Post-Apocalyptic SciFi Romance
Population, Book 1 (Abel and Kane)
Saltlands, Book 2 (Abel and Kane)
Generation 1, Book 3 (Diego and Pia)
Brianna, Book 4 (Lahve and Candy)
more to come!

Brothers: Interracial Dark Mafia Romantic Suspense
The Hunting Town, Book 1 (Knox and Mer, Dixon and Sara)
The Hunted Rise, Book 2 (Aiden and Alina, Gavriil and Ify)
The Hunt, Book 3 (Anatoly and Candy, Charlie and Molly)

CPSIA information can be obtained
at www.ICGtesting.com
Printed in the USA
LVHW010129300122
709583LV00008B/996